CW00493533

FALLING FOR PROVENCE

ALISON ROBERTS

Boldwood

First published in Great Britain in 2024 by Boldwood Books Ltd.

Copyright © Alison Roberts, 2024

Cover Design by Lizzie Gardiner

Cover Photography: Shutterstock and Adobe Stock

The moral right of Alison Roberts to be identified as the author of this work has been asserted in accordance with the Copyright, Designs and Patents Act 1988.

Every effort has been made to obtain the necessary permissions with reference to copyright material, both illustrative and quoted. We apologise for any omissions in this respect and will be pleased to make the appropriate acknowledgements in any future edition.

A CIP catalogue record for this book is available from the British Library.

Paperback ISBN 978-1-83617-307-6

Large Print ISBN 978-1-83617-306-9

Hardback ISBN 978-1-83617-304-5

Ebook ISBN 978-1-83617-305-2

Kindle ISBN 978-1-83617-308-3

Audio CD ISBN 978-1-83617-299-4

MP3 CD ISBN 978-1-83617-300-7

Digital audio download ISBN 978-1-83617-303-8

Boldwood Books Ltd
23 Bowerdean Street
London SW6 3TN
www.boldwoodbooks.com

For my dad, who showed me that magic can lie between the covers of a book xxx

1

An ancient stone wall was almost touching the passenger side of the car Eleanor Gilchrist was sitting in.

'I can't get out.'

Not that it really mattered when she wasn't sure she particularly wanted to get out.

'You can get out my side.' There was a note in Laura's voice that warned Ellie her sister's patience was wearing thin. 'If I don't park this close, we'll block the road. But you can wait here while I have a wee look. Maybe the satnav's got it wrong.'

She opened the driver's door, got out and walked a few steps to stand in front of a gate. She stood so still, for so long, that Ellie wriggled out of the car, wondering what was wrong.

Laura words were almost a plea. 'This can't be right...'

Ellie pulled at a scramble of ivy that suggested it had been a very long time since the solid, iron gate in front of them had been opened. 'I think it is... Look.' She rubbed at the chipped surface of a glazed, ceramic tile attached to a crossbar to reveal lettering that was faded but still legible.

La Maisonette

'Aye... that's it. That's the name on the legal documents.' Laura peered over the garden wall. 'No wonder they called it "The Small House".'

Ellie followed the direction of her sister's gaze. Through the rusty bars of the gate, above the knee-high grass and overgrown hedges of a long-neglected garden and past a shed where an enormous padlock was hanging from a stable door, was a dwelling that had been built of the same, rough-hewn, golden-brown stone as the walls of both the garden and the other side of the road.

La Maisonette had been built a long time ago. Probably several hundred years ago, Ellie reckoned. Having been born and bred in Scotland, she was no stranger to historic stone dwellings, but she'd never seen anything like this. Golden rock instead of grey, and soft rounded edges rather than careful squares. A roof that looked like layers of old split terracotta drainage pipes and nothing like the neat slate tiles of her mother's cottage. The colours of Oban reflected the mist and rain and chill of a Scottish climate. This house had been gently simmering in the sunshine of countless French summers.

Ellie found a smile. 'Ripe for restoration, perhaps?' she suggested.

'Is that supposed to be funny?' The sharp look from Laura was suspiciously close to a glare.

Ellie's smile faded as she closed her eyes. Until now the slightly awkward inability to feel comfortable in her oldest sister's company had been disguised by the busyness of airports, car rental arrangements, navigating in a foreign country and the tension of driving on what was the wrong side of the road for them both. There was nowhere to hide now, as they stood alone together on this quiet road on the outskirts of a medieval French village, and the effect of adding a deeply disappointing reality to the day seemed to have put a spotlight on what neither of them wanted to talk about.

Why on earth had Ellie allowed herself to be persuaded – or had it actually been bullied? – into coming on this flying visit from Scotland to the south of France? Did her family really think a mini-break was going to change anything? That undiluted exposure to Laura's attitude that you could get over anything with a bit of determination and self-discipline was the push that she needed to start embracing life again?

To be fair, Laura Gilchrist was probably not currently thinking about how disappointingly feeble Ellie was proving herself to be. It was more likely that she was racking her brains to find some aspect of this property that could make it possible to offload as soon as possible. She'd already had to cross off a quick commute from the nearest airport at Nice and direct access to one of the desirable French Riviera beaches.

'Sorry.'

The apologetic murmur was enough for Ellie to open her eyes again.

'It's okay.'

And it was. She knew that Laura had shouldered the vast majority of the stress that was associated with this unexpected journey. But Ellie still found herself pressing her lips firmly together – partly so that she didn't say anything else that might annoy Laura and make this time together even less pleasant but also to stop herself smiling again. Because it *was* kind of amusing that their destination clearly deserved the euphemistic 'ripe for restoration' tag line her sister's estate agency often employed for properties that looked uninhabitable.

That La Maisonette was in such a neglected state was a relief, in some ways. Maybe they could just turn around and go home now and leave this problem for someone else to sort out.

Blood-red poppies and bright white daisies were scattered though the long grass on the other side of the gate, and spears of lavender drooped over what might be a cobbled pathway leading to the dark arch of a wooden door. Ellie drew in a deep breath, searching for the scent of the lavender, but something else was much stronger.

'I can smell lemons,' she said. Again, she had to stifle the way her lips wanted to tilt into the beginnings of a smile. Could there be a more appropriate situation to invoke the proverb that when life gave you lemons you should make lemonade?

'Oh?' Laura blinked, as though being dragged back from a daydream. Or more likely a daytime nightmare about how difficult it was going to be to make something good out of this twist of fate. 'I guess there might be a lemon tree somewhere.'

She unlatched the iron gate. 'Let's go and find out.' She uttered those words with the same tone she might have used for 'Let's get this over with, shall we?'

The gate, still caught by tendrils of ivy, didn't want to budge, but Laura's push was, admittedly, a bit half-hearted.

'I'll do it.' Ellie grasped the bars and shoved hard to break the ivy strands and shift the gate over a tangle of weeds. 'You don't want to get rust all over your nice new dress.' She wiped her hands on her jeans, oblivious to any streaks, and slid sideways through the narrow opening. Another tug from the inside made the gap big enough for Laura to step through without getting a mark on the pale olive-green linen of her figure-hugging dress.

In a silence redolent of the increasing distance between them, the two sisters picked their way towards the heavy wooden door. The elaborate carving of the door hadn't been visible due to the shade from the tangle of an overgrown climbing rose clinging to the stone arch, and Ellie's fingers automatically traced the outlines of one of the four-petalled flowers carved into the centre of each wooden rectangle.

She snatched her hand back as if she'd been caught doing something she shouldn't, and her fingers began curling into a fist, not unlike the shape of the solid door-knocker fixed to the central panel. 'You've got the key?'

'Of course.' Laura opened her handbag. 'It would be hard to lose something this big.'

The huge iron key didn't want to turn.

'I wonder how long it's been since Uncle Jeremy came here.'

Ellie made a huff of sound. 'I didn't even know we *had* an Uncle Jeremy until last week.'

'Aye... well...' Laura shrugged. 'It was Dad's side of the family. We never saw any of them again after he vanished.' Her tone hardened. 'We never *wanted* to.'

The flash of almost forgotten childhood bewilderment, laced with fear, grief and that shameful edge of relief that could never be admitted, got released in the wrench Ellie gave the key. The lock turned with a definitive clunk that seemed to give weight to Laura's statement. Nobody wanted a reminder of Gordon Gilchrist. Nobody wanted anything to do with this holiday house they had unexpectedly inherited from his brother simply because there were no other living relatives to be found.

Dust motes danced in the streak of sunshine the open door was providing, but the room was still dark with the windows shuttered. There were massive rough-hewn beams on the ceiling, and the interior of the walls had been smoothed with white-washed plaster, some of which had crumbled enough to reveal the stones that formed the outside of the house. Matching stones created an open fireplace with a blackened interior, but there was no hearth in front of it, perhaps because the entire floor was covered in hexagonal terracotta tiles. To one side of the fireplace was a family of three differently sized pottery jars that had small handles and, oddly, were only glazed on the top half. The biggest pot was knee high, and the dark, golden glow of its limited glazing was part of the spectrum of ochre that included the terracotta of the floor.

'It has a certain charm, I suppose,' Laura conceded. 'We'll have to sell it fully furnished, though. Imagine trying to move *that*...' She waved a hand at a cupboard that looked like an enormous wardrobe, with carved doors and brass inlays. 'Although... it's obviously an antique.' Her breath came out in a snort. 'The furniture might turn out to be worth more than the house.'

Ellie stepped towards the cupboard, resisted tracing the intricate pattern of flowers, leaves and bunches of grapes with a fingertip, and pulled the door open. Heavy shelves were stacked with bowls and plates in the same warm, earthy tones that were clearly intrinsic to this house. The uppermost dishes and the shelf space between the stacks had a film of dust peppered with mouse dirt.

Laura's high heels tapped on the tiles as she moved to the kitchen. She twisted one of the old taps, which coughed and spluttered and then released a stream of rusty water. With a grimace, she turned it off.

'Looks like a French version of an Aga, here,' she said, turning away from the sink. 'A wood burning version. I wonder if there's actually any electricity.'

'Doubt it.'

Laura reached for a wall switch and a bulb sprang to life above her head. 'I wasn't expecting that.'

'Maybe someone didn't get the memo and forgot to disconnect it.'

'Let's hope there isn't a huge power bill waiting for us some-where, then.'

'Nobody's been here, so why worry about it?'

'Somebody's got to. We can't all float through life and hope that problems just magically melt away.'

Laura's earlier apology for snapping wasn't repeated, but Ellie ignored the barb despite the unfair suggestion that any approach to dealing with a personal struggle as soul-destroying as hers had been could ever be dismissed as something as carefree, or pleas-ant, as 'floating'. But saying anything would mean she had to talk about it, and that was the last thing Ellie wanted to do.

She tried the light switch beside the crockery cupboard but nothing happened. Walking past a table to one of two pairs of tall doors, she opened them and then pushed at the shutters behind the doors. One creaked ominously and then sagged to catch on the ground as the top hinge gave up any attempt to continue supporting it.

'*Oh...*'

'What is it?' Laura abandoned the kitchen but didn't forget to switch the light off. She shaded her eyes against the much brighter sunlight, stood silent for a long minute and then let her breath out with an approving hum.

'Well, that's something positive. Nice view.'

'Mmm...' But Ellie was no longer looking at the craggy outline of mountains or the green wash of acres of forest or even the bright streak of blue just a little deeper than the sky that was the glimpse of the Mediterranean in the distance. Her gaze was on what was directly in front of them – a stone-flagged terrace and ornate metal candle holders, like tall miniature houses, that sat on the stones amongst even higher weeds and hung drunkenly from the branches of an overhanging tree. This space looked abandoned and totally forgotten. A secret garden that had been alone so long there was nothing left but a sense of... what... loneliness?

Despair, even?

Ellie tried to shake off the claws of an unpleasant sensation she was only too familiar with. She knew that the best thing to do was to move, so she walked across the terrace. 'That's why I could smell lemons,' she said. 'It looks like there's an orchard.'

The steep slope of the garden had been terraced with stone walls, and flat spaces were filled with the dark green foliage of the trees. Bright yellow lemons glowed amongst the leaves and lay on sparse grass beneath. The heel of Laura's shoe speared one of them as she went further into the garden.

'Oh, *yuck.*' She used a stick to scrape the overripe fruit from her shoe. 'I'm not going any further. That must be the boundary, anyway.'

She was pointing at a sagging wire fence at the end of this terrace. The slope beyond was gentler and there were olive trees instead of lemons. Shorter grass gave the impression that the land was less neglected, so they assumed it was part of the neighbouring property. A flicker of movement under the shade of one of the olive trees made Ellie blink.

'Oh,' she said again. 'Look! Donkeys.'

The shapes blended into the shade of the tree, but two huge shaggy heads were pointed in their direction, four long ears pricked forwards with mild curiosity. One of the ears twitched again.

But Laura was already turning away. 'I need to get some photos,' she said. 'We haven't even seen the bedrooms yet. Or the bathroom.' Her voice faded as she went back into the house. 'If there *is* one...'

* * *

Laura began scrolling through the photos she'd taken as soon as she'd had enough of her lunch. Ellie was sitting opposite her at a table in an outdoor restaurant tucked away in a small square behind the cathedral in Vence, a short drive from the house. It was surprisingly warm for early summer, but they were shaded by the generous leafy fans of an enormous chestnut tree. The shade was also making it easier to see the photos.

'The bedrooms aren't a bad size. Shame there's only two of them.'

'The bedrooms are tiny, Laura. They barely fit anything more than a bed and a wardrobe.'

'One of those beds was a *double*.'

'An antique double. No more than a large single by today's standards.'

No adult would have been able to use the child-sized single bed in the other upstairs room, and just a glimpse of a high-sided wooden cot had been enough to make Ellie turn away instantly.

'Some people love that old furniture. We can sell it as fully furnished, right down to the linen and cutlery. Ready to walk into and bask in all the delights this area has to offer. Or as an investment, to rent out to all the other people who are desperate for a summer holiday on the French Riviera.'

Ellie had to laugh. 'Are you kidding me? It's been neglected for years and years. There were *bats* in the bairn's bedroom. Pigeon poo all over the floorboards in the other.'

'It can't have been that long. The washing machine in the basement doesn't look more than about ten years old.' But Laura shuddered. 'I hate bats.'

'It's not habitable. It's filthy. The electricity's dodgy, and there's barely any water.'

'It probably just needs some new fuses and some of that stuff that cleans out pipes. And a professional clean. I'll put it all on the list to discuss with the agency rep we're meeting later.'

'It's miles from anywhere.'

'Oh, for God's sake, Ellie, why are you being so negative?' Laura's temper was clearly still fragile. 'Look where we are! It took us less than ten minutes to drive here and Vence is gorgeous. A market town that's got everything, with the bonus of a medieval centre. I'll bet there's any number of famous artists that have lived here. We need to find the tourist office and pick up some brochures.'

'And the food...' she added, breaking a short silence just as Ellie was about to apologise because she *was* being negative, wasn't she? 'You can't tell me that slow-cooked daube de boeuf wasn't the most delicious thing you've eaten in a long time.'

Ellie's eyes dropped towards the bowl in front of her which, unlike Laura's, had been scraped clean. Or, rather, wiped clean with shreds of the fresh crusty bread that had filled the small basket.

'And St Paul de Vence is just down the road. Even *I've* heard of that town. Apparently, it's a living museum, and I'm looking forward to checking it out after we meet the agent there.' She checked her watch and then signalled to the older man who seemed to be both the owner and waiter.

'*L'addition, s'il vous plaît.*'

Laura's French might be rusty, given the number of years since she'd spent her gap year in Paris, but it was a lot more than Ellie could remember from her high school classes. What she did remember, however, was that she'd loved listening to the language. Hearing snatches of conversation around them from the local diners, and as they'd wandered through the medieval heart of this small town looking for somewhere to eat, was reminding her of the sheer musicality of this language – how it felt like hearing the opening bars of a long-forgotten but once-favourite song. And maybe there was a genetic reason for that.

Inheriting a house hadn't been the only shock for the Gilchrist sisters in the last few days. They'd discovered they had French blood themselves. It was a confession from their mother, Jeannie, on a subject none of them had ever had the courage to force her to talk about: her husband's family, who'd all turned their backs as the police gave up searching for a man who clearly didn't want to be found.

'*Your grandmother on your father's side was French. She only shifted to Scotland after she got married and had her children. She came from somewhere in the south.*'

The way back through the narrow streets of the old town to where they'd finally found somewhere to park the car took them past purple blooms of a wisteria foaming over the edges of a high stone wall. Past a fountain shaped like a giant urn pouring water into a pool with edges that reminded her of the flowers carved into the front door of the house they'd been to see.

Their house. Temporarily, anyway. A third share of the proceeds from its sale was likely to be life-changing for all three of the Gilchrist girls. Enough for a house deposit. Enough to float through life for a while, perhaps?

To get far enough away from the past to be able to forget?

Round the corner from the fountain, they bypassed the large central town square with its finely gravelled surface, perfect for the group of men who were engrossed in a game of boules to one side. What appeared to be the main road through the town was a little wider but still cobbled. Someone came out of a boulangerie with three baguettes poking out of their paper bags, and they had to skirt around two women who'd stopped to talk, their small dogs blocking the rest of the footpath. Most of the shops were closed and shuttered.

'I can't understand why the French still hang on to these ridiculously long lunch breaks,' Laura muttered. 'Don't they realise how much business they're losing?'

'Maybe they don't care,' Ellie suggested. 'Money isn't the driving force for everybody, you know.'

'It is when you've got a bunch of kids to feed and clothe,' Laura snapped back. 'Ask Mam how that was for *her*, sometime.'

Ellie slowed her steps a little. Or maybe Laura sped up. The distance was increasing between them, anyway, both emotionally and physically. By the time Ellie got into the car, Laura was drumming her fingers on the steering wheel, impatiently.

Ellie sighed. 'I don't want to fight.'

'Neither do I.' Laura started the car and backed carefully out of the parking space. 'Look, I know how awful it's been for you. And we've all done our best to help you get through it, but everyone's been tiptoeing around you for more than six months now and that hasn't helped, has it?'

'Oh... you mean I should just snap out of it?' Ellie didn't want to talk about it. She could feel it pressing in on all sides, and it still had the power to suffocate her. 'I'm dealing with it, okay? In my own way and my own time.'

'Mam thinks it's time you saw somebody. She's worried about you, Ellie. We're all worried about you.'

'Thanks for your concern.' Ellie stared out of the window. They were leaving Vence behind them up the hill, and there was nothing but forest on both sides of the winding road. 'But I'm fine. I'm looking after myself, aren't I? I'm eating. I'm sleeping. I'm working.'

'When was the last time you picked up a paintbrush?'

'You should be pleased I've given it up. Haven't you always said I was dreaming if I ever thought I was going to make a living as an artist?'

'Part-time work in a retirement home is the other end of the spectrum.' Laura glanced at the satnav and began to slow the car. A turn off the main road before they reached the entrance to the walled, medieval part of St Paul de Vence was indicated to find the address of the estate agency they were heading for. 'And the lease on your apartment is due to run out when? Next week?'

'Couple of weeks,' Ellie muttered. 'And yeah... I know I haven't found a place I can afford yet, but Mam says I can move back home for a bit if I need to.'

'That would be a backwards step and you know it. You're twenty-nine years old, Ellie. You need to stand on your own two feet.' The car jerked as Laura hit the brakes, having spotted the sign that told them they'd reached their destination.

'Look,' she said, her tone gentling after she'd stopped the car and turned to face her sister. 'We all loved Jack. We all shared your grief when he died. I know I've never had a baby of my own and I doubt I'll ever want to, so it's fair to say that I know nothing about what you've really gone through, but... but you've still got your whole life ahead of you and you can't just throw that away. And you're well rid of Liam, who never came close to making the grade as a decent boyfriend let alone a life partner. You've got the chance to make a whole fresh start.'

'Look out!' Ellie had to warn Laura not to open her door as she saw a huge motorbike approaching from behind at speed. Then it slowed down too fast and came to a halt just ahead of them. The rider dismounted and pulled off a motorbike helmet to reveal shaggy, dark hair. It reminded Ellie of Liam's hair.

Liam... the first man Ellie had ever fallen in love with.

The first man who'd broken her heart.

Or had that honour gone to the father who'd simply walked out of her life without any explanation?

How many times could trust be stolen, Ellie wondered, before you decided that maybe you didn't even want to try and find it again?

'Think about how passionate you were back in art school days.' Laura said. 'Being a single mother was never part of that dream, was it?'

Liam... the man who, as soon as he'd learned she was pregnant, had repeated history by simply walking out on her without saying a word.

'Dreams change.' Ellie released the catch on her safety belt and reached to open her door. 'And sometimes they die.'

2

The two sisters were standing outside the estate agency again less than an hour later.

'I thought that guy on the motorbike was delivering a pizza or something,' Ellie said. 'Who would have thought that *he's* our agent?'

'If Noah Dufour was any more laid back, he'd be horizontal.' Laura was looking uncharacteristically dazed. 'At least he seems to know what he's talking about. I didn't realise that real estate is so complicated here with all the fees and taxes and legal requirements.'

'I wasn't really listening then,' admitted Ellie. 'When Noah asked if we were all in agreement about selling as quickly as possible, I was thinking about the other night.'

That hastily called family meeting.

'We'll have to sell it.' It had been Laura who'd taken the lead, of course. *'It's not as if any of us can afford the upkeep on a holiday house, let alone the cost of getting there on a regular basis. Anyone disagree?'*

'Fiona's not here. She should get a say.'

'*Fi might think it's a grand idea to keep it, Mam,*' Laura had warned. '*She never seems to pass up an opportunity to be difficult these days, does she?*'

'*Let's try calling her,*' Ellie had suggested. But she'd known how unlikely it was that the call would be answered.

'*We'll go for a majority, then.*' Laura had announced. '*Fi'll get some money eventually and that will be a far more useful inheritance than a share of a house nobody else wants. I'll do some research, find the best local agency and get the ball rolling.*'

The best local agency had been that of Noah Dufour, and it had been a relief to hand over the big iron key and the task of disposing of something none of them wanted. Now they could enjoy a bit of sightseeing before the flight they had booked back to Glasgow tomorrow morning.

'Shall we leave the car here and walk down to the old part of St Paul de Vence?' Ellie suggested.

'Good idea. I could do with a bit of fresh air. That office reeked of cigarette smoke. And red wine.'

They reached a tiny chapel on a bend in the road which gave them a clear view of the old town, and, by tacit consent, they paused to look at the jumble of ancient stone buildings piled inside the impressively high walls. A square tower that stood out against lower rooflines had to be a church.

Laura didn't seem to be focused on the view, however. 'It could be a year or more before the place sells by the sound of how slowly things are likely to happen. Unless we do something to speed the process up...'

Ellie could feel her sister's gaze shift to settle on her rather than the view.

'Are you sure you don't want to stay and do some of the cleaning and tidy up the garden and make sure things like the broken shutter is fixed? It would probably only take a few weeks.'

'*No.*' The word came out more sharply than Ellie had intended. 'I don't even want to see the place again, let alone stay in it.' She shook her head to emphasise her negative response. 'I don't speak French, Laura. I wouldn't even know where to go to buy a broom or cleaning products. I don't want to drive on the wrong side of the road. I... just don't want to...'

... to be even more alone than she already was?

In a house that had a baby's cot in one of the bedrooms?

'Fine.' Laura gave up with a shrug. 'Let's go and see if we can find a wee gift to take home for Mam, shall we?'

They crossed the main road, walked past another large, gravelled square with another game of boules happening in one corner and then started the climb up to the gap in the medieval ramparts to enter the old town. Stone walls crowded in on either side. Shop signs hung on metal brackets. Vines with their roots in huge terracotta urns scrambled up to reach wooden shutters. The contents of tourist-type shops, with racks of tee shirts and baskets of lavender- or violet-scented soap, edged onto the walkway and every second space seemed to house an art gallery.

But Ellie was looking down at her feet.

Not because she wasn't interested in what was around her. Or because she didn't want to talk to her sister.

It was because she'd never seen cobbled streets quite like this.

Between edges of larger cobbles, small, flat stones had been used – the kind you might find on a beach or riverbed. Some were set deep into the grey cement on their sides and others were lying flat to make patterns of flowers.

It was a simple but very effective technique, and, with every turn, a new twist appeared. A flower with a terracotta centre was amongst flowers with pale centres and a larger circle enclosed the whole bouquet. Around another corner, darker stones had been placed to form a flowerpot that held a trio of blooms on long stalks. Some flowers had sparse petals that made them look like daisies, but others had so many petals it made her think of the kind of flowers her grandmother had loved, like dahlias and chrysanthemums.

Completely unexpectedly, it stirred something in Ellie.

Interest.

Inspiration, even? How long had it been since she'd felt even a flicker like this?

'I'd like to try that,' she said aloud.

'What... these chocolates?' Laura was peering into a window display. 'They look amazing, don't they? You'd think they were olives, but it says they're almonds. And those ones look like little pebbles. Let's get these for Mam. Chocolate-covered almonds are her favourites.'

'You get them. I'm going to sit here for a minute.'

Ellie perched on the edge of a large, deeply pitted stone step. She was close enough to the ground to reach down and trace the outlines of the cobbled flowers nearest to her feet. They'd been so carefully set that the surface was smooth enough to be easy to walk on, and there were people walking past who seemed oblivious to the artwork beneath their feet.

Who had laboured over the placement of thousands of small stones so long ago? Ellie could imagine herself doing it. Selecting shades of grey that would accentuate the design. Placing a pale stone in the centre and then darker ones for the petals. There was a surprising variety of colours when you looked more closely. Shades of red to orange and yellow fading to cream, but the effect was as harmonious as the myriad colour combinations you'd find in a cottage garden like the one her mother took such pride in.

'Hullo? Earth to Ellie?'

'What?' Ellie blinked as she looked up.

'You were away with the fairies. You didn't even hear me, did you?'

She scrambled to her feet. 'What did you say?'

'That maybe we should head back.' Laura was already leading the way back to the gap in the ramparts. 'I'd like to see if the tourist office in Vence is still open, so I can get some information. I'm planning to write the copy for the advertising myself. Noah's English is excellent, but I know the market at home and how to pitch something like that house.'

That house.

Their house.

'Are there any rivers around here?' Ellie threw a last glance over her shoulder as they left the cobbled streets behind them.

'I have no idea.' Laura's gaze was bewildered. 'Does it matter?'

'Not really.'

Her homeland had plenty of rivers. Beaches that were made of countless millions of stones. Ellie knew she could be taking photographs of these patterns, but she resisted taking her phone from her pocket. Because she knew it was unlikely that the images in her head were going to fade anytime soon? Maybe she would prefer to tap into these memories than hold a two-dimensional print that could become a barrier to something more significant.

But would a memory alone recapture this spark of connection? The way that touching them had? These paths were part of this place, and maybe the tiny glow of whatever it was that felt like a glimpse into the soul of the person she had once been was about more than simply a pattern. It might be connected to the sense of history that was as unique to this part of the world as the language and the smells and the softness of the sunlight and warmth. Different instruments but all playing their part in the same concerto?

They were almost back at the estate office, where they'd left the car.

'I'm going to pop back in and ask how soon the house might be ready for some marketing photographs to be taken. I think I'd better come back to supervise that myself.'

'You could ask for the key back, too.'

Ellie was almost as surprised by her own quiet words as Laura. They were enough to have stopped both of them in their tracks.

'Why would I do that? You said you didn't even want to see the house again, let alone go inside it.'

'I think I've changed my mind,' Ellie said slowly.

'Oh, my God...' Laura was watching Ellie intently, her eyes widening. 'Is it the idea of staying and cleaning up the house that you've changed your mind about?'

That wasn't the reason that was prompting this crazy impulse, but Laura didn't need to know that. Whatever that flicker of connection had been, it was too tiny and fragile to expose to any external influence in case it was instantly extinguished.

It wasn't that Ellie *wanted* to stay, exactly.

It would be a terrifying idea if she let herself think about anything other than taking this first, tentative step. But she knew that she *needed* to stay.

That she needed to find out if that spark had been real. If there was the possibility that all of her dreams hadn't died forever.

'Yes... I think so.' The words came out as no more than a whisper. Then she cleared her throat. 'Only for a while,' she added, because that made it feel not quite such a huge decision. 'Maybe just for the summer.'

* * *

'I hate rushing off like this.' Laura pulled back from Ellie's hug the next morning to look down at the bags by their feet. 'I'd help you carry it all inside, but I have no idea what the traffic will be like near Nice and I've got to get the rental car back. Unless you want to change your mind and keep it? I could get a taxi.'

Ellie shook her head firmly. 'I'm not going to drive here. I'd forget which side of the road I'm supposed to be on and kill somebody. Me, probably, but it would be worse if I killed somebody else. Besides, how expensive would that be? You've already spent enough, and you're going to be covering the costs of this renovation.'

'I don't mind. I'll get it back when the house is sold. How are you going to get to the shops?' Laura waved her hand at the bags. 'That food won't last long and the supermarket in Vence is miles away.'

'I can get a bus. The main road's not that far.'

'I suppose so.' Laura turned towards the car but then stopped again. 'You've got the key?'

Ellie patted the back pocket of her jeans. 'Yep.'

'And you've got Noah's card? With his phone number? You'll ring him later, won't you, if that plumber he called hasn't turned up to sort out the hot water?'

'Aye.' The card was in her pocket along with the key. 'Now get going or you'll miss your flight. You don't want to be late for that awards dinner tonight.' She stepped forwards to give her sister another brief hug. 'Good luck. I reckon you're going to win a gold medal for your sales record this time.'

'I'll call you. And I'll get some of your clothes packed up and your laptop and anything else that looks useful and get them couriered tomorrow, okay?'

'Okay. Go!'

But Laura paused again on the other side of the road. 'Do you really want to do this, Ellie? Are you going to be all right?'

'I'll be fine.' Ellie sucked in a deep breath as she heard the tiny wobble in her own voice. She summoned a smile. 'I'm going to make lemonade.'

'What? Oh... from the lemon trees?'

'No.' Ellie's smile widened as she caught a sudden flicker of something new.

Courage, perhaps? Hope, even?

'From life,' she said.

* * *

There was no point in putting any of the groceries away until there was somewhere clean to put them, so Ellie found a shady spot behind the shed to keep things out of the sun.

The house felt different as she entered it today, maybe because she knew what she would find. Or perhaps it was because she was alone and she wasn't about to escape anytime soon. If this was going to work, she needed to find a connection to this house. To start caring about it at some level.

Finding a small fridge tucked under the wooden benchtop was a good start, and, surprisingly, it was cold enough inside for the small metal freezer compartment to be coated with white ice. Maybe Laura was right and there was going to be the less pleasant surprise of a large electricity bill in the near future. The shelves were far from clean, however, and Ellie knew she would need more than paper towels and a spray product to tackle the grime. Was she going to have to find kindling and work out how to get a wood-fired cooker going in order to have some hot water available?

No. Hidden under a large wooden breadboard was an electric cooktop with two hotplates. She held her breath as she turned one of them on and didn't let it out until the plate began to glow red. Then she twisted the top of the brass tap over the sink as far as she could, hoping that the spluttering and rust would eventually run its course. By the time she located a cast-iron pot in one of the cupboards, the water was definitely clearer, although the sputtering continued. She half-filled the pot, put it on the hotplate and went back outside to find one of the bags of cleaning products that Laura had selected from the supermarket that morning. She needed a scouring pad and bleach and cloths.

An hour later and the interior of the fridge looked hygienic enough to put food inside. She rescued the bag that contained milk, cheese, butter and ham and then went back for the bottle of wine. She had just closed the door on her culinary treasures when her phone beeped.

> About to board

Laura's text read.

> But I've been online to pass the time. Make sure you're home for a delivery late this afternoon xx.

More food? Or maybe some more clothes, Ellie thought. That would have been a brainwave. Who knew that cleaning out one small fridge could have made her tee shirt and jeans quite this grubby?

She looked even worse a few hours later, when she'd emptied kitchen cupboards, scrubbed them out, washed all the pots and put them back. She hadn't stopped to eat anything, she realised. The crockery cupboard needed to be next on the list so that she had something clean to put food on to and eat it with, but she was tired already and needed to do something about where she was going to sleep.

Oh, help...

It wasn't as if there was any choice about which bedroom she would use, because she knew she couldn't even set foot in the one with the baby's cot, but pigeon poo on the floor was almost as off-putting as bats hanging from a curtain rail. Was she going to find some new horror when she went to put clean sheets on the larger bed – like mice nesting in the mattress?

Ellie sank onto the cushions of the huge old leather couch in the living area. The combination of fatigue, hunger and a glimpse at the scale of the challenge she had taken on was suddenly over-whelming. Especially when she could feel every mile of the distance that was now between her and everybody she loved. Or even knew, for that matter. She was alone in a country populated entirely with complete strangers, most of whom she wouldn't even be able to communicate with.

Squeezing her eyes tightly shut was the only way to stave off tears that could end up being an admission of defeat. She'd made a start, she reminded herself. She had food in a clean fridge and clean pots and pans and basins in the cupboards under the sink. A small corner of the house was useable, and all she needed to do was gradually expand that area.

Cleaning the entire crockery cupboard wasn't urgent. She could simply wash a single plate. And one wine glass. The thought of a cold glass of the local rosé she had chosen from a bewildering variety on offer in the supermarket was becoming increasingly appealing. She didn't even have to make the bed today. It was already quite apparent that this couch would be more than comfortable enough to sleep on.

A bath was going to be essential, however, so Ellie kept her fingers crossed that the tradesman Noah had called would appear. She would never be able to summon the energy to carry multiple pots of hot water up the stairs to try and fill that old clawfoot bathtub, and, anyway, it needed scrubbing out and bleaching before she could even start. Imagining the effort that the task would entail made her sink back against the cushions of the couch, her eyes still firmly shut.

Her swirling thoughts gradually subsided and it was impossible to resist the lure of escaping completely into sleep. Just for a minute or two...

* * *

Startled into wakefulness by the sound of a truck stopping on the road outside the house and a door slamming, Ellie had a moment of confusion about where she was and what time of day it was. As reality rapidly dragged her back into the present, she noticed that the light had changed, softening into early evening. At the thought that this could be the arrival of the person who could supply her with the luxury of a hot bath, she had a hopeful smile on her face as she hurried to the front door.

'Mademoiselle Gilchrist?'

She recognised her surname and nodded. 'Yes.'

'*Signez ici, s'il vous plaît.*'

Ellie didn't understand a word, but having a form and a pen thrust towards her made the meaning clear. Except... why would she need to sign something before any repairs to the hot water system had been made? The truck didn't look like a tradesman's vehicle, either, she realised. It was large enough to be blocking the narrow road, and a car was already waiting behind it.

'Um... Sorry... what is this about?'

The young man's sigh, along with an exasperated expression, let her know that he couldn't be bothered with someone who couldn't speak his language. An impatient toot from the waiting car added to the tension.

'*Venez avec moi*,' he commanded, leading the way to the truck. He waved at the impatient driver that he was blocking. '*Un moment*,' he shouted, and then shook his head, waving a dismissive hand in Ellie's direction. '*Anglaise*.'

It was patently obvious that the irritation was being explained by her nationality. Ellie felt her cheeks flush as she waited for the back door of the truck to be flung open.

'*Voilà*.'

'Ohh...' Ellie pressed her hand to her open mouth. So this was Laura's surprise? It was... fabulous. Her family might be a long way away, but this felt like an encouraging hug. She wasn't really alone, was she? Her lips curved into a smile that wobbled a little. 'It's... beautiful.'

Her reaction seemed to have diffused the atmosphere. The waiting driver was climbing out of his car to peer into the truck himself.

'*Oh là là*,' he exclaimed.

It was the first time Ellie had heard the exclamation, which was such a cliché, in real life and it took her back to French classes in high school, where she and her friends had decided it was the most hilarious response to anything at all until the novelty wore off. The memory brought another smile and a soft huff of laughter from her lips. When she took the pen and swiftly signed the delivery form, she actually received a smile from the delivery man in return. He jumped into the truck and handed her surprise to his unexpected assistant from the trapped car, who set it onto the roadside in front of Ellie.

It was a bicycle.

Not just any bicycle. This one was retro style, bright red, and it had a basket on the front.

Ellie searched for her schoolgirl French.

'*Merci*,' she said. '*Merci beaucoup.* It's... *magnifique*...'

The two men nodded, spoke to each other and then shook hands. Within seconds, the truck rumbled to life and took off along the road. The driver of the car waved as he followed. The sound of the vehicles receded into total silence, but Ellie was still standing there, holding the handlebars of the bicycle.

This was, quite possibly, the best present anyone had ever given her.

She could go as far as her legs would be able to pedal. She'd have to do it on the wrong side of the road, but she could go wherever she wanted to go. Into the nearby small village of Tourrettes-sur-Loup for daily requirements like bread or cheese. Into Vence if she needed a supermarket. Back to St Paul de Vence, maybe, to spend more time on those cobbled streets. To a river, even, to fill the basket with stones of her own choosing...

It was a stroke of genius on Laura's part, and it pretty much wiped the slate clean of all the criticism and disappointment that had accumulated for too many years. In that moment, Ellie had never felt so much love for her oldest sister. She wasn't trapped in this sad, dirty little house.

It felt like Laura had given her freedom.

3

Ellie propped the bicycle against the wooden door of the shed and stood there for a long moment, admiring it. Then she took a photo with her phone, texted it to Laura and added a message to tell her that she was the best sister ever.

The response was instant.

> You're welcome. Chose the colour to match your hair. Don't forget to stay on the right side of the road!!!

The boost to Ellie's morale carried her back into the house. Into the kitchen, where she spotted a baguette sitting on the recently scrubbed wooden breadboard. Her stomach growled a reminder that she hadn't eaten since breakfast, so she broke off a large chunk of baguette and prised it open. She folded in a slice of the juicy ham Laura had chosen from the supermarket delicatessen and added some wedges of a soft Camembert. As a final touch, she spread a generous amount of Dijon mustard, squashed the roll a little flatter and then took her first bite.

Oh, *wow*.

There was nothing like hunger to make something astonishingly delicious. The bone-deep weariness from a long day of physical labour sprinkled with dollops of some rather intense emotions seemed to add another condiment. Or perhaps it was that the flavours were so quintessentially French and she was eating it looking out onto that incredible view that could only be the south of France. A view that was now tinged with the first colours of what promised to be a long and gentle sunset.

There was only one thing that could make this experience even better. A glass of rosé. Oh, and maybe sitting down to eat it. Not inside, though. Right now, that terrace wasn't looking like a trap to suck someone into a vortex of loneliness. It looked like the perfect place to watch a sunset paint its magic onto an endless sky.

It wasn't that lonely, either, Ellie decided some time later. Having swallowed the last mouthful of her sandwich and chased it down with the rest of the wine, she went back inside to refill her glass.

Such a pretty pale pink. Like that first flush of the sunset that was now deepening into a much more intense colour, with streaks of gold that might become orange very soon. She took the glass with her as she wandered outside again, towards the lemon orchard this time, as if she wanted to step closer to the rapidly darkening silhouette of the nearest mountain.

No. It wasn't lonely.

It was... peaceful.

So peaceful it felt like nothing she had ever experienced before. The warmth of the air around her was as comforting as a snuggly blanket on a freezing winter's night. The light was gentle on her eyes, and the silence, only occasionally broken by the call of a bird, was utterly different to the silences she had been living with for so long.

It wasn't punishing her with what was missing from her life.

It felt as if it was soothing her with the promise of a new beginning.

The sun was low enough now to give the air the soft, misty quality Ellie had noticed yesterday and made her think of classes back at art school, exploring paintings by some of the masters, like Matisse or Chagall.

Of course it did. There'd been a good reason why so many famous artists had lived and worked in this part of France, and it probably had a lot to do with this light. And the landscape. She took another long moment to soak in the postcard-perfect scene. Not that she'd ever try to capture it on a canvas herself. Ellie's focus had always been on smaller details – like that lemon she could see nestled amongst the glossy foliage of the nearest tree in the small orchard.

She walked closer. Close enough to touch the skin of the lemon. To bend her head and inhale the sharp, clean scent as she cupped the fruit in her hand. Overripe, the lemon fell from the tree at her touch, so she stooped to pick it up. She spotted another lemon not far away, so she picked that one up as well.

A couple of steps and there were more – still firm enough to be good. With her wine glass still in her other hand, Ellie couldn't pick up any more fruit, so she started making a small pile. She would bring a bucket out in the morning to collect them, and maybe she really would make some lemonade.

Ellie finally reached the sagging fence. The shadows were long and deep, but it was still easy to spot the two donkeys – in the same place as yesterday, underneath that olive tree – on either side of the boulder.

Wait...

That boulder hadn't been there yesterday.

It was an effort to pull her brain back from the peaceful,

dreamy space it had embraced. Ellie narrowed her eyes and tried to focus. It wasn't a boulder. She could see something poking out from the rounded shape because it was pale and almost gleaming as the last rays of the sun touched it. Even so, it took a minute to recognise what she was seeing because it was so unexpected.

A small, human foot.

'Oh, my *God*.' Adrenaline flooded Ellie's body and her wine glass slipped, unheeded, from her hand.

It was a child. Right between the large bodies of two potentially dangerous animals. Within inches of hooves that could cause serious injuries. Ellie remembered the horrific bruises her sister Fiona had received on one occasion, when she'd been kicked by a horse. Her own unfortunate incident with a pony, as a young child, had instilled enough fear to make Ellie instinctively keep her distance from anything equine.

But she had to do something now.

It wasn't hard to climb over the fence, which was simply a few strands of smooth wire suspended between what looked like upright tree branches. With her heart in her mouth, Ellie slowly approached the donkeys. As their heads swung in her direction and those long ears pointed forwards, her heart rate increased noticeably. They could turn in an instant, couldn't they? Getting ready to kick or bite her. Trampling that small child without even noticing.

'Shhh...' she said aloud, even though they weren't making any noise. 'It's okay, donkeys. I... just want to... you know...'

Save that child's life.

She could see a little face now, as well as the foot. A pale face, with a sweep of dark lashes beneath closed eyes and a tumble of dark, curly hair. A toddler, maybe around three years old?

Ellie kept moving. Slowly, so that she didn't startle the donkeys into making a sudden movement. She didn't dare make direct eye contact with them, but she could feel them watching her. She was close enough to touch one of them now and, as she leaned down, could feel the brush of air as it flicked its ears.

'Don't move,' she whispered through gritted teeth. '*Please*, don't move.'

She touched the child's shoulder, but he didn't wake up. Her mouth dried instantly. Had he already been hurt? Was he even *alive*? No. She couldn't let herself sink into that horror or she wouldn't be able to move at all. Crouching, she slid one hand behind the small body and scooped him into her other arm, drawing him out from between the shaggy bellies of the donkeys. Then she straightened, carefully, and took a step back. And then another. The nearest donkey took a step towards her, and that did it. Ellie turned and fled back to the fence, clambered over it and then stopped. Her breath was coming in short gasps and she was shaking like a leaf, but the child in her arms was still sound asleep. Or was he unconscious?

And then it hit her with far more effect than any kick those donkeys might have delivered.

She was holding a child.

The first time she had done so since her own child had died.

But this little boy – she was sure he was a boy despite those astonishing eyelashes and perfect Cupid's bow of a mouth – was alive. She could feel the warmth coming from small, bare limbs and the huff of his breath against her neck. It was impossible not to be aware of the dewy softness of his skin or the smell of his hair. Unable to stop herself, Ellie pressed her cheek against the dark curls and closed her eyes as she drew in a long, shaky breath.

The child stirred in her arms, and Ellie jerked her head back in time to see two large, very dark eyes appear. A flash of fear came and then morphed into surprise, and then, to her astonishment, those perfect little lips curved into a smile.

'*Maman?*'

Oh... that single word, so clear it was like a bell in the silent evening, could have been spoken in any language and it would have pierced her heart like a spear. Ellie couldn't say anything, but her arms tightened a little around the boy as tears sprang to her eyes.

It became even more heart-rending when two small arms came up to wrap themselves around her neck and that curly head rubbed the space beneath her collarbone to find the most comfortable spot to snuggle into before the little body went limp again.

Oh... *God*...

The *feel* of this child... The smell of him...

That small snuffling sound of breathing through a nose that was squashed against her skin.

Ellie had never wanted to hold a child again because she'd known how unbearable it would be.

Because she'd never be able to hold her own baby again.

She couldn't move.

Couldn't think.

Where had this child come from? Where was his mother?

Worse... was he even real, or had her mind somehow conjured up a waking fantasy? Or, perhaps, a nightmare? Aye... the sound that now tore the quiet evening apart definitely pushed it into nightmare territory.

'*Hé!*' The raw bark of sound was startling enough to make her flinch. '*C'est quoi ce merdier? Qu'est-ce que vous foutez?*'

The voice was male. And furious. A figure was striding through the olive grove, right past the donkeys as if this man had no fear whatsoever of the large animals.

Tall. Dark. Fierce. With a look on his face that made Ellie step back a pace. She heard the crunch of glass under her foot as she stepped on the wine glass she had dropped but there was something much louder happening inside her head.

Words that couldn't be ignored.

He knew...

Somehow, he knew that she shouldn't be allowed to hold this child. That she couldn't be trusted to protect him because she hadn't been able to protect her own.

No. That was a daft thought, and Ellie needed to cling to reality in what was already an overwhelming situation. This man had never seen her before. He knew nothing about her. They didn't even speak the same language. He was still shouting at her. In French.

'I don't understand,' she said desperately. 'Who are you?'

He stopped, just on the other side of the fence, and glared at her. His mouth opened, closed, and then opened again.

'You're *English*?' He made it sound like the ultimate insult, much the same way that the bicycle delivery man had managed to do.

'Erm... Scottish, actually.' Was it possible this tension could be diffused by tapping into centuries worth of rivalry and animosity between Scotland and England?

He ignored her. 'What are you doing with my son?' The French accent was stronger than Noah's had been, but his words were perfectly clear. 'Give him to me at once.'

It was such a relief to hear someone speak her own language that Ellie smiled at him, despite his obvious fury.

'He's your son? Oh, thank goodness. I had no idea how I was going to find out where he belonged.' She knew she was babbling as she stepped closer to the fence. It wasn't just relief at being able to communicate, she was being absolved of having to make decisions when her brain had been totally fried by the shock of what had just happened. 'I just found him... asleep. Right beside those donkeys... At least I think he was only asleep...'

Strong arms were wrenching the child from her arms.

'*Theo?*'

The little boy woke up again. And stared up at his father. '*Papa...*'

A stream of incomprehensible French followed, but it was clear that this man was checking to see if his son was uninjured. Ellie could sense the intensity of the scrutiny being given. She could still feel his anger but, curiously, it was at complete odds with how gentle his hands were as he ran them over the small, chubby limbs right down to each little finger and toe.

He looked very different to the sort of men Ellie was used to seeing. His features were clearer somehow. More defined. Especially that nose. He looked... French but had neither the groomed, sophisticated elegance so often associated with both French men and women nor the kind of rock star, scruffy chic that Noah portrayed. This man was a craggier version of the sophisticated end of the spectrum. A bit more tousled and casual but still with that indefinable sense of style. In the very short amount of time she'd been with him, Ellie had also detected an even stronger whiff of something like aloofness, or even arrogance, that told her she was intruding into a world where she definitely wasn't welcome.

Ellie was uncomfortably aware that she must look a right mess with the corkscrew curls of her hair escaping her braid, and her filthy clothes. Good grief... she probably smelt awful, too. She edged back as she heard from the man the expulsion of a breath that was redolent with relief, and she knew exactly how he must be feeling. She was about to ask whether everything was all right and express her own relief when the stranger simply wrapped his arms around his son and turned away. After two paces, however, he turned back.

'Fix your fences,' he snapped. 'They are unacceptable.'

Ellie's jaw dropped. He was blaming her for his son having been in danger when she had risked her own life to rescue him? Where the hell had *he* been?

'He wasn't on my property,' she told him defensively. 'He was where you are now.' Within touching distance of those donkeys, but, again, he didn't seem to even notice them.

He was still glaring at her. 'You are the new owner of that house?'

'Erm... yes... I just moved in today.'

'This *is* your property, then. *Your* fence. Your fence on the other side, too, where it joins my property, and that is in the same state of shameful repair.'

Oh, help... this wasn't the best way to be meeting her first neighbour, was it? Ellie could understand why he might be so angry.

'I'm sorry... I didn't know.'

'*Donc*... now you do.'

He turned away again and kept going, but Ellie was still processing what he'd said and she could feel a new, sinking sensation in her stomach.

'Excuse me,' she called.

He either didn't hear or was choosing to ignore her, but she had to try again.

'The donkeys,' she shouted. 'They're yours, yes?'

He still didn't pause, but she could hear his response floating back through the olive trees.

'Of course not. They are also yours.' The hand that appeared in the air gave a very Gallic gesture of exasperation. 'Now you can finally start taking care of them yourself. *J'en ai marre.*'

He vanished into the lengthening shadows on the far side of the olive grove.

Very slowly, Ellie shifted her gaze to something closer.

Disconcertingly close now. As if underlining the information that had just been delivered, the donkeys had moved closer while she'd been watching the man and child retreat. They were almost within touching distance on the other side of that inadequate fence. Standing very still again, as if they were all in the middle of a game of Fairy Footsteps, a game she remembered from her primary school playground that involved sneaking up behind the back of whoever was 'in' and trying not to get caught moving as that person turned around. They were staring at her, their ears pricked forwards.

It had to be her imagination, but Ellie had the distinct impression that they were both amused by her new predicament. Smiling, even.

* * *

The potential malevolence of smirking donkeys, along with the echoes of that angry male voice, followed Ellie back into the house, but the ache in her chest that was making it difficult to breathe was due to the muscle memory of holding that small boy in her arms, and she was afraid that that ache was going to escalate into the kind of pain she'd actually hoped was becoming part of the past.

But there were other things to worry about now.

Like what she was supposed to do about the two wild donkeys that had apparently come with this house.

And the fact that it was dark. What did those bats do once night fell? Wake up and fly around the house? Bite people and give them rabies?

Ellie's first instinct was to call her mother. Or one of her sisters. She picked up her phone, but her fingers fumbled the swipe and the screen remained blank. She still felt shaky, she realised. And if she heard a comforting voice, she would probably burst into tears, and she could just imagine the flurry of calls or texts that would ping between members of her family after that. If Fi hadn't already been informed of developments, she'd be dragged into the situation now, and Ellie could almost hear snatches of the conversations.

I knew she wouldn't be able to cope.

It's hardly a surprise, is it? She's barely been coping for months and now she's alone in a foreign country.

Who would have thought there'd be a wee bairn next door, though? Poor Ellie... that's just cruel.

But what are we going to do?

I suppose I'll have to organise a ticket for her to get home. Oh... I wonder if I can get a refund on that bike?

I really thought that this might be the answer...

Well, it isn't, is it? Look at the mess she's in already. She's too scared to even go upstairs because of the cot and the bats and now she's had a stooshie with a neighbour.

What's the big deal with a couple of donkeys, anyway? If she wasn't so pathetic, she'd pull herself together and get on with it.

Don't be so mean. She can't help it...

Ellie scowled at her phone and then dropped it onto the kitchen bench beside the half empty bottle of rosé. Maybe she *was* pathetic, but she didn't need people talking about it behind her back. Even imaginary conversations. She didn't want her mother lying awake tonight and fretting about her, either. She'd probably talk to one of the doctors at the medical centre she worked in about getting her an appointment with someone who could dish out antidepressants.

She didn't want to go home with a cloud of failure hanging over her.

She didn't want to ask for her job at the care home back when she'd only just resigned. Or to go back to her flat to help with the clean up when so many unhappy memories had seeped into the walls there.

The only thing Ellie really wanted right now was the escape that sleep could bring. It would only take one more glass of wine and she'd be out like a light if she curled up on the sofa again. But she did need a blanket – something that she could pull over her head if the bats came visiting. She eyed the staircase. There were blankets in the bedrooms.

It took even more courage to get up that staircase than it had to approach the donkeys to rescue that child. Ellie remembered the fierce expression on her new neighbour's face as she hesitated. That dose of contempt when he'd realised she wasn't French. If he could see her now, he'd think she was pathetic as well as being a scruffy and unwelcome foreigner.

Did she care what he thought of her?

Not at all.

But maybe it was time she should start caring what she thought of herself again.

Ellie took a deep breath, lifted her chin and started climbing. She hurriedly slammed the door shut on the bedroom where the bats – and that cot – were and went into the other room to pull the cover and a pillow from the bed. Her heart was still thumping when she got back downstairs, but there was something else cutting through the disaster that her evening had turned into.

It was pride, she realised. It might have been a small thing, but she had done it, so she wasn't entirely pathetic. And the bats were trapped behind the door, so she wouldn't have nightmares about waking up to find them tangled in her hair.

The kaleidoscope of her day had images chasing themselves through her head, too fast to catch and keep, as she lay down a short time later and pulled the light cover over herself. Endless pots of hot water, including the last one that she had used to wash herself as best she could and rinse out her underwear. Dirt and dust. Hearing someone actually say *oh, là là* and the promise of freedom that gleamed like the paintwork on that bicycle. The taste of the fresh baguette and the sweet softness of the sunset. The intensity of that man's glare and the shape of that small body in her arms.

The precious *feel* of a living child...

Oddly, as Ellie drifted into sleep, she realised that the ache hadn't become any worse after all.

It hadn't even made her cry.

4

The hours flew past the next day.

A courier had arrived in the morning with the suitcase that Laura had dispatched and, not long after that, Mike the plumber had turned up. Having assumed that any tradesmen Noah might dispatch would be French, it was pleasantly astonishing to find that Mike was English. A huge, genial Londoner, he had made the daunting task of making this house more habitable suddenly seem a whole lot easier.

'You'll have hot water by tonight, love,' he promised, after a quick tour of the issues in the house. 'And we'll get those pipes running a bit better. I don't do glass, but I can get the bats out, put a board over that window and find you a glazier. We'll need to get someone else to check the electrics, but I'll see what I can do about that broken hinge on the shutter while I'm here.'

'That's great. Thank you so much.'

'No worries. Any chance of a cuppa before I get started?'

'Yes, of course.'

Mike looked around in the living area as Ellie busied herself in the kitchen making a pot of tea. When he touched a wall, shards of plaster crumbled and rained onto the floor. 'This needs to be fixed as well. It will all need to be stripped off and replastered.'

'I could probably do that,' Ellie said. 'If I can find where to go and get supplies.'

'Any *bricolage* shop would have them.'

'*Bricolage*?'

'Hardware shop, love. DIY and house and garden supplies. Paint, tools, commercial cleaning stuff.' Mike was smiling. 'My favourite shops. Like Aladdin's caves, they are. There's a good one as you go into Vence from this direction.'

'Good to know. Do you take milk?'

'Yeah. And three sugars, ta.'

Ellie handed him the mug of tea. 'I might go and have a look at the *bricolage* later. I probably need a special cleaner for the tiles on this floor.'

Mike looked down. He tapped a tile with the toe of his boot. 'These are called *tomettes*,' he told Ellie. 'Traditional but not so popular now. You could replace them. Or cover them with vinyl or laminated wood.'

'*No!*' Ellie was surprised at her vehemence. 'I really like these tiles.'

'But some of them are broken. And they're old-fashioned and... so dirty. It'd be a lot of work to clean them.'

'I can do it.' Ellie felt suddenly protective of the floor covering. 'I think they'd look amazing when they're all cleaned up.'

'It's your house, love.' Mike shook his head and drained his mug. 'I'd better get my tool bag and get on with sorting out this water heating.'

Ellie watched him walk back out to his van. Yes. This *was* her house – for now, anyway. And she was going to make it as beautiful as she possibly could. She fetched a dustpan and brush and stooped to sweep up the plaster fragments Mike had loosened.

Had it been his criticism that had done it? The suggestion that La Maisonette was old-fashioned and in need of so much work?

She'd certainly felt the need to defend this poor, neglected little house despite her own misgivings. Maybe she was also defending herself for having taken up the challenge.

Whatever it was, it had given her exactly what had been missing when she'd come back to this house alone.

A feeling of connection.

* * *

Cleaning the bathroom after Mike had left a few hours later took a very long time. Long enough for the water in the reconnected tank to have heated and provide the most enjoyable bath Ellie had ever experienced. Having the prospect of fresh clothing to put on afterwards seemed like another luxury, and, wrapped in one of her new supermarket towels with another providing a turban to cover her wet hair, she started unpacking the suitcase.

Finding that some of the available space had been used to pack a selection of her old art supplies, like sketchbooks, pencils and paint, was a less than pleasant surprise. Who'd thought that was a good idea? After one attempt, months ago, nobody had tried again to suggest that reconnecting with an old passion might be therapeutic, and this seemed like an even less subtle push. They simply didn't understand, did they? How could anyone have any inclination to be creative when their heart had been ripped out and their soul left to bleed to death? Ellie left the art supplies in the suitcase, zipping it shut firmly after pulling out the clothing.

There were, fortunately, also some nice surprises in what Laura had chosen to pack for her, probably because the last time Ellie had needed summer clothing she hadn't been able to fit into anything she owned, thanks to her post-pregnancy shape. Maybe that was why she selected a pretty summer dress that she had forgotten she even owned, because it had been relegated to the back of her wardrobe for so long. The blue, daisy-spangled fabric of the calf-length skirt swirled around her bare legs as Ellie stepped out into the evening sunshine to comb the tangles from her damp hair, and it made her remember dressing up as a child in one of her mother's old dresses – the way she had suddenly felt grown up and feminine.

The follow-on thought, that it was a shame she hadn't been wearing this dress last night, made her pause for a moment, her comb only halfway down the length of her hair. She pulled a little harder through the next tangle, but the sharp tug didn't quite erase the disturbing image of that angry Frenchman from her mind. Those dark eyes. The tousled hair.

Those gentle hands as he checked out his small son...

It was only then that Ellie remembered the glass she had stepped on and broken last night when her furious neighbour had been storming towards her.

She needed to pick up those pieces. Finding a container for the shards, she went through the lemon orchard towards the fence.

Had the donkeys been expecting her? They weren't standing under the olive tree this time. They were standing right beside that droopy wire fence, their huge heads hanging over the top.

Ellie's heart rate picked up, but her steps slowed and then stopped.

She stared at the donkeys. Tufts of grey hair stuck out at odd angles, making them look totally unkempt, especially where it hung over their eyes. She could see stripes of dark brown on their shoulders that matched the short manes and straggly tails, but it was their ears that really caught her attention. The dark rims made them look even bigger and they were filled with pale fluff that looked invitingly soft. Their muzzles were pale as well, as if they'd dipped those massive heads too far into a bucket of cream.

They didn't seem to mind the attention they were receiving. They stood there silently, at peace with the world, and, oddly, Ellie could feel that sense of peace enclosing herself as well. Becoming part of the whole scene, with the solid stone retaining walls dividing the slope of the garden behind her, the scent of lemons and the soft evening light.

Tentatively, she reached out her hand.

'Do you bite?'

A flick of one of those extraordinary ears was the only response.

She touched the closest donkey on its neck, just below its ear. The hair felt coarse as she stroked it, but she could feel the warmth of the skin beneath and it reminded her of the warmth of that little boy's limbs in her arms last night. Warmth from another living creature.

The donkey's eyes drifted shut as she stroked it, giving Ellie the impression that biting her wasn't being considered as an option. The other donkey was still watching, but it was a patient look, as if it was waiting for its turn to get patted.

'In a minute,' Ellie promised. 'I need to find that glass first. Someone might step on it.'

Like a small boy with bare feet, perhaps?

It wasn't easy to find the broken glass in the long grass, and then she had to be sure she had collected all the pieces. As she carefully shifted the stems of grass and wildflowers, she kept glancing back at the donkeys.

'You haven't got much grass on your side of the fence, have you? And where's your water? I'm sure you must need water.'

She could hear the echo of her neighbour's parting words, telling her that now she could finally start caring for these creatures herself. But how was she supposed to do that? Apart from a tabby cat that had turned up on the doorstep and decided to stay, pets hadn't been a part of the Gilchrist family's lifestyle because there hadn't been enough space. Or money. She'd toyed with the idea of having a dog, once, but a student lifestyle had made that impossible and then she was totally absorbed by starting her career and that morphed into falling in love with Liam which, of course, meant that she hadn't needed anything else to make her life perfect.

Yeah... right...

Ellie's breath came out in a huff. How naïve had she been to believe that fairy tales like that happened in real life? Especially against the background of her own family history.

She dropped what appeared to be the last piece of broken glass into the container. Then she curled her fingers around a clump of grass and broke it free. She went back to the fence and held it out.

'Are you hungry?'

It was the donkey that she hadn't patted that stretched out its neck. This one had more pale hair around its eyes, as if someone had used a thicker brush to outline them. Its lips were pale as well and they wobbled as the donkey carefully explored and then accepted the few blades of grass. Ellie watched them disappear into its mouth, feeling the gentle tickle of the lips barely touching her fingers, and then she offered a handful to the other donkey. A minute later, she was picking more grass, trying to avoid the stems of the poppies and daisies sprinkled through it in case they were poisonous.

'Do you need something else?' she asked. 'Like hay?'

Four dark eyes looked back at her. She was the one who was supposed to know, but she didn't. She knew absolutely nothing about what these animals might need.

Ellie found her phone in the pocket of her dress. She sent a text message because her sister, Fiona, didn't often answer her phone, but she was the person that Ellie needed advice from. Horse mad from her early teens, Fiona's first job had been in a stables and she now worked as a farrier. Donkeys were just small horses, weren't they?

To her surprise, her phone rang moments after she'd sent the text.

'You've got what? Two *donkeys*? What were you thinking?'

'I didn't buy them. They were just here. Abandoned, maybe. The neighbour's been looking after them.'

'What are you going to do with them?'

'I have no idea. But, in the meantime, I need to take care of them. They don't seem to have much grass. Do I need to give them hay or something?'

'They don't need much grass. They can founder easily if they get too much. You could give them some straw.'

'Isn't that the same thing?'

'No. Straw is just stalks. Fun to eat but no nutritional value. Have they got water?'

Ellie looked along the fence line and then walked a short distance. 'Yes... there's a concrete tub thing.'

'Is the water clean?'

'I can't tell. It's getting darker and it's in the shade of an olive tree.'

'It's probably full of leaves and old fruit, then. You'll need to clean it out. What sort of condition are their feet in?'

'What?'

'Donkeys need their feet trimmed regularly, same as horses. If it doesn't get done, they keep growing until they get crippled. Like... you know, how Turkish slippers curl up at the ends?'

Ellie walked back and peered over the fence. 'I can't tell. They look kind of like they've got their toes splayed a wee bit.'

'They probably need trimming, then. You'll need to find a farrier. And a vet. They'll need worming as well.'

Ellie sighed. 'I'll add a vet to the list, then. Along with the glazier and handyman and everyone else I have to find and talk to in a language I don't even speak.'

There was a moment's silence.

'You okay, El? Did Laura get too bossy and push you into staying to clean that place up when you didn't actually want to?'

'No... no, it was my idea. She's helping by paying for it all. She said she can wait till the house sells to get her money back. And it's okay. Really. It's... it's a nice place to be. It's just... well, I'm having to sort weird stuff out. Like what to do with these donkeys.'

'There must be a donkey sanctuary in France, or at least an animal rescue society. I could have a look online for you, if you like.'

It sounded like a good plan. But the donkeys were staring at Ellie again. They didn't look threatening any longer. They looked kind of sad. As if they knew she was planning to abandon them just like at least one other person already had. They weren't really a big problem, were they? Not right now, anyway.

'What do they like to eat?' Ellie asked. 'For treats?'

The silence felt surprised this time. 'Carrots would be good.' Fi's voice had softened a little. 'And I've heard that they really like ginger biscuits. You're not getting attached to them, are you?'

'Of course not. I was a bit scared of them at first, to be honest, but... they seem kind of nice. You know, kind of friendly.'

'I guess it must be a bit lonely for you there.'

'It's... different. But it feels like a good place to be right now. I don't know... Peaceful. And it's so warm.'

'Lucky you. It's been pouring here today. Feels more like winter than anything close to summer.'

'You should come over for a weekend or something.'

Fiona laughed. 'And what... bring my hoof clippers and a file?'

'That's a *grand* idea. I bet you could find some cheap tickets. You're good at that sort of thing. I'll pay for them, if you like. It would probably be cheaper and a whole lot easier than trying to find a farrier here.'

'I'll think about it. I'm pretty busy at the moment.'

It felt like a warning not to push things too far. So did the way Fi suddenly needed to end the call. 'Gotta go... things to do... Bye.'

Ellie stood there for a few moments after the call had ended, looking beyond the donkeys to the fence line at the other end of the olive grove. There were more trees in the distance that interrupted the view of another old, stone house but she could see that the shutters were still open. Was that why her skin prickled, as if she could sense someone watching her?

The same someone who had told her, in no uncertain terms, that she could finally start taking care of *her* donkeys, *her*self. The echo of his tone was enough to make Ellie raise her chin a little. To reach out and pat the donkeys again.

'I've got this,' she told them. 'You'll see. Tomorrow I'm going to clean out your water trough. And I might even go into town and buy you some carrots.'

* * *

He should have stepped away from the window the moment he'd spotted her, but it felt like his feet were caught in quicksand.

Even his breath had caught, long enough to make his chest feel uncomfortably tight.

Mon Dieu... She could have stepped straight out of the frame of some Pre-Raphaelite painting by someone like Rossetti.

That flowing dress, which an evening breeze was catching just enough to make it caress her legs. The same puffs of air were playing with the long, loose spirals of her hair, and the last true glimmers of sunshine were setting it on fire. This new neighbour of his was undeniably an extraordinarily beautiful young woman, and, for the first time in what felt like for ever, Julien Rousseau's body was stirring with the ripple of a sensation he recognised only too well.

Attraction? No, it was stronger than mere sexual interest. This was more like desire...

She couldn't see him, of course. Not that she was looking, because she seemed to be talking on her phone, but even if she did look this way, this upstairs window was partly screened by trees, was too far away and the room he was in was dark, apart from the soft light beside the bed in which his small son was now soundly asleep.

Julien had only come in to check on Theo, as he always did, but something had drawn him towards the window – possibly a remnant of remorse that he'd been so uncharacteristically rude to his new neighbour last night? He had, in fact, been contemplating going over there this evening, after Theo was asleep. He could have taken a bottle of wine, perhaps, and made an apology. He had no doubt that she would understand how upset he had been to find that his son had vanished from the house while he'd been caught by an emergency on the other end of his phone.

That embryonic intention had just evaporated. He didn't want to go anywhere near this woman after the signals his body was giving him.

She was *English*, for God's sake. Like his wife, Sarah, had been. Well, Scottish, but that was close enough. Too close for comfort, anyway, and more than enough to make this stranger completely off limits.

Bon Dieu... Sarah had cured him of ever wanting a committed relationship again, even with someone who didn't have an English accent.

With an effort, Julien turned away from the window, his gaze automatically seeking that small face on the pillow with the sweep of dark lashes against perfect skin and a mouth that naturally curled up at the corners to make it look like Theo was smiling, even in his sleep.

His chest was tight again, now, but it had nothing to do with any woman. This child was *so* precious. He could feel an echo of the fear that had propelled him from the house last night when he realised that the toddler wasn't where he'd last seen him, falling asleep in front of a favourite cartoon on television. The emergency call regarding a deterioration in the condition of one of his young patients had required his full attention, and he hadn't noticed the minutes ticking past. He'd pretty much forgotten that his mother had gone out this evening and wasn't providing the automatic back up in childcare for situations like this.

The horror of finding Theo's blanket an empty puddle of fabric on the floor and the back door open had only been outdone in intensity by the jolt of relief when he'd spotted him across the olive grove in that woman's arms.

But then that faint sound had carried in the stillness of the evening. His son's voice uttering just a single word.

Maman.

It had broken his heart and made him snap. Had he tapped into his fear and let it morph into anger because he had an easy target? Was he already feeling the guilt of failing to look after his son well enough? Or had he subconsciously recognised a threat to the stability of the new life he had created here, and he knew he had far more to protect than simply himself?

Whatever. He wasn't going to spend any time trying to analyse something that was already over and done with. What was more of a concern was Theo's wellbeing.

Had he really thought his mother had miraculously returned from the dead?

It was only now that Julien remembered an impression he'd got when he'd first seen his son in the woman's arms. It was only now that he realised what it was that had seemed obvious about the way she had been holding Theo. Cradling him against her body with the kind of protective intensity that Julien would automatically associate with a mother.

Had Theo felt that? Had it made him remember his own mother? Surely not. He'd been only a baby when Sarah had died.

It was possible, however, that such a young child could be aware of something missing from his life. Something that couldn't be replaced by even the most loving father and grandmother.

Merde. Julien pushed his fingers through his hair, closing his eyes for a long moment. It didn't matter whether he never saw the woman next door again.

Something had changed... and he didn't like it.

Pas du tout.

5

It came out of nowhere.

Maybe she would have seen it coming if she hadn't been enjoying herself so much on her first excursion on the red bicycle. Ellie hadn't needed to risk the main road to get to the village of Tourrettes-sur-Loup, and she'd just had a delightful hour or more exploring a village that she found even more appealing than St Paul de Vence. It didn't have the flower-cobbled streets, but it was just as charming and... more real, somehow. Real people lived here, and there were everyday shops to be found when she returned to the central square.

A boulangerie to get some fresh bread. A fromagerie, where she'd found eggs as well as new cheeses to taste, like the tempting-looking Époisses and the intriguing Morbier with a dark line through its centre. An *épicerie* was the last shop she visited, with an impressive array of fresh fruit and vegetables, including some delicious-looking carrots with their greenery still attached.

Her eye had been caught by the way the carrot tops, poking out of the basket, were catching the breeze, and her confidence in recapturing her bike riding skills was far greater on her return trip. Enough to make her increase her speed on this downhill slope so that she could feel the wind in her hair and not just see it in the carrot tops.

Ellie had had a great big smile on her face. Until it happened.

Until her peripheral vision had caught the small, hairy dog shape that was doing a kamikaze bolt across the road. Ellie jammed on her brakes, yanking on her handlebars at the same time, in an attempt to avoid a collision, and she'd felt the loss of her balance even before her front wheel clipped the dog. She heard its yelp of pain seconds before she toppled sideways into the stone wall and gave her own yelp. She also heard the skid of a car braking too swiftly behind her and, a second later, the sound of rapid footsteps.

'*Ça va? Vous êtes blessée?*'

The bicycle was being lifted from her body, but Ellie kept her eyes closed a moment longer. Because that voice sounded disturbingly familiar, and it wasn't simply that he was speaking French.

'Oh.' The voice was closer now. 'It's *you*.'

She opened her eyes. Yep. There was that intense stare again. She pushed herself up on one elbow.

'I could have run over you,' he said. 'What happened?'

'There was a dog...' Ellie sat up. 'He ran out in front of me. Oh, help... I hit him.' Her gaze skimmed the pile of produce that had spilled from her basket. The wrapped cheeses, broken eggs, scattered carrots and the baguette that had slipped from its bag to land in the dust of the road would have to wait. Where was the dog?

It was hunched beside the wall. Shivering. If holding one front paw in the air wasn't enough of an accusation, the expression in its eyes certainly was. This small, nondescript animal could not have looked more miserable.

'Are *you* hurt?' The note of concern in his voice was enough to make Ellie's gaze swerve back to her neighbour in astonishment. It sounded genuine, and she also had the impression that he hadn't stopped staring at her.

'I... I don't think so.'

'You're bleeding.'

His hand caught her wrist, tilting her arm so that Ellie could see the blood on her elbow.

'It's just a graze.'

'Can you bend your arm? Wiggle your fingers? Does anything hurt?'

Ellie bent her arm and wiggled her fingers. Her elbow could well be bruised, but any discomfort was overridden by the sensation of that loose grasp on her wrist. The awareness of skin on skin was intense enough to be disturbing, and she pulled away from the touch. He let her go instantly.

She turned to look at the dog again. 'I think *he* might be hurt, though...' A horrible thought occurred to her as she realised how close to her gate she was. 'He's not *your* dog, is he?'

'*Non.*' With a sigh, the man straightened and walked the few paces it took to reach the dog and crouched beside it. Ellie got to her feet and watched as he cautiously patted the animal on its head and then ran his hands over its body. It made her think of him checking out his own son after he'd wrenched him from her grasp. It was a focused attention, as if he knew exactly what he was doing. He left the dangling paw till the end and had barely touched that leg before the dog yelped in pain.

'It could be broken,' he said. 'He needs to go to a vet.'

Ellie bit her lip. 'It's my fault,' she said. 'I have to help him.'

'Yes.'

'But I don't know about vets here. Do they come to your house?'

'Not usually.'

'Is there a vet in Tourrettes-sur-Loup? Or in Vence?'

'I'm not sure of Tourrettes. I certainly know one in Vence. A friend of mine, in fact.'

Ellie eyed her bicycle, which was now propped against the stone wall. 'I guess he's small enough to put in my basket. Erm... could you possibly tell me the address of your friend, the vet?' She swallowed. 'Please?'

There was a long silence. Then he closed his eyes for a long moment. The sigh this time, as he opened them again, was even more heartfelt than the last one had been. A defeated sound?

'I will take him,' he said. 'As I said, the vet is my friend.'

It could have been an easy way out of this new dilemma, but Ellie shook her head. 'This is my fault. I'm the one who's responsible, so I will take care of him.'

She could feel the muscles in her jaw tightening and knew her tone was defensive. Would he recognise that she was belatedly responding to his unfair demand about assuming responsibility for donkeys that she hadn't even realised were on her property?

Maybe he did. He stared at her for a long moment. Then he shrugged. 'You can come too. Put your bicycle in your garden and then get in the car. I need to make a call. Don't touch the dog. He's injured,' he added, as Ellie opened her mouth to say something else. 'He might bite.'

Ellie picked up the baguette and carrots but ignored the rest of the mess on the side of the road. It took only a minute or two to wheel her bike a little further down the road and tuck it behind the wall of the shed with the stable door. As she turned back, she saw that her neighbour had taken off his jacket to wrap it around the dog. She heard the yelp of protest as he was carried to the car and put on the back seat.

He was holding the front door open for her. Further down the road, a woman had come to her gate. His gate, Ellie realised, because it was just on the other side of the olive grove. The woman lifted a hand, and the man raised his own and shouted something in French. The response was faint but didn't sound angry.

'Is that your wife?' she asked, as he got behind the wheel of the car.

His expression was unreadable. 'No,' he said curtly. 'My mother.'

Ellie winced. It was no wonder he was offended, but how could she have guessed someone's age from that distance? And what was someone *his* age doing living with his mother, anyway?

They drove towards Vence, onto the main road that Ellie had chosen to avoid on her first bicycle ride and in the opposite direction she had taken to go to Tourrettes-sur-Loup, in silence. An increasingly awkward silence.

Ellie decided she had to break it.

'My name's Ellie,' she said, finally. 'Ellie Gilchrist.'

He didn't shift his focus from the road. 'I'm Julien,' he said. 'Julien Rousseau.'

'Pleased to meet you, Julien.'

Her automatic response drew a huff of sound from him that was almost amusement.

'Thank you for doing this,' she added. 'I realise it must be very inconvenient.'

'It's my lunch break so it's not interfering with my work. I suspect you would have only had another accident if you'd tried to take the dog in your basket.'

Ellie didn't respond. He had her pegged as a complete nuisance, didn't he? Someone who had put his son in danger because her property had inadequate fencing. Someone who couldn't ride a bicycle safely and ran over dogs. Someone completely incompetent.

'He may have a *puce*. The vet will be able to find out who he belongs to.'

'A... what?'

'A *puce*. A small electronic device. I don't know its name in English.'

'Ah... a microchip?'

'*Oui. C'est ça.*'

It was Julien who broke the next silence, albeit reluctantly, as they got caught up in traffic entering Vence.

'Besides... I think I owe you an apology,' he said. 'I was not very polite when I first met you.'

The sound Ellie made was somewhat strangled as she changed her mind about agreeing with him too readily.

'I was... worried about my son.'

'I understand... I was worried about him, too, when I saw him so close to the donkeys.'

'The donkeys are very gentle. Theo adores them. That was why we started looking after them. Gave them names.'

'You gave them names?'

He nodded. 'Coquelicot and Marguerite.' He slid a sideways glance towards Ellie. 'Because of the flowers.'

She must have looked blank. 'A *marguerite* is a daisy,' he added. 'I forget the word for *coquelicot* – I must be losing some of my English. The flower for remembrance?'

'A poppy?'

'*Oui. C'est ça.*' Julien nodded. 'Poppy.'

'Daisy and Poppy,' Ellie echoed. 'Cute names.'

'They are French donkeys.' His tone was a reprimand. '*Coquelicot* and *Marguerite*.'

'Mmm.' Ellie wasn't going to argue. 'Did you know the

previous owner of the property?' Her tone was tentative. It felt disloyal, in a way, to be asking about someone who had caused her mother obvious distress.

Julien shook his head. 'We moved into our house less than a year ago. We were told that your house had already been empty for some years. Nobody knows where the donkeys came from.' His sideways glance was vaguely accusatory. 'I didn't know that the property was for sale. There was no sign.'

'It wasn't for sale. It belonged to an uncle I'd never met. He died recently and my sisters and I inherited the property. I'm staying here long enough to get it tidied up, and then it will go on the market.'

His grunt in response sounded approving. Because his nuisance neighbour was only temporary? Ellie wasn't really offended. He might not like her, but he was going out of his way to help her right now, wasn't he? It was a relief to be with someone who could speak her language and... okay... she had to admit that his accent was a delight to listen to.

'Where did you learn to speak such good English?' she asked, as he took a turn that went downhill, past a sign that advertised the municipal swimming pool.

'I spent some years in England at boarding school. I also went to university there. Before I came back to go to medical school in France.'

'Oh... you're a doctor.' So that explained why he looked as if he knew what he was doing checking a small boy for injuries. It also explained why he had been concerned about the graze on her elbow. That it had been a purely professional interest in her wellbeing felt disappointing for some reason.

What wasn't disappointing was that Julien took charge as they entered the veterinary clinic. She would have been totally lost trying to communicate, so she just stood to one side, listening to the flow of conversation. The two men seemed to know each other and had a lot to talk about initially, but then things got quieter as the vet examined the dog and used a scanning device to try and locate a microchip.

Julien didn't interrupt the conversation or examination to translate anything for her, so Ellie waited patiently at one side of the consulting room until she found herself the object of attention from both men.

'The dog does not have a *puce*,' Julien told her. 'And the clinic knows that there's no room at the local rescue centre because they had reason to speak to them about another dog earlier today.'

'Okay.' Ellie nodded. 'Is his leg broken?'

'No. Sprained, probably. And he has a badly bruised paw.'

He exchanged a meaningful glance with the vet. 'Christophe has already exhausted any means to care for a dog like this with the one they had earlier. He says that most vets would suggest that the kindest thing to do would be to euthanise him.'

Ellie's jaw dropped. '*Kill* him? Because he's got a bruised paw?'

'He's old,' Julien told her. 'Possibly more than ten years. And he's clearly been homeless for some time. He's too thin and he's very dirty.'

Ellie looked at the dog. He was certainly scruffy, and he had the saddest eyes she had ever seen. He was still shivering, but he'd been surprisingly brave during the examination and had only whimpered rather than yelped when his leg had been touched. And he hadn't shown any signs of wanting to bite anyone.

The dog looked back at her. He had odd ears, she noticed. One stood straight up but the other was bent and it almost made it look as if he was winking at her.

She looked at the vet, who smiled sympathetically. She looked at Julien, who shook his head in response.

'I do not want a dog,' he said. 'My life is complicated enough as it is.'

Of course it was. He was juggling parenthood with a demanding career. He lived with his mother. He'd been caring for a pair of donkeys that didn't even belong to him.

'There must be someone who would want him,' she said. 'I can't have a dog, either. I won't be here for very long.'

Julien spoke to the vet again. A short exchange that ended with a shrug by the vet.

'It's possible that a space at the rescue centre, or with one of the people that help by fostering unwanted pets, could become available before long. A notice could be put up here to see if someone wants to offer him a home but... in the meantime, there's simply no way the clinic can help.'

Ellie looked at the dog again.

If she didn't do something, this small, unhappy animal might not be alive for much longer. She couldn't let that happen. Not just because she felt responsible for what was happening. It was more that she had an opportunity to cheat death, even if it was only for a scruffy, homeless dog.

'Fine,' she said. 'I'll take him. Until somewhere more permanent can be found.'

The vet was smiling again, this time with approval. Relief, even? He hadn't wanted to put the dog down, had he? Christophe might have ended up taking him home himself if Ellie hadn't offered, but it was too late to find out now. He was speaking to Julien quietly.

'He's not going to charge you for this appointment,' Julien translated. 'He'll bandage the leg, and you can bring him back to be checked next week if he's not a lot better.'

Ellie smiled back at the vet. '*Merci beaucoup*,' she said.

'You'll need some food, I expect?' Julien added. 'And maybe a collar and lead? They have supplies here for sale.'

Ellie nodded slowly. She might not have enough cash on her, but hopefully she could use her bank card here. Not that she'd expected to see her savings eaten into quite like this, but, now that she'd made the decision to save this sorry little dog, what else could she do?

And it wasn't just the dog...

Ellie suppressed a sigh as she followed Julien out of the consulting room. She'd been up early this morning to clean out the trough in the olive orchard, emptying it of water and scraping out the sludge at the bottom before refilling it. She had been pleased with the quality of water the donkeys now had to drink, but she was now remembering other things Fi had mentioned.

'Could you please ask if they have what is needed to treat donkeys for worms?' She asked Julien. 'And possibly the name of a farrier? My sister tells me their feet will need attention.'

'They are fine for the moment. I had Christophe check the donkeys when we first realised that nobody was looking after them. They had their feet trimmed not so long ago.'

'Oh...' Ellie bit her lip. 'We owe you some money, then.'

Julien shrugged. '*De rien* – it doesn't matter. You didn't know. And it was my choice. As I said, Theo was very taken with the animals when we arrived, and... and he needed something to be happy about.'

He turned away to speak to the girl behind the reception desk and she pointed towards large bags of dried food against a wall. Ellie was left out of the conversation again, but she wasn't even thinking about dog food.

What had happened, she wondered, to make Julien's son so unhappy at such a young age?

And then she remembered those big brown eyes looking up at her. The fear in them that had become something very different. Something like surprise and then trust. Hope, even.

That single word that had pierced her heart.

Maman.

* * *

They put the dog onto the back seat of the car again for the ride home, but, before they had even pulled out of the veterinary clinic's car park, he squeezed through the gap between the front seats, climbed onto Ellie's lap and then lay down, pushing his nose into the crook of her elbow.

Julien's sideways glance came with a half-smile. 'I think he knows who saved his life.'

'I'm only going to be looking after him for a bit. Until I can find him a proper home.'

'Of course.' But Julien sounded unconvinced.

'I can't *keep* a dog,' Ellie insisted. 'I don't even know how long I'm going to be here. Or where I'm going to live when I go home again.'

The weight of the dog in her lap wasn't unpleasant, and she could feel his warmth as they sat in a small traffic jam on the narrow street leading back into the centre of Vence. It was reminiscent of the kind of comfort a hot water bottle could provide when you had a tummy ache. The smell of the dog was less pleasant, however, as was the chill of a small, damp nose against the bare skin of her arm, but when Ellie moved, so did the dog, which released more of its dubious odour. Giving up, she stroked the wiry fluff on his head.

'He needs a name,' she murmured. 'I can't keep calling him "the dog".'

'Everyone needs a name,' Julien agreed.

'Like Coquelicot and Marguerite.' Ellie was pleased with herself for remembering to use the French version of the donkeys' names. 'You're good at naming animals. What would you suggest?'

Julien shrugged. The traffic was moving again towards the main square of the town. 'Spot?'

Ellie ran her hand across more of the spiky, tousled hair on the dog's body. There were ginger patches, including his ears, but the rest was a dirty white colour. 'He hasn't got any spots. He's very scruffy. Maybe that would be a good name.'

Julien seemed to be concentrating on the available space to pass a large van that was double-parked beside the square. Looking up, Ellie was astonished by how different it looked to when she and Laura had wandered past. There was no room for any quiet games of boules to be happening today. The square, bordered by huge, leafy plane trees, was crammed with people around stalls with bright awnings of red and yellow and white.

'What's going on?'

'It's market day, that's all. Every Tuesday and Friday. They'll start the evening markets for summer soon, though, on Tuesdays, and they go on till about the end of August.'

Ellie could see trestle tables laden with produce as they drove slowly past. Clothing hung from rails at other stalls. People queued for what looked like hot food. A bright blur of flowers as she turned her head to catch a last glimpse. A lot of the people didn't look like tourists. There were women wheeling trolleys as if this was a normal shopping day for them, and many people had brought their dogs. It was a vibrant scene – the beating heart of a genuine French market town.

'I'll have to come one day. It looks fun.'

Julien increased his speed as soon as he reached the main road.

'I hope you still have time for lunch,' Ellie said.

'It doesn't matter. I can pick up some socca at the market. My clinic is on the other side of the Grand Jardin so it's very close.'

'Socca?'

'A local speciality. Try it when you go there. It's very good.'

Julien got out of the car when he stopped beside her gate, coming round to open the door for Ellie. It was a courteous gesture that made her feel curiously shy.

'Thank you so much.' She held the dog in her arms as she climbed out of the car, and then she looked up to meet his gaze. 'For everything.'

He held her gaze for a heartbeat. And then another, which made it suddenly more significant than it should have been. It was Julien who looked away first.

'I'll get the food. For... what did you decide his name was?'

'I don't know. He's a French dog. He needs a French name. Like the donkeys. What's the French word for scruffy?'

'*Miteux.*' Julien opened the gate and waited for Ellie to enter first. 'But it can also mean... what's the word... sleazy, perhaps?'

'That's no good, then. He doesn't look sleazy.'

'Maybe Leo? Or Max or Felix?' Julien put the bag of food down beside her front door. 'Pascal?'

'Hmm... I like that. Pascal it is.' Ellie crouched to put the dog on the ground. Her elbow was starting to ache. Not that she was about to admit that. The pain wasn't just reminding her of the fall; her skin was remembering the touch of Julien's hands as he'd checked her arm to make sure she hadn't broken it. If she showed any signs of being in discomfort, he'd probably consider it his duty to check it again, and that didn't seem like a good idea.

Maybe naming this dog wasn't such a good idea, either. She

was only going to foster the animal for a short time, not adopt it, and giving it a name seemed to suddenly give it more of a personality or something. But her gaze was caught by the small, scruffy face as she released her hold. The personality was already there, wasn't it?

Pascal was sitting, his bandaged leg held carefully above any contact with the ground, looking up at her with his lopsided ears. And then his tail moved from one side to the other and back again, in a slow, slightly tentative, wag – as if he had been considering *her* personality as well and was showing his approval. Or possibly that he had forgiven her for running him over.

'Oh... he's actually quite cute.' Ellie couldn't help smiling as she straightened. 'Did you see that?'

Julien was smiling, too. A real smile, this time, and... what a smile it was. It gave him crinkles at the corners of his eyes and dimples in his cheeks.

'*Très mignon*,' he agreed. 'Very cute.' Again, he seemed to hold her gaze for a millisecond too long and, again, he was the one to look away first. Abruptly. His smile was fading even before he turned.

'I have to go,' he said, his tone crisp. '*Bonne après-midi*, Ellie.'

Ellie blinked at what seemed like a curt dismissal. He was a curious mix, this man. There was kindness there, that was certain. How many people would give up their lunch break to help a stray dog? Or look after someone else's donkeys because his son was fond of them? He had a smile that could light up his face and an intensity in his eyes that did something odd to her body, but he could shut those glimpses away as swiftly and conclusively as pulling shutters closed on a window.

Leaving her feeling like she was missing the view?

She watched his car sail past his own gate. Maybe he'd been

annoyed by realising that he'd lost the chance to spend any of his lunch break at home.

Or maybe he was simply annoyed by her. Because she spoke English. Or because she had inadequate fences on her property. Or perhaps because she was intruding on the life of a person who preferred his privacy.

She looked down at her newly named companion, who was still sitting there, gazing up at her. The moment he caught her gaze he wagged his tail again, and a little bit more of Ellie's heart melted, albeit reluctantly.

'We kind of need to say a proper thank you, don't we, Pascal?' She opened her door. 'Maybe I could get those fences fixed.'

It would be the gesture of a good neighbour but more than that as well – it could be seen as a symbol of respecting boundaries and privacy. Both physical and personal? Reassurance that Ellie wasn't about to cause any more disruption to Julien's life than she already had, perhaps.

That he was safe?

Aye... As safe as she intended to keep herself.

6

—————

'Here...' Ellie was carrying bowls to where Pascal had curled up in the corner of the living room, near the French doors. 'Here's some food and water. I'm sure you must be hungry and thirsty.'

Pascal didn't move. He wasn't looking at her either, but Ellie knew he'd been watching her every move since she'd brought him into the house. Perhaps he needed to feel a bit safer before he accepted the food and water?

'Would you rather I left you alone to eat?' She paused to consider her new housemate. 'A blanket or something for you to sleep on would be more comfortable than those hard tiles. Or maybe an old towel, because that would be easier to wash and you kind of smell bad.'

It felt slightly ridiculous to be speaking aloud to an animal like this, but Pascal's upright ear twitched as if he was listening.

'You need a bath,' she added. 'But I can't do that while you've got your leg all bandaged up. If I took the bandage off, I wouldn't know how to put it back on properly.'

Julien would know how to do something like that...

Ellie gave herself a mental shake. Good grief... It was only about fifteen minutes since she'd seen her neighbour, but she was already inventing an excuse to see him again? Like a teenager with some sort of crush?

'You'll just have to smell bad for a while,' she decided aloud. 'But I'm not going to sleep anywhere near you. I reckon it's time I sorted out a bedroom.'

Armed with a broom, dustpan and brush, and a piece of fabric large enough to protect her from breathing in any horrible dust, Ellie climbed the narrow stairs. She knew, from the brief glance when she had first explored this house, that the two bedrooms were almost identical in shape, with sloping, beamed ceilings, wooden floors and whitewashed walls. She knew that Mike the plumber had shooed out the bats and covered the broken pane on the window in the second room with a piece of wood, but she wasn't ready to open the door that she'd slammed shut so decisively on that first night. Besides, the room with the larger bed had a window looking out onto the garden and the view beyond, so it would have been her first choice anyway.

The iron frames and vertical rails of the bed were painted an odd green-tinged black, and two horizontal brass rails at the top of both the head and foot ends were separated by circles and moulded columns that were thinner versions of the ornate knobs on the four corners of the bed. They were tarnished and dusty. The mattress was covered by what looked like very old lace. Probably handmade, Ellie thought, as she inspected the intricate flower patterns separated by cobwebs of tiny chain stitches, so it would need careful washing by hand. The feather-filled duvet looked clean enough but smelt musty, so Ellie carried it outside and threw it over one of the smaller lemon trees to bake in the afternoon sun for a while, even though she knew she wouldn't be in need of its warmth at night.

She stripped the sheets off as well and took them down to the washing machine in the basement. Laura had bought a new set of sheets in the supermarket the other day, but whoever had purchased the linen for this cottage clearly had a taste for something more luxurious, and these felt like pure cotton with a high thread count. How lovely would they feel, freshly washed, bleached by sunshine and infused with the scent from the lemon trees as they dried?

Ellie took the feather pillows outside as well, but throwing open the shutters and windows to air the room was the best that she could do for the mattress. At least there was no evidence of it being inhabited by mice. It was also inner-sprung and didn't look too ancient. Had this been her uncle's room? A chest of drawers with an inset pattern of branches and leaves, a marble top and very ornate handles offered no clues because it was empty, the drawers lined with old wallpaper. A huge mirror with a brass surround crested by a fleur-de-lis motif startled Ellie as she looked up while closing the drawers.

Taking a second glance, she tried to figure out what felt so different. The wispy curls escaping from her braid were familiar enough, as was their fiery colour. Her hazel brown eyes still looked sombre. So did the set of her mouth. Were her freckles more obvious, perhaps due to the first kiss of the French sunshine? Or was it that she just hadn't looked at herself properly for a long time because she didn't want to see a reflection of how she felt.

Maybe that was the difference.

She *felt* different.

Not like someone who was dragging herself through the remnants of a life and struggling to find a way through broken dreams. Here, she was someone with a purpose. A house to coax back into life. Cleaning and renovations that needed to be done and a terrace and garden to tackle after that. But first things first.

Ellie turned away from the mirror to find the broom she had propped in the corner and then started sweeping. Whatever pigeon population had been in here seemed to be long gone. The droppings were attached to the floorboards like concrete, and she had to use the back of the broom to break them free before they could be swept up. The effort required was enough to let her know that her elbow had definitely been bruised as well as grazed.

And that was enough to remind her, again, of Julien's touch on her body as he'd examined her injured arm. Only, this time, it wasn't just confined to the memory cells in her skin. Ellie could feel it somewhere much deeper, down low in her abdomen. It took her a moment or two to recognise the sensation that only ever came from physical attraction. Because it was so long since she'd experienced it?

No. More likely because she hadn't expected it. And didn't want it. She had chosen to stay in France because she needed to rediscover herself. *By* herself. For heaven's sake, a big part of why she was at such a low point in her life was down to the last man she had allowed to share it. She wasn't about to make another mistake like that.

She also wasn't about to let Liam sneak back into her thoughts. As Laura had reminded her, she was well rid of him. It was probably quite timely, mind you, to remind herself that it was physical attraction that had started that whole train wreck of a relationship.

As a distraction from thoughts she didn't want to gain traction, Ellie attacked the floor with even more enthusiasm, holding her breath to avoid inhaling the dust, and she soon had too much mess to fit into the dustpan. On her first trip downstairs to empty it, she found that Pascal had moved from the corner of the living room. He was now lying close to the bottom of the staircase.

'Did you have some food?' she asked him. 'And water?'

She checked the bowls as she went outside to empty the pan under a lemon tree, but they seemed undisturbed, and that worried her a little. She didn't just have a property to spruce up, she had unexpectedly gathered some other beings to care for. Even if they were only abandoned donkeys and a stray dog, she had responsibilities to think about other than purely personal ones.

Surprisingly, it didn't feel like an unwanted burden.

Because this was a temporary situation? Because they were animals, rather than people? Or was it because they, along with this property, meant that she had to think about things other than herself?

When she came downstairs to empty the last of the mess she had scraped from the floorboards, Pascal got up and followed her, limping badly. Ellie slowed her steps, paused by the bowls and waited for the little dog to catch up.

'Water... See?' She stooped, wetting her fingers and then holding them out. 'You must be thirsty by now, aren't you?'

Pascal sniffed her fingers, and then, a heartbeat later, a pink tongue appeared and licked them. Thoroughly. While Ellie wiped her fingers on her jeans, he took another step towards the bowl, lowered his head and began to lap up the water. As she returned from the lemon orchard to find the little dog delicately extracting a single piece of kibble from the bowl and then crunching it between his teeth, she found herself smiling, a little bemused by how such a small thing could feel like a significant achievement.

That she had figured out how to work the washing machine was also very satisfying and, while the sheets were drying in the sunshine, Ellie took hot water, a scrubbing brush and a couple of old towels upstairs to finish cleaning the floor of the bedroom. By the time she was done, the linen was dry, and she climbed the stairs yet again to remake the bed. This time, Pascal followed her. He didn't come into the bedroom but positioned himself by the door to see what was going on.

The new fitted sheet from the supermarket, with its elasticated corners, would have been easier to put over the mattress, but she knew how delicious this crisp cotton would feel against her skin tonight, especially with that faint hint of lemon that she caught as she shook out and smoothed the sheet. Folding and tucking in the 'hospital' corners she, along with her sisters, had been taught at a young age gave her a pang of homesickness, so she took a photo of a neat corner and texted it to her mother.

> I remembered, see? Just as good as a fitted sheet.

> Proud of you

> But hope you're doing more interesting things than housework all the time.

Ellie considered her reply, her gaze roaming until it caught on the small face peering around the edge of the door, a black nose resting on a bandaged paw. Should she tell her mother that she had run over a dog that she was now fostering? Or that she had had a disturbing moment of finding her less-than-friendly neighbour attractive?

> It's all good

> I'll have a glass of wine and enjoy the sunset when I've finished making the bed. It's gorgeous here.

That seemed to finish the conversation, and Ellie decided later, as she fluffed up the pillows and stuffed them into their clean cases, that maybe she shouldn't have added that last sentence. This inheritance, and the reminders of a former life, had been obviously unwelcome for her mother. Upsetting, in fact. Although the catastrophic disintegration of her marriage and the struggle to raise her young daughters alone had been decades ago, so surely it should have lost its power to derail such a hard-won contentment, if not happiness?

Homesickness was laced with something that felt like a warning. A bad relationship or an inability to escape the past could really taint the rest of your life, couldn't it? Ellie was finally realising how close she had been to letting that happen to herself. Her family had been right to be worried about her.

They'd been right about something else, too.

What had been intended as simply a two-day break in another country had unexpectedly become life-changing. And maybe Laura telling her to start standing on her own two feet had provided the motivation to dig deep and find some determination and self-discipline. Perhaps that push had been exactly what she'd needed, because it was beginning to feel as if it was at least possible to start embracing life properly again.

And, even if it was only a possibility, it felt remarkably good.

7

_____

Ellie woke at first light the next day and lay there for a moment letting her skin remember the bliss of getting into this bed last night.

She'd had a bath, shaved her legs and then slathered them with moisturiser because she hadn't forgotten that, while freshly laundered sheets were one of her favourite things in life, having smooth legs definitely took the experience to the next level. Well... she _had_ forgotten, to be honest. Or perhaps she had simply pushed pleasures like that out of her life because they seemed too irrelevant or too self-centred or something.

She moved a leg to recapture the sensation of the crisp cotton, her heart missing a beat when she encountered an unexpected obstacle in the space behind her knees. Her head jerked up from the pillow.

'_Pascal..._ how did you get there?'

He didn't lift his head, or even open his eyes, but his tail thumped the bed slowly, and Ellie sank into her pillow again with a sigh.

'Dogs aren't supposed to sleep on beds,' she told him. 'Especially smelly dogs.'

Against the backdrop of a dawn chorus gathering more participants outside her open window, Ellie thought about what she was going to do with her day. It took a moment to decide what day of the week it might be.

'It's Saturday,' she finally said aloud. 'Because there was a market happening yesterday, and Julien said they only happen on Tuesdays and Fridays, didn't he?'

Saying his name aloud made it almost seem as if he was in the room.

Her bedroom...

Getting out of bed was the best way to step well away from that line of thought. Ellie lifted Pascal down so that he wouldn't hurt his leg.

'We've got a busy day ahead,' she informed him. 'After breakfast, we're going to have a go at that wall in the living room. There's no point in cleaning the floor if we're just going to make a whole lot more mess, is there?'

It didn't feel silly talking to a dog any longer. Even the use of the shared pronoun felt perfectly natural. The donkeys, as other living creatures, were all very well and quite likeable but they were out of sight most of the time. This new companion was right by her side. He had even snuck upstairs during the night to stay close, and Ellie liked that. By the end of that day she found that she was liking it enough that any hovering mist of loneliness at being in a foreign country by herself had virtually evaporated.

The only mist around her this evening consisted of particles of plaster that were everywhere. On her skin, all over her clothes and right through her hair. It wasn't finished by any means, but the reward of uncovering the stone was irresistible, and Ellie had barely stopped for anything more than a glass of water or a quick bathroom break all day.

'Why would they have covered them up with plaster?' Pascal hadn't seemed bored by the repeated question as more and more stones were scraped and then scrubbed. 'They're gorgeous.'

It was past time to stop scraping now, however.

'I need a bath,' she announced. Stooping to pat the dog, Ellie could feel the grit in Pascal's hair. '*You* need a bath, too. What are we going to do about that?' She straightened up with a grin. 'Reckon we need a glass of wine and a think.'

The terrace was rapidly becoming Ellie's favourite part of this property, even in its totally neglected state. She loved this view. She could let herself relax as her gaze rested on that endless horizon of the sea in the distance, enjoy the soft green of the forests, feel inspired by the towering rocks of the mountains and finally search out the glow of nearby lemons in the fading light.

The dark shape moving amongst the lemon trees at the far end of the orchard was decidedly more disconcerting, and she could feel her heart miss a beat. Had one of the donkeys escaped from the olive grove?

No. The shape quickly became human and, even before it was close enough to recognise anything, Ellie knew it was Julien. A faint alarm bell sounded in the back of her head, reminding her how disturbing it had been to feel attracted to her neighbour, but her heart was overriding the warning. After skipping that beat it was speeding up now, and perhaps it was an increase in blood flow that was creating a tingle that made it feel like her whole body was coming alive.

* * *

He'd never been this far into the neighbouring property before. The only time Julien had even crossed the fence on the other side of the olive grove had been that evening he'd rushed to snatch Theo out of Ellie's arms.

Fear had morphed so easily into anger, hadn't it? And he'd directed that anger at a woman who hadn't deserved it. Ellie Gilchrist had a gentle soul. Maybe a part of him had recognised that the moment he'd seen her cradling his son, but he hadn't wanted to see it. Hadn't wanted to find her attractive in any way.

But he hadn't been able to forget the way she'd been so determined to save the life of that scruffy little dog yesterday. He'd seen the moment her heart had truly been captured, as well, in the expression on her face when the dog had wagged its tail.

That smile...

He'd stopped himself from going to see her last night even though it had been easy to think of an excuse – like checking to see that the injury to her elbow hadn't been more serious than he'd thought, or that the dog hadn't chewed the bandage off its leg, perhaps. His latest motivation had taken him by surprise and seemed like such a good idea he'd started walking in this direction before he'd had time to talk himself out of it.

'Ellie!' He called out as soon as he saw her standing outside on her terrace in case she was frightened by someone approaching at this time of the day. '*C'est moi*... Julien.'

As he stepped closer, he thought he must have already frightened her. She looked like a ghost, standing there so still with her face as white as a sheet. The little dog was standing beside her. Pressed against her leg, in fact, as if he was preparing to defend his new owner.

'*Mon Dieu*...' Julien stopped as soon as he reached the flagstones of the terrace. 'Ellie... what's happened? Are you all right?'

She was holding a glass of wine, he noticed. Not something

that people normally did if they were injured or unwell. He peered at her more closely.

'What *is* that? On your face...'

'Plaster dust.' Ellie was looking embarrassed. 'Aye... I know. I'm filthy. I... erm... wasn't expecting a visitor.' Her eyes widened as her expression changed. 'Oh, my God... Theo hasn't gone missing again, has he?'

'No... not at all. He's with my mother. And *her* mother. She takes him to visit once a week, and it's a mountain village a fair drive away, so they always stay the night.'

It was fascinating to watch the change in Ellie's features yet again, as relief wiped out any anxiety. Unlike many women – unlike *Sarah* – she'd never be able to hide how she truly felt about something, would she?

'Oh...' He could see indecision now. And the note of shyness in her hesitation was unexpectedly appealing. 'Would you like a glass of wine?'

'I don't want to inconvenience you. I just came over because I thought of something. I might know someone who would be able to give the dog a home. My grandmother, in fact.'

'Oh?' Ellie didn't look nearly as pleased as he'd thought she might. She actually turned away. The dog turned with her, as if this was an exercise in obedience. 'It's no inconvenience,' she said. 'I'll get you a glass.'

He followed her to the door and then stopped again. He could see where the plaster dust had come from. Furniture had been moved to one side of this room, and a large section of the wall had been scraped to reveal the stonework beneath.

'You've been busy.'

'Aye...' Ellie was in the kitchen, pulling a cork from a bottle. 'The plaster was starting to fall off anyway. I was going to plaster it again and give it a fresh coat of whitewash, but I think I'd prefer to see the stone. It's beautiful, isn't it?' She came back and offered him a glass. 'I hope you like rosé. It's the only sort of wine I have at the moment.'

'*Merci*...' Julien raised his glass. '*Santé*...' He shifted his gaze back to the wall. 'I think you're right,' he said. 'The stone will look much better in its natural state.'

'It's going to take me a few days to finish the job.' Ellie shook her head. 'Come outside. You don't want to get this dust all over you. Pascal and I need a bath. I was just wondering how to do that when he's got that bandage on his leg.'

Again, Julien followed the pair. 'He's not limping nearly so much today. We could take the bandage off and see how he goes.'

There were wrought-iron chairs and a small table on the terrace, and the glow of the sunset was caught by ornate Moroccan metal candle holders. Rusty holders, Julien noted. And the weeds amongst the stone paving were brushing his ankles.

Ellie had noticed what he was looking at. 'One of my next jobs,' she told him as she sat down. 'Can you imagine how gorgeous it will be out here when it's done? With dozens of candles glowing and maybe some fairy lights in the tree?'

It was Ellie's eyes that were glowing right now, and it was impossible to look away.

'Champagne on the table,' she added. 'With two glasses. And... a wooden board with a wedge of some lovely cheese and bread and olives...'

She was painting a picture with her words. A romantic fantasy kind of picture. Suddenly, it was easy to look away, and the noncommittal sound that he'd intended to make came out sounding more like disparaging.

Not that Ellie seemed to have noticed. 'How rude of me,' she exclaimed. 'I've got some cheese. And bread... I don't know about you, but I'm starving. We didn't get round to stopping for lunch.' She was on her feet again. 'I'll be right back.'

It would have been rude to refuse, but Julien felt less than comfortable at this turn of events. He took a long swallow of his wine. He'd only intended to speak to Ellie for a minute or two and then get on with his evening. There was a stack of medical journals on his desk that he wanted to read, and he always looked forward to sinking into his favourite leather chair in his library on the quiet Saturday nights when he had the house to himself. Sitting outside amongst weeds and rusty garden ornaments, having an *apéro* with his foreign neighbour had certainly not been on his agenda.

Curiously, however, as he drained his glass Julien realised he didn't want to leave just yet.

What was it about this woman that was so intriguing?

She must have splashed some water on her face while she'd been in the kitchen, because he could see her skin between fainter streaks of dust – and some of those charming freckles that were an echo of the colour of her eyes. The smile on her face was satisfied as she placed a wooden board on the table.

'There we go. I'll just get the wine.'

Ellie vanished again, the dog still her shadow. Julien looked at the board. How could someone make such ordinary things, like thin slices of baguette, a round of cheese, a handful of olives and what looked like ham rolled into small cigar shapes, look like the most appetising array ever?

She held the wine bottle up as she returned, a silent invitation to have his glass refilled. Julien didn't say anything, either, as he held his glass out. It was definitely too rude to refuse this hospitality now that Ellie had gone to so much trouble. Besides, he still hadn't apologised properly for the way he'd treated her the night they'd met. He waited until she was sitting and had taken a sip of her wine. And then he waited a bit longer, to let her use a slice of bread to scoop up some of the soft Époisses that was starting to ooze into a puddle on the board and then eat it. When she tilted her head back a little and closed her eyes with the pleasure of the taste, he found himself smiling. Finally, he waited until she opened her eyes again.

'I didn't explain properly,' he said quietly. 'About why I was so impolite when we first met. My mother had gone to have dinner and see a movie in Vence with a friend, so I was at home by myself with Theo. It's not often that she can do something for herself like that, because I work at a hospital as well as in my clinic, and I am often on call. That can be difficult without someone else to help care for a child.'

Ellie was nodding. 'My mother's a nurse. She used to work in a hospital, and sometimes her shifts meant that my oldest sister had to look after us. She didn't get to go out with her friends nearly as much as most teenagers.'

'I wasn't on call that night,' Julien continued. 'But there was an emergency at the hospital. One of my patients had a serious allergic reaction to a medication, and there was only a junior doctor available to manage the situation. It was very tense, and I needed to concentrate, so I took the call away from where Theo was watching a favourite cartoon. He was wrapped in his special blanket and almost asleep, so I didn't want to frighten him with my tone of voice as I gave rapid instructions.'

Again, Ellie nodded. Her gaze was fastened on his face as she listened. Her focus made it seem as if what he was telling her was the only important thing in the world in this moment. As if *he* was also that important?

'I can't say how long I was on the phone,' he admitted. 'For a time, it looked as though the child might stop breathing. Might die, even. It took too long, anyway, and when I went back to get

Theo, all I found was his blanket that had been dropped on the floor. I looked for him in the other rooms and I called out for him but...' He touched his chest, 'I could feel, in my heart, that he wasn't in the house, and that was when I began to panic.'

Ellie's eyes had widened. It was almost as if she could feel that panic herself. Again, despite no evidence, he had the feeling that Ellie had an intimate understanding of what it was like to be a parent.

'And then I saw that the back door to the garden was open. It is almost always locked, that door. I didn't know if Theo had opened it himself and gone outside, or perhaps someone had come inside and taken him, so I was even more afraid. And then...' Julien paused and took a deep breath before saying any more. 'Then I saw him in your arms, and you looked as though... as though something was terribly wrong... and... and I heard what Theo said to you...'

'He thought I was his mother.' Ellie's voice was no more than a whisper, and Julien thought he could see a shimmer of tears in those huge eyes.

'His mother died,' he told her. 'When Theo was not even a year old.'

'Oh...' The intake of breath was a shocked gasp. 'I'm so sorry, Julien...'

He liked the way his name sounded on her lips, with that Scottish lilt that made it sound very different to the way it did on the lips of someone who'd attended a prestigious school in London, as Sarah had. He liked the way she was still so focused on him, and it was easy to see that her instant distress on his behalf had darkened that golden brown of her eyes.

'She must have been so young. What happened?' Ellie pressed her fingers to her mouth as her expression morphed into chagrin. 'But that's none of my business. I do apologise.'

A movement of Julien's hand deemed the apology unnecessary. 'It was a car accident,' he said. 'And yes, Sarah was young. Only thirty.'

'My age,' Ellie said softly. 'Or it will be, on my next birthday.'

The comparison was a timely reminder that he should go. That he definitely shouldn't be so intrigued by this woman. By the way her face was such an open book. By how much she enjoyed her food. Because he already knew she had a big heart.

'She was also English.' His words were cool.

'I'm Scottish,' Ellie said. But then she shook her head as though dismissing the reminder as irrelevant. 'You had your first baby,' she added. 'That's such a tragedy. Poor Theo. He must miss his mother so much.'

Yes... it was tears making her eyes shimmer.

'*Carrément*...' Julien didn't translate the murmured word, assuming that the sound of agreement would be enough. He didn't trust himself to say any more right now, in any case. Would Ellie be this sympathetic if he told her the truth? That his beautiful English wife had been with her lover in that car. That she'd been leaving him. That he sometimes thought that Theo was better off because he never needed to know that his mother had been so willing to abandon him.

No... He'd already learned that it was easier to protect yourself if you kept an emotional distance from other people and he had no intention of getting close enough to anyone to reveal the truth. It was preferable to let them assume that he had suffered a life-shattering tragedy by having his beloved wife, and the mother of his child, ripped from his life. The spectre of an irreplaceable soulmate had also proved helpful when he wanted to extract himself from a friendship that was threatening to become too intense.

Oui... Ellie looked as if she was thinking about how devastated he would always be by losing the love of his life. A single tear escaped and rolled slowly down the side of Ellie's nose. The strength of the urge to reach out and catch that tear with his thumb caught Julien by surprise. So did her next words.

'I know how hard it is.'

He couldn't look away from her gaze. 'You've lost someone?'

Ellie nodded. 'My baby,' she whispered. 'My son.'

So he had been correct. She was – or had been – a mother herself. He could hear the catch in her throat as she took a breath. His own breath had caught in his throat.

'His name was Jack, and he died when he was just six months old.' She must have seen the shocked question in his eyes. 'It was a cot death. Unexplained. He... he just went to sleep and never woke up.'

She looked away from him. Took a deeper breath, clearly collecting herself. Then she took another sip of her wine. 'It's why I'm here,' she added, in a brighter tone. 'We found out about inheriting this house on the day that would have been Jack's first birthday. I think that's why my sister came up with the idea that we needed to see the property for ourselves, and my family decided it would be a good distraction for me.'

'And is it?'

'I think it is.' The slow smile that tilted the corners of Ellie's mouth was like a glimpse into what really mattered. 'I think I'm falling in love with this house. I *want* to love it, which is actually a big thing because I've avoided having feelings about anything. I didn't want to start loving something and then lose it, you know? But it feels okay to love this house. I want to bring it back to life.' She caught her bottom lip between her teeth. 'That sounds silly, doesn't it?'

'No.'

One word, but it covered a whole raft of what he already knew about Ellie. The ability to bring something – even a house – back to life would have to be healing after losing something so important to death. *Bien sûr...* that was why she had been so determined to save Pascal. He could remember the shock on her face at the suggestion of euthanising the little dog.

Even more clearly, he was remembering the look on Ellie's face the first time he'd seen her. Holding his son. She'd seen Theo asleep on the ground, and Julien knew how still and pale his child could look. He'd stood beside the cot and held his own breath on occasion, waiting to see the rise of that small chest, hovering in a space that was close enough to feel the claws of panic almost touching his skin. Ellie would have been sucked into that space far more easily having had the horror of holding her own dead child.

It was heartbreaking.

And he'd been so harsh with her.

Julien wanted to get to his feet. To take Ellie into his arms and hold her. To tell her that he was even more sorry now. That he understood. That he cared...

That was enough to stop him moving, because something else Ellie had said was striking a chord. That she hadn't wanted to start loving anything else that she might lose. He was even more firmly in that space. Apart from his professional concern for patients, Julien had no room in his life to care about anything new. He especially didn't want to care about a stranger. A woman. An *English* woman. Or Scottish. *Peu importe...* it didn't matter.

And okay... maybe he was finding this woman attractive, even when she was caked in plaster dust, wearing shapeless clothing and had crazy curls of hair escaping in all different directions. But being attracted – thinking about making love, even – was one thing; caring was quite another, because it might be only a step away from falling in love, and that was never going to happen again. Because he was never going to allow it to happen again. Julien emptied his glass in one swallow and then got slowly to his feet.

'I must go. I really only came to tell you about the possibility of a home for Pascal with my grandmother. It doesn't have to be now. It could be when you go back to Scotland.'

Ellie nodded. 'Thanks. I'll keep it in mind.'

'How long—' Julien cleared his throat '—are you planning to stay?'

'I'm not sure.' Ellie also got to her feet. 'There's an awful lot to do to the house, but I expect it will be just for the summer.' She smiled, as if it was a relief to have changed the subject so definitively. 'But it's kind of hard to know when summer ends here, isn't it? Compared to Scotland, it probably feels like summer for most of the year.'

Julien took a step towards the darkness of the path he needed to follow through the orchard but then paused as he turned his head. 'Our last evening summer market happens around the end of August. The schools go back after that, and it feels like summer is officially over.'

'That sounds like enough time for what I need to do here. And having a deadline is always a good thing.' Ellie straightened her back, her gaze drifting towards the house as if she was already making plans. 'I like it.' The way she nodded her head and spoke more quietly made it seem as if she was talking to herself. Making a promise?

'I'll stay until the last summer market,' she said.

8

The plaster dust turned out to be a blessing in disguise, having forced Ellie's hand in giving Pascal a bath. He was actually a much whiter dog than she'd realised, and, when she'd sent a photo home, the general consensus was that his genetic heritage had to include at least some West Highland terrier, which made him at least partly Scottish. Her mother even suggested that she could bring Pascal back with her when she came home.

'*A wee dog is good company,*' was all she'd said.

And Ellie had said nothing, partly because she hadn't wanted to say the first thing that had crossed her mind – that a dog was not a substitute child – but also because a part of her quite liked that idea. She had to admit she liked the weight of the small body against her legs as she slept and the way she woke to find Pascal gazing at her, as if the world would only start turning once she was ready to begin her day. Julien's grandmother could always find another dog to rescue if she needed company, couldn't she?

The trust Pascal had already bestowed on Ellie was tested somewhat the first time she'd put him into the basket on the front of the red bicycle and wobbled up the slope of the road, but, only a day or two later, he was sitting up straight with his nose tilted to catch the breeze as they came down again. There was no room to put any purchases into the basket, but Ellie had solved that problem by purchasing a small backpack. It was becoming routine to buy fresh carrots along with any other supplies and then to find the donkeys waiting by the fence in the mornings, at the end of the track she took through the lemon grove. Pascal kept a respectful distance, a pale shape against the trunk of the nearest tree, as he waited for the next part of their day.

There was so much fruit on the trees that some branches were in danger of breaking, and Ellie had snapped a few ends off yesterday morning and taken them inside. She'd discovered a collection of old, white jugs when she'd cleaned out the crockery cupboard, and she'd filled the largest one with the branches of bright green foliage and their ripe fruit. Today, she'd taken the time to gather the daisies and a few poppies that were still flowering amidst the long grass around the house, and those had gone into a smaller jug.

The results of both floral efforts were so pleasing that Ellie stood there for some time, simply admiring them. The confidence that she could capture the simplicity and beauty of the arrangements with her paints or pencils was no more than a passing thought, but the fact that it sparked interest was... well, it was quite exciting, to be honest. As if another part of her was trying to come back to life, like the part that had woken up when she'd realised the effect that Julien's touch on her skin had created. That it was possible to be attracted to a man again – something she hadn't considered remotely likely ever since Liam had walked out over a year and a half ago.

It was too hot to feel like moving too soon after a now-favourite lunch of ham and cheese baguette, and the terrace was pleasantly shaded by the trees. Pascal was sound asleep amongst the weeds at her feet, but Ellie noticed his ear twitching repeatedly, irritated by the leaves of what looked like a type of dandelion. She grasped the weed and pulled, finding it came out easily from the mix of sand and soil between the flagstones. Pascal, showered by the debris that came off the roots of the plant, got up with a sigh and moved further away. Ellie kept pulling at the weeds. She'd waxed lyrical to Julien the other night about how gorgeous this terrace would be when she'd cleaned it up properly, so maybe she'd better make a start, in case he came back again another evening.

Within a few minutes, Ellie found herself sitting on the flagstones, the weed-pulling an automatic task as her thoughts drifted back to that evening and the... intimacy of them both sharing such personal revelations. Her first impressions of Julien had been so wrong, hadn't they? No wonder he'd reacted the way he had when she'd spoken to him in English. The tortured look on his face, when she'd sympathised with how much Theo must be missing his mother, made it more than clear that the person who really missed Sarah was the husband who'd adored her enough to want to spend the rest of his life with her and create a family.

And Sarah had been English!

What a shock it must have been for Julien to hear Ellie speaking her language. It would have dragged him back to the time the unthinkable had happened and he'd lost his wife, and their son had lost his mother. To make it even more of an emotional bombshell, he'd found her with *their* son in *her* arms.

But, in a way, there was something rather poignant about that now that they both knew how much they had in common. They both knew what it was like to suffer a huge, personal loss in their lives.

It was impossible for it not to have brought them closer.

Ellie let herself sink into the warmth that that thought gave her as the pile of weeds grew taller. It felt inevitable that an internal warmth like that was going to morph into something rather more intense, but the flicker of attraction was not unpleasant. Her cells might be waking up from a hibernation deep enough to have felt like death, and that was okay. Rather nice, in fact.

And perfectly safe. Even if Julien had moved on enough to have female companions, it seemed most unlikely that he would be looking for a replacement for his wife. Ellie, of all people, knew that grief had its own timetable and couldn't be rushed. But, on the other hand, the way he'd been looking at her the other evening, the way that attraction had increased so suddenly, had made her think that she was seeing a reflection of what she was experiencing herself. That he was, at some level, attracted to her. What if...?

Ooh...

Did she dare follow that thought?

Okay... what if they *were* both attracted to each other? Was she anywhere near ready to follow that through? Would it be such a big deal if she was? It wasn't as if she was going to be here very long. It would be nothing more than the kind of holiday romance a lot of people had when they went to, say, Spain for a couple of weeks, or on a cruise.

What if a total absence of any kind of intimate physical connection with another human might be having far more of an effect on her wellbeing than she'd realised? Ellie hadn't been kissed since the moment she'd discovered she was pregnant and Liam couldn't get away fast enough. She hadn't felt the touch of a man's hand for over a year and a half. Had the dark space of mourning the loss of her baby been made worse because that had been missing from her life?

Dipping her toes into a romantic pool might be the perfect way to take a really significant step forwards in living her best life again, and how happy would that make her family? If nothing else, it was definitely not unpleasant to toy with the idea.

Dusting off a bit of sand from her bare arm, after she'd thrown another handful of weeds onto the pile, made Ellie's thoughts a lot less coherent because all she could think of now was the touch of Julien's hand on her arm when he'd checked her grazed elbow, and the curl of blatant desire in her belly was sharp enough to make her catch her breath.

He'd said that his mother took Theo to visit his grandmother once a week and that they always stayed the night, which meant that there would be another occasion before very long when Julien was on his own in his house on the other side of the olive grove. If she saw him again, she could suggest another glass of wine on the terrace, perhaps. Dinner, even? He'd gone too soon to even taste that wonderful cheese last time.

If he did come back, Ellie wanted this terrace to look fabulous. Despite the heat, she pulled at the weeds even faster. She'd brush all the cobwebs off the candle holders later and put candles on tomorrow's shopping list. She might need to go into Vence to find an item like that, but... Ellie straightened after throwing her next handful of weeds, stopping to count days on her fingers. Tomorrow's Tuesday, she realised market day in the main square in Vence. Didn't Julien say that his rooms were nearby and that he often bought something for his lunch at the market?

A local speciality that he recommended she should try because it was good. What was it, again?

Oh, aye... Socca.

* * *

The sign was hand-painted, standing on a counter in front of a white-domed pizza oven on a trailer:

Socca
2.50 € la part
Le plateau de 5 parts, 12.00 €

Visible flames and the glow from the wood fire within suggested that, while this might be a great way to make a living in the depths of winter, it was hot work for the middle of a summer's day. It was also obvious that this local speciality was popular. A little before midday, having left her bike in a stand on the edge of the square, Ellie joined the queue in front of the socca stall. Pascal, on his lead, was sitting almost on top of her feet, which made it a little awkward to edge closer to the front of the queue.

She could see more of what was happening as they got closer. The owner of the stall was working hard, with two wide, shallow cast-iron skillets taking turns in the oven. When one came out, it was left to steam on the counter for a minute while he prepared the next, scraping out anything stuck, brushing the base with oil and then ladling three scoops of a thin-looking batter into the pan before pushing it into the open mouth of the oven and turning his attention back to the already-cooked platter with its browned top and slightly blackened edges.

He set out five paper plates and then used a square piece of plastic to divide up what looked like a huge, slightly overcooked pancake. A large triangle went onto each plate, and then a second one to make a generous portion. Ellie watched the interactions with customers, noting that most chose to have salt and pepper sprinkled on the top and that some had their plates wrapped in foil but others took them with no foil and began eating them straight away.

'*Une part?*'

'*Oui. S'il vous plaît.*' Ellie smiled and nodded, handing over her money and hoping that she'd chosen the right response to a rapid-fire question she hadn't understood. She was picking up a few words and phrases of the language now, but the speed with which French people spoke and any background noise or distractions made it so much harder.

'*Le sel et le poivre?*'

Ridiculously pleased with herself for picking up the word for pepper, Ellie nodded and smiled again. '*Merci.*'

'*Et vous mangez tout de suite?*'

This was another moment to nod and smile, and Ellie figured out the meaning as she received her plate with no foil. She followed the example of people she had been watching and moved to a bench seat to eat her lunch straight away, and, by the time she sat down, she could feel the weight and heat of the socca coming through the plate despite the layer of paper serviettes she'd been given. She tied Pascal's lead to the end of the bench, and he sat directly in front of her feet this time, his expression much easier to understand than the French she'd been listening to around her.

'Might be a bit hot for you,' she told him. 'I'll test it, shall I?'

She tore a piece off the edge of one of the triangles and put it in her mouth. It *was* very hot. It was also unexpectedly delicious. Crispy on the outside, soft in the middle and delightfully savoury – salty, peppery and smoky. It was burning her fingers as she tore tiny pieces off, but it was too good to wait and let it cool.

Ellie actually forgot the little dog waiting hopefully at her feet as her senses were hijacked. It wasn't just the taste and smell of the socca. She was listening to the bustle of the busy market in front of her and taking in everything she could see. They were mostly food stalls in this part. A dreadlocked woman presided over a large vegetable selection. There was a long table with baskets of differently flavoured olives, a smaller one that sold eggs and one in between that had huge wheels of cheese. Further away, near the socca oven, Ellie could see a stall that had great slabs of nougat, and beyond that was a bright splash of colour from rows of flowers and plants. Everything was shaded by the red and yellow canvas awnings, and it was crowded. Men, women, children and dogs. Tourists and locals. There was music, as well, with a man playing jazz on a saxophone near the flower stall, and the sound was a soothing background to the kaleidoscope of things to look at: people shopping, tasting samples of food, meeting and greeting friends and often stopping to talk, creating an obstacle that others negotiated with the ease of practice. The queue at the socca stall had doubled in size, and Ellie felt lucky she'd joined it when she did.

Lucky to be here at all, in fact. This was another one of those moments like she'd had in St Paul de Vence when she'd been captured by the mosaic flowers in the cobbled streets. The new culinary experience of the socca would always be an integral piece of this place and this moment in time, and it was sealing itself into Ellie's memory banks as something she knew she would treasure for years to come.

It wasn't just Pascal's desire to share her food that Ellie had forgotten. When she saw the tall figure emerge from the crowd to walk towards where she was sitting, she remembered that Julien worked nearby. The surprise of seeing him was enough to make her heart skip a beat and then increase its speed – the same way it had when she'd recognised him coming towards her through the orchard that evening. Ellie could feel the beat of it in her throat.

'Is it good?' Julien's eyebrows were raised as he sat beside her on the bench. 'You like socca?'

'*So* good... I *love* it.' Ellie's smile felt too wide. 'It's my new favourite thing. I may have to come here every market day.'

'I came to get some myself, but that queue... *pfft!*' The sound of dismissal was so French it made Ellie's smile get even wider.

'Please, have some of mine while you wait.' She held out the plate. 'The pieces are much bigger than I expected.'

Julien hesitated, and, oddly, Ellie found herself holding her breath. Maybe because he hadn't eaten any of that hastily prepared platter the other evening, if this offer was also rejected, she might need to take it as a sign that an offer of something more significant than food would not be welcome. And, because she had that thought in her head, when he did reach out and tear off part of the remaining triangle, it felt almost like a silent conversation. The way he held her gaze as he folded the socca and put it in his mouth felt like an acknowledgement that any attraction here was, indeed, mutual.

It was only a heartbeat of time, but Ellie knew it had the potential to change her world dramatically. Until the next beat of time when the moment was completely shattered. As was the whole ambience of the market with the shrill sound of a woman's scream, so close that Ellie shot to her feet, the paper plate slipping, unheeded, to the ground. She stared in the direction of the sound, trying to make sense of the movement of people. Some were frozen to the spot, also staring. Heads were turning and some people were running towards the disturbance, which appeared to be beside the olive stall. And then, as people moved, Ellie saw the hunched figure of a young woman with long, dark hair. She was picking something up from the fine gravel of the town square. A small child in a summer dress, whose head fell back as she was lifted, her limbs also unnaturally floppy.

In the split second it took to process what was happening, Julien was already moving towards the woman and child with long strides that closed the distance so fast Ellie barely had time to drag in a breath. He seemed perfectly calm, she thought, as he reached out for the child. The woman was too distraught to speak, but other people seemed to be trying to tell Julien what they'd seen. More than one was pointing at baskets of olives in the shade under the trestle table – within easy reach of a passing child.

She saw the way he was checking to find out whether the child was breathing, and then he was covering her mouth with his own to try and deliver a life-saving breath. Once, twice... Ellie's gaze was fixed on the little girl, unconsciously stepping closer as she desperately watched, willing that small chest to rise.

But, even from this distance, she could see that it wasn't moving.

The child was as still as a stone.

Exactly the way Jack had been that dreadful morning.

Ellie was holding her own breath now, and her cry was silent.

'Please...'

9

'*Appelez le SAMU!*'

Julien knew that, as soon the nearest stall holder got through on the phone and told the *Service d'Aide Médicale Urgente* they were coming to a child who was choking, they would send one of their advanced life support units, staffed by a doctor and nurse or highly trained paramedic. In the meantime, he knew he had only a short window of time to save this child.

He scooped the little girl into his arms and turned her face down with her head lower than her chest, flattening his hand so that he could apply back blows that might be effective enough to dislodge whatever was blocking her airway. But when he tried another rescue breath, it was clear that the air was not reaching her lungs.

He could still feel a pulse in her neck, but that window of time had just become smaller; unless he could clear her airway, her heart would stop beating. Julien got to his feet with the child still in his arms. He could get to his consulting room in less than sixty seconds, and he had all the equipment he might need there, like a defibrillator to manage a cardiac arrest, special forceps to try and remove the obstruction, and even the surgical items that would enable him to create an airway in the child's throat if necessary.

The concerned crowd of onlookers parted as he told people to tell the ambulance crew where to find him, and, as he started moving, Julien noticed two things. One was that the mother of this child was standing very still, frozen with shock. The other was that Ellie was also watching – a reflection of that shock on her own face.

'Come,' he told Ellie, as he strode past. 'Follow me and bring the mother. She needs to be with her daughter.'

As did Ellie, he realised. Both these women needed to see that everything possible was being done to save a young life.

Assistance was also valuable, with his clinic being empty of staff for the lunch break. He laid the girl onto the white sheet covering the couch in his consultation room and called Ellie closer.

'I need you to do chest thrusts,' he told her. 'Like this.' He took her hand and placed it on the child's chest. 'Push with the heel of your hand. As fast and as deep as this.' He held her hand under his as he demonstrated. 'It will help to keep her heart going and might dislodge the obstruction.'

It also made it possible to step away and find and prepare the equipment he needed. He chose a curved blade to snap onto the handle of a laryngoscope and clicked on the light to make sure it was working. Then he reached into a cupboard that had emergency kits and found a small-sized pair of Magill's forceps. Like an elongated and angled pair of scissors with blunt, circular ends, these forceps were specifically designed to be used in airways to guide the placement of tubes or to remove foreign objects.

He slid a rolled-up towel beneath the girl's shoulders to tilt her head into the best position.

'Stop for a moment,' he instructed Ellie.

The bright, focused light from the laryngoscope, with its blade holding the tongue out of the way, was his best chance of seeing and removing a foreign object. And he *could* see something... As he picked up the forceps and felt his entire body tensing as he focused, Julien could feel a similar tension radiating from Ellie. She was holding her breath. The mother was just as still. The crew from the ambulance were stepping through the door, and they, too, stopped so as not to disrupt his task. It felt like the entire world was holding its breath.

He slid the forceps into place and closed them carefully, but as he tried to pull the small, slippery object clear, it escaped the grip of the metal. He could hear his own breath escape in a hiss of frustration at the same time, and he glanced up, knowing that the SAMU doctor would be ready to step in and perform the surgery needed if this didn't work. The instant nod he received told him that his silent message had been received.

One more try...

As his gaze brushed Ellie's on the way back, it was his turn to receive unspoken communication.

You can do this... Please...

It took only a split second, and then Julien was aware of nothing but the need to guide the forceps into place, take the time needed to get the best grip possible and then to pull very slowly and very carefully until... *yes...*

The sound of the child taking a first, desperate gasp of air in too long a time happened at the same time he lifted up the forceps holding the large, firm green olive. The cry from the child's mother was almost lost in the sound of other voices as the emergency crew stepped in to help provide oxygen and assess their young patient to ensure she was breathing adequately.

She was doing even better than that. She was regaining

consciousness, at first confused and frightened, but then she saw her mother and reached out with both her small arms, and her first word cut through every other sound in the room with piercing clarity.

'*Maman.*'

* * *

Oh, God…

That word. With all its connotations and, on this occasion, the overwhelming relief that was more than enough to bring tears to Ellie's eyes as she stepped further back to allow the medics to do their job. She could understand nothing of what was being said, but it was obvious they were comforting the mother as they did things like listening to her daughter's chest. Everybody was clearly very happy with the outcome of this crisis, but it appeared that they were going to take both mother and child away – presumably for a more thorough check in a hospital – so, in what seemed like a very short space of time, Ellie found herself alone with Julien.

She needed to say something. To tell him how incredibly impressed she was with his ability to save a life. That she knew exactly what it would mean to that young mother, but she knew she would burst into tears if she tried to say anything. And maybe she didn't need to, because the expression in Julien's eyes suggested that he understood completely how she was feeling about the crisis she'd just witnessed.

More than that, even. That, because he knew about Jack, he understood how it had made her feel when she'd been holding his son in her arms and he'd opened his eyes and said the same thing this child had said when she'd woken?

Maman.

Mammy.

Julien didn't say anything, either. He took a step towards Ellie. And another. And then he simply took her into his arms and held her. She could feel his warmth. The beating of his heart against her cheek. The strength of his arms as he tightened his hold when she did burst into tears. And still he said nothing. He didn't move – as if he had all the time in the world to hold her. To comfort her. To let her know that he understood.

To tell her that it was okay? That she was safe?

Ellie wanted all the time in the world. She didn't want to move. She'd never felt quite this safe in her life and... it was a feeling that was so powerful it was impossible to pull away from it. Far more powerful than any physical attraction she'd discovered to this man, in fact.

You could fall in love with someone who could make you feel this safe.

For a heartbeat, all Ellie wanted was to sink into that feeling. To let herself start falling, even, knowing that the process would be anything but painful. The triggering of an internal alarm might have been entirely silent, but it was palpable enough to make the hairs on the back of Ellie's neck prickle.

Safety was only an illusion, wasn't it? It could get snatched away in the blink of an eye and, the more you believed in it, the more shattering it was when that happened. Falling in love might be deliciously painless, but losing it could tear your heart into a million bleeding pieces.

Ellie couldn't allow it to happen again. She was nowhere near ready to even think about it happening. She felt as though she wouldn't survive another loss of someone she loved, so she couldn't afford to trust any impression of safety. With an enormous effort, she pushed back. Julien released her instantly, but

Ellie made the mistake of looking up as she stepped out of his embrace.

Dark, dark eyes. So full of compassion that she was caught all over again. He did understand. Of course he did – he'd lost someone he loved that much, too. And, while that connection of shared loss was a layer of attraction quite apart from anything physical, the combination – in the aftermath of an emotional rollercoaster of fear and relief – was proving to be an irresistible force. Was Julien also aware of it?

He seemed to be. His expression was changing as he held eye contact, and then his gaze dropped to her lips, and Ellie knew he was thinking about kissing her.

And, heaven help her, she *wanted* him to.

So much.

Too much.

She'd avoided feeling anything this strong in a very long time. She'd known that panic would be close behind, and she could feel it now, snapping at the heels of any thoughts of letting herself give in to a longing this powerful.

She had to escape.

'I have to go,' she said. Inspiration sprang from sudden anxiety as she turned swiftly away from Julien. 'Oh, my God... I left Pascal tied up to that bench.' She was already halfway to the door. 'I hope he's still there.'

10

––––––––––

The relief of finding the little white dog curled up and asleep in the shade beneath the bench had been oddly overwhelming. Ellie hid her face against his scruffy curls for a moment or two while she regained her composure, but she still needed to swipe a tear away as they headed back to where she'd left her bicycle.

The relief of getting back to what was her safe space in this temporary new life was also huge. Walking into this small, solid, golden-stoned house felt like walking into a mother's hug.

It felt like home.

But it was a home that was very different to anything Ellie had ever known before. This was nothing like the cluttered bustle of growing up with her sisters, with the sound of laughter interwoven with the sharp tones of yet another dispute between the girls or the authoritative tone of Mam, or Laura, taking control. It was nothing like the frequent silences of living above that rented studio with Liam, either. Not the creative kind of silences when they were both immersed in the art that had been a huge part of the attraction between them, but the ones where it was dangerous to say or do anything because eggshells would get broken, and it would always, always be Ellie who got hurt by the shards of those shells.

This room, with the golden glow of stonework, the rich red of the floor and the tantalising streaks of sunshine finding their way through the bars of the shutters, offered a silence that was imbued with a sense of... peace, that's what it was. Ellie crouched to detach Pascal's lead and then found herself sitting on the cool tiles, wrapping her arms around her knees and closing her eyes as she breathed in exactly what she needed in this moment: an opportunity to step back from the emotional rollercoaster, with the drama of that choking child and that desperate desire to stay in Julien's arms, and to find a calm place in her head – and her heart. To sink into the stillness that hung in the air in here and seemed to offer the promise that everything would be okay. That *she* was going to be okay. That life would feel like it was really worth living again. All she needed to do was to breathe in the sense of peace that was the result of a unique alchemy of components that she was only just beginning to identify, and to take one step at a time.

She'd felt it before, without being able to identify it, when she'd known that she needed to stay here, because she'd felt the possibility of finding the person that was still buried in the aftermath of soul-destroying events. She'd felt the magic of a particular combination of elements, and it was a magic that could shift its shape. It could be a glow of inspiration. This sense of peace. Hope for the future.

The polite scratch of a small paw against the doors to the terrace got Ellie to her feet, but she could still feel that stillness, even as she began moving again.

'I think it's going to be okay,' she told Pascal as she let him outside. 'What do you think?'

He was heading towards the nearest lemon tree in the orchard but paused at her questioning tone and looked back. Ellie knew it was hot and that Pascal was panting, but it looked, for all the world, as if he was smiling at her. As if he agreed.

She was aware of another wash of that relief she'd felt seeing him still tied to the bench, curled up safely asleep beneath the seat. How awful would she have felt if he'd somehow become untied and run away in fear? That anxiety had been disturbing because it suggested that she might still be capable of feeling the warmth and protectiveness and relief that only came when you cared deeply about someone or something. When you loved them. And that would mean that Pascal had somehow found a chink in the armour she was relying on to protect her heart.

That didn't ring the same alarm bells that the thought of falling in love with Julien had, however, because this was just a small dog, not a person. And it was only temporary. She would be leaving France and Pascal would have a new home with Julien's grandmother. Surely it was safe enough to enjoy something that would only be a memory soon? Like so many things that were making it feel that this tiny patch of the earth was custom-made to heal her soul – the soft light and colours, the musical drift of the language and the taste and heat of socca straight from the oven. Pascal was a part of that mix in his own right, and she would never forget sitting in the square with him today or being in this tiny orchard with this deliciously fresh scent of lemons. The more memories like this that she could hold close to her heart in the future, the better.

Ellie followed Pascal further into the orchard, stooping to pick up some of the fruit. Maybe she was also searching for enough distraction, for more distance, to prevent her thoughts returning to the drama of the market.

'I'm going to make some lemonade,' she decided. 'And lemon honey. And... what else can you do with lemons?'

The Internet provided an answer to that question when she and Pascal curled up on the sofa to escape the intense mid-afternoon heat.

'Limoncello,' she read aloud. 'A sweet, smooth drink that can be sipped straight from the bottle you keep in the freezer will bestow the tang of lemons to sparkling water and can be shaken into cocktails that will be a favourite party tipple. Wow... that sounds quite a bit more exciting than lemonade, doesn't it?'

Pascal's tail thumped against the worn leather of the sofa.

'It says that the lemon skin is the most important ingredient, and they have to be the right sort of lemons, like the ones that grow on the Amalfi Coast in Italy. I'm guessing we have the right sort of lemons here – we're not that far from the Italian border, are we?' Ellie lapsed into silence, making a mental list of other ingredients she'd need to buy, like vodka and sugar.

She needed to write this recipe down so she didn't have to go online to find it again, and the only paper she knew she had was that sketchbook she'd left in the suitcase Laura had sent over. It was only natural to pick up the case of pencils that had been packed with it, to save her hunting for another writing implement. As a teenager Ellie had had a bit of a passion for calligraphy, and it was a skill she'd used ever since if she had something like a card to write. It was too hot to do anything too energetic in the way of house or garden improvements at the moment, anyway, and taking her time to add the curls and flourishes to these words should be an enjoyable distraction.

Pascal had taken up the spot on the sofa beside her again, and Ellie was getting quite used to sharing what she was thinking aloud.

'Six ripe lemons, freshly picked. Well, that won't be difficult, will it?'

Ellie brushed her fingertips over the familiar texture of the cold-pressed watercolour paper. A4 size was rather too big to write a recipe on, but she was reluctant to cut it into smaller pieces. Instead, she found herself planning a way to fill the entire space in a way that could turn it into something special, which could become a gift. Picking up an HB pencil, she softly outlined a title, thought about how much space would be needed to write the list of ingredients and the instructions and then began to sketch a lemon tree branch in the centre of the paper. She had the vase on the kitchen table to glance at as she drew the fruit and stalks, and the leaves with that little curl at the end. Her case was full of watercolour pencils and the brushes she used to activate them with water, and they were the perfect medium for this subject. By the time Ellie was happy with the shading of the yellows and greens she was using and she'd added the smudge of darker marks and lines of small imperfections, she'd almost forgotten about the text she wanted to add, but it was a welcome change to switch to a calligraphy pen and write with the kind of focus that produced letters to rival the neatness of a digital font.

She knew the recipe off by heart by the time the afternoon light was softening into evening, and she had been so immersed in what she was doing that it was still filling her mind as she wandered outside. The percentage of alcohol in vodka was not something Ellie had ever taken note of, but 95 per cent sounded rather a lot. She needed to go to the *bricolage* shop again because she needed a couple of bottles, firstly to put the lemon rinds and alcohol together to shake occasionally for a week, and then to filter the addition of the syrup before leaving the concoction for another three weeks until it was ready to drink.

It would be nearly a month before she could taste it.

A good chunk of the time she had available to finish reno-vating the house. Laura was thinking of coming back for a weekend about then, to check on progress and take photographs of anything that might be ready and suitable for the advertising campaign. Ellie needed to make another list. Not ingredients this time, or the steps of a recipe, and there would be no reason to illustrate a description of the work still needing to be done on the house and garden. It would be a waste of time to make a list like that into an artwork.

An artwork...?

Ellie found herself standing very, very still. With her eyes closed. Because that was what she had done with the recipe, wasn't it? For the first time since Jack's death she had lost herself in the process of creating something beautiful. It had snuck up on her, disguised as a practical task to record information she needed, and perhaps it had been her need for distraction from any thoughts of a child who nearly died or a man who could potentially steal her heart that had led her back to doing something she'd thought could never provide satisfaction. Or pleasure.

Maybe she hadn't wanted to find that satisfaction, let alone any pleasure.

Because she didn't deserve it?

Because she had failed as a mother and been unable to protect her precious baby even as he slept so close in his bassinet, right beside her pillow.

No wonder it had been overwhelming to find that Pascal had still been tied safely to that bench today. She'd almost witnessed another mother facing the loss of her child and... and she'd felt the touch of being held in someone's arms.

Feeling protected.

Safe...

It was all too much, and whatever peace she'd found in coming home to this house was suddenly shattered. Ellie didn't want to feel protected. She didn't want the warmth of being cared for that much. Or of car*ing* that much. Because she didn't want the fear that came with it. She could never face the grief of losing it again, and the only way to stay completely safe was to avoid the risk.

She opened her eyes. She picked up that sheet of paper with its soft colours and beautiful words, crumpled it into a ball and dropped into one of the half-glazed pots beside the fireplace so that it was out of sight. She had to blink hard to clear the tears that were gathering, but Ellie knew that if she let them start falling now, they might never stop. She tried to focus on what was right before her eyes, to bring herself into the moment and escape both the past and any fear of the future, and she found herself staring at the floor. At the hexagonal tiles that Mike had called *tomettes*. She was noting the range of shades of terracotta and the cracks and chips and wondering if they had always had such a matt surface or whether they had just been neglected for a very long time.

The afternoon heat still hung heavily in the air, but Ellie's need for a task that could keep her entirely in the moment overrode any reluctance to engage in physical effort. Within a very short time, she had a bucket of hot, soapy water, a scrubbing brush and a pile of old towels. She was ready to scrub. One tile at a time, if necessary, and she would keep going until every single one of them was as clean as she could possibly make it.

Despite how often she had swept this floor, there was enough grime caked onto the tiles to make it necessary to replace the water in the bucket again and again. When the scrubbing brush proved inadequate for the task, Ellie switched to a pot scourer. Her knees hurt from kneeling on the unforgiving surface, her fingertips turned into prunes from being wet for so long and she had curls of her hair stuck to her face with perspiration. The dust from where she had been chipping away the plaster covering on the stone wall added an extra layer of dirt – and maybe it would have been more sensible to have waited until that renovation task had been completed – but she wasn't going to stop, because this was helping.

This was the safest thing she had done all day.

She could allow herself to care about how clean a collection of ancient tiles was. To care about bringing an old house back to life so that it could be sold more easily and relieve her family of a burden they didn't need or want. What Ellie couldn't do was to allow herself to care too much about someone else's child who'd nearly died. About a small dog that was going to go and live with someone else in the near future. And, maybe especially, about a man who'd reminded her of what it felt like to be held.

And cared for...

* * *

'So... what did you think?'

'About what?' Laura sounded as though she had the phone on speaker. Ellie could hear the shuffle of papers and the scratch of a pen that suggested her sister was multitasking as she took this call.

'About the photos I sent. The floor.'

'Oh... right. Those old tiles.'

'*Tomettes*. A really traditional flooring in France. Sometimes they're square, but they're almost always hexagonal in Provence. I scrubbed them yesterday, and today I went and found a special polish for them in the *bricolage*.'

'The what?'

'*Bricolage*. A hardware shop.'

'Ah... No wonder that's a word I never added to my vocabulary.' Laura gave a huff of laughter. 'I have zero interest in DIY.'

'Can you see how shiny they are now?' Ellie was holding her

phone over the tiles. 'It's amazing what you can see when you look closely. The variation in shading is astonishing.'

'You've done a great job. I like the stone wall that's getting exposed, too. I think it's about time we took some photos and started the advertising campaign.'

'But there's still so much to do.' Ellie found she was fighting a wave of something that felt like alarm. 'I've still got a huge list. I've got Mike the plumber who's said he'll come back soon with a builder friend to look at all sorts of small jobs like repairing that shutter. I haven't started on the front garden, and the glazier hasn't even been yet to put in the new window upstairs. It's not ready. It might take weeks longer.' It suddenly struck Ellie that she was nowhere near ready, either. She didn't want to even think about the house being sold yet. About having to leave. 'There's a boundary fence that needs fixing as well.'

The boundary fence between herself and Julien...

Okay, maybe that task would be better left for as long as possible.

'That's okay. We'll just photograph the bits you've done. I need a meeting with Noah, anyway. We're making good progress on the brochure, but there are some things I want to see for myself.'

'Like what?'

Ellie wasn't listening properly, however. By shifting her gaze just a fraction, she could see those pots by the fireplace. She knew that crumpled ball of paper was still in one of them, a reminder that she had been irresistibly drawn back to doing something that she loved. Something that was a part of her and not simply a way to make a living.

'Like the Rosary Chapel in Vence that Matisse considers to be his greatest work,' Laura said. 'There's a mosaic work in the cathedral done by Chagall, and did you know that one of Vence's claims to fame is that it has the smallest cathedral in France?'

'No. I didn't know that.' Ellie's feet seemed to be moving without any instructions from her brain, taking her towards that set of pots. She pulled the crumpled ball of paper from the pot and put it on the table so that she could smooth it out.

'So—' Laura cleared her throat, signalling a brisk change of subject. 'There's a good reason for me to pop over, just for a day or two. I'll let you know when I've scheduled it. There's a useable spare bed in the house, isn't there?'

'Mmm... well, there's a bed, but it's very small.' Ellie could feel a knot of anxiety forming in her belly. She hadn't been in that room again since she'd slammed the door shut. If Laura wanted to use it, she'd have to force herself to go in there and clean it up properly. 'The window needs fixing, too,' she added hurriedly. 'And there's just a board there to keep the bats out at the moment. I'll give Mike a call tomorrow and see if I can speed up the glazier coming.' She cleared her throat. 'Do you want me to clear that room out and see if I can buy a bigger bed?'

'No... don't do that. It's a good marketing move to have a room set up for kids.' But Laura's hesitation revealed that she understood exactly why it would be hard for Ellie to sort that issue. 'Don't worry about it,' she added, quickly. 'I'll sort that room when I come. I can always sleep on the couch,' she added. 'Or go back to that little hotel we used in Vence. In fact...' There was an uncharacteristically dreamy note in Laura's voice now. 'I think I might rather like to stay there again.'

Ellie let her breath out slowly. Maybe she should feel hurt that her sister didn't really want to sleep under the same roof, but she was too grateful that she wasn't going to have to deal with that room. She could already feel that unpleasant knot beginning to unravel.

'We do need to get the window fixed, though.' Laura sounded crisp and organised again. Back to normal. 'It would be great if you could find the time to have a go at that wilderness of a front garden, as well. I can see a great photo op with your bicycle propped up on the stone wall by the front door – maybe with a bit of the iron gate in the shot too. Just to make it a bit arty, you know?'

'Aye...' Ellie was smiling. Not at the thought of contrived 'arti-ness' in a photo, however. She had completely forgotten about the upstairs room because she was looking at her watercolour sketch of the lemon tree branch, with its leaves and fruit, and the care-fully crafted words that danced on the paper around it. To her surprise, it didn't feel threatening any longer. In fact, she liked the way it made her feel. As if there was a tiny piece of her own soul smudged into this crumpled sheet of paper, which was how she'd always known whether what she created was something she could be proud of.

'Anyway...' Laura's tone suggested the conversation was being wound up. 'I'll be in touch.'

Ellie was ready to go, too. 'I'd better get started on everything that needs doing before you arrive. I think I'm going to be a wee bit busy.'

'Can you manage? It's not going to be too much, is it?'

'*Au contraire*,' There was satisfaction to be found tossing in a French phrase. 'I think I'm ready for a bit more of a challenge.'

Because a challenge would mean less time to think about other things.

Like having to leave this place sooner rather than later.

Like handing over Pascal for someone else to look after him for the rest of his life.

Like Julien...

* * *

It was proving disturbingly difficult to stop thinking about her.

Julien knew he should apologise. Again. But not for being impolite this time – quite the opposite, in fact. He'd been too... warm? He'd held Ellie in his arms because the urge to comfort her had been overwhelming.

She was far more courageous than he'd given her credit for. When that choking child had recovered consciousness and cried out for her mother, Julien had been aware of a sharp pain in his own chest – as if his heart had cracked wide open, even though he knew perfectly well that that was a medical impossibility. It seemed as if he could share what Ellie had to be feeling in that moment. It made no difference that her own son had not been old enough to start calling her *Maman*; it was the meaning of the word and the darkness that would always be there for her, having lost something so precious.

It was the word that she'd heard from his own son when she'd been holding him in her arms. And, on top of all the huge emotions that were already there, the word had been a cry of victory for a small girl who had come terrifyingly close to death.

Ellie hadn't run from facing such a difficult situation. She'd embraced it. She could have coped with it all without any support from anyone else and, if he hadn't offered her that comfort, she probably wouldn't have cried in front of anyone. But he couldn't have *not* held her then. The urge to offer that comfort, the need to protect, had been as powerful as any he ever felt for Theo. Or Theo's mother.

The people he loved the most.

That said something about the attraction this woman held for him, which made it imperative he didn't get too close, but what had he done then?

He'd very nearly kissed her, that's what he'd done.

Merde... It was no wonder that Ellie had been so eager to get away from him. Why she seemed to have been avoiding him since then. Or was he avoiding her? The end result was the same, in any case, and was probably for the best for both of them, but it was frustratingly difficult not to be thinking about her. He'd caught glimpses of movement at the small house, and it wasn't just Ellie who was busy working there. He'd heard the sounds of hammering when he'd come home for lunch and the shouts of masculine voices. He'd seen the vans of tradesmen parked further down the road and, on one occasion, heard the drift of laughter that he could swear included the sound of Ellie's voice.

She was getting on with what she was here to do – bringing that old house back to life. And then it would go on the market to be sold and she would go back to Scotland and vanish from his life. Julien could forget about her. Perhaps he could also forget the shame that came with the knowledge that he'd come so close to taking advantage of a distressed woman. Nearly kissing her in a way that would have had nothing at all to do with comfort and everything to do with sheer physical attraction. Perhaps even more than mere physical attraction?

That was a disturbing thought.

He'd been blown away by understanding how courageous Ellie was and the glimpse he'd had of just how much she was capable of caring. She had a generosity of spirit that made her seem completely trustworthy, but, thanks to bitter experience, Julien knew better than to rely on his impressions when it came to trusting women.

He could, however, trust his instinct in feeling the need to apologise in some way. For his own pride, he wanted Ellie to know that he hadn't been trying to use a tense situation to try and seduce her into something she had no wish to happen.

Except...

There'd been a moment there. A long moment that was not only imprinted on his memory but, when he recalled it, also felt in his body as an odd tingling sensation that started in his gut and reached the very tips of his fingers and toes. It was not a sensation that he recognised, but it was not unpleasant. Far from it. It was like a mix of anticipation – excitement even – and... hope. For what, he had no idea.

Hope for the future, perhaps. For life in general and for the ability to trust again?

Just a moment. No more than the space of a few heartbeats, but it had been enough to see, or possibly just feel, something he hadn't expected to see.

Ellie had *wanted* him to kiss her.

And, if they'd both wanted it to happen *that* much, maybe it was inevitable that it *was* going to happen.

Maybe just once would be all that was needed.

To find out if there was a reason why it seemed so very important.

11

It was Bert the builder who suggested breaking the padlock securing the stable door of the shed in the front garden of La Maisonette.

He'd turned up with Mike the plumber to tackle the list of handyman jobs that needed to be done, and both men were in the kitchen as Ellie made a pot of tea to go with the lunch she was providing. Their attention was initially caught by the huge bowl of lemons on the table.

'I'm thinking of making some limoncello,' she explained. 'I just need to find out where I can buy a bottle of 95 per cent alcohol.'

'You'll have to go across the border for that,' Mike told her. 'But it's easy to buy in any pharmacy or supermarket in Italy.'

Ellie's breath came out in an amused huff at the idea of finding the time for a day trip to Italy. She led the way out to the terrace. 'It's just an idea.'

'I've got a mate who lives down south. I'll see if he's coming up this way and he could bring you some.'

They talked about selling the house as they ate cheese and ham baguettes.

'It'll sell fast,' Bert said. 'It's got a garage, which is a big plus on narrow roads like this one. Like hen's teeth around here, garages are.'

'It's just a shed,' Ellie said. 'The door is on the side, in the garden.'

Mike shook his head. 'I reckon that ivy on the road end is covering one of those metal tilt doors. Or maybe an old wooden one. It'd be worth uncovering that.'

Ellie laughed. 'Thanks. I'll add it to the list.'

'We could take a look inside while we're here,' Bert suggested. 'I've got bolt cutters. Big ones. They'd cut through that padlock like it was butter.'

'Only if you've got the muscle to use them,' Mike laughed. He flexed an undeniably impressive bicep. 'Reckon I'd better do the cutting.'

Ellie topped up the mug of tea on the wrought-iron table in front of Bert, who was half Mike's size and probably a couple of decades older. He was also a craftsman builder, and he'd just finished expertly repairing the broken shutter and stopping the basement door from catching when it was only half open. Ellie was more than happy with his work, and she smiled at him now.

'That's not a bad idea,' she said. 'I could get a new padlock with a key from the *bricolage*. It would be nice to have somewhere safe to store my bike outside, although I'm still not sure it's big enough to be a garage.'

'And it might have a fair bit of stuff in there already,' Bert warned. 'Sheds like that often get used for storage if people rent out their houses over summer.'

'I don't think this house has been lived in for a long time,' Ellie told them. 'But it might explain why I haven't found anything personal here. No photos or books or... I don't know...' She shrugged. 'Drawers full of letters or old birthday cards or whatever.'

'No time like the present.' Mike drained his mug of tea and grinned at Ellie. 'I'm getting curious myself, now. Shall we go and see if there's a family skeleton or two in the shed?'

Oh... he had no idea how close to the bone that phrase actually went. Did Ellie want to discover family stuff that had an unwelcome genetic link to her own family? In a way, it had been a relief not to find anything personal in the house, because it might have included a glimpse into her father's life and stirred up old memories best left undisturbed.

Except those memories had already been disturbed by the inheritance of this property from her father's brother, hadn't they? And the shed would have to be cleaned out prior to sale, anyway. As a bonus, this was a new distraction. Despite the energy she'd been devoting to the renovations, it seemed to be getting harder to keep her thoughts from straying back to Julien. To stop herself imagining what might have happened if she hadn't panicked and pushed him away so fiercely. To think about the path that a single kiss could have led them both down...

'Let's do it.'

Pascal got up from the shady corner he'd found under the tree and followed Ellie as she led the way through the house and into the front garden.

While Mike and Bert went to fetch the bolt cutters, she busied herself pulling ivy away from the door hinges and pushing aside any new doubts about whether this was a wise thing to do. For heaven's sake, the shed was probably empty.

It wasn't, of course. Why would anyone have used such a heavy-duty padlock to secure an empty shed? What was inside wasn't what any of them were expecting, however, and they all entered the shed to have a closer look.

It was a car. One that Ellie recognised, thanks to an ex-boyfriend who'd been a car fanatic.

'It's a Citroën, isn't it? A 2CV?'

'Sure is,' Mike said. 'In great condition, too.'

It was possibly the cutest car Ellie had ever seen. Bright red – almost the same shade as her bicycle, with headlights sitting on top of the front mudguards, like eyes.

'Be worth a bit,' Bert added. 'Even more if it still goes.' He opened the driver's door and climbed in. 'The key's in here.' He turned it but there was not even a sigh of response from the car. 'Dead as a dodo,' he declared.

'Prob'ly just needs a new battery,' Mike suggested. 'I've got a mate who's a mechanic. I could get him to come and have a look if you like?'

Ellie was tracing the slope of the bonnet with her fingers, leaving tracks in the thick layer of dust. Stroking the protruding headlight was irresistible, too. 'I don't need a car. I can get everywhere I need to on my bike.'

'What about the beach?' Mike was edging around the little car to get to the passenger side. 'Or a trip north to see the lavender and sunflower fields in bloom in a couple of weeks?'

Mike's enthusiasm was contagious, but it wasn't persuading Ellie to learn to drive on the wrong side of the road. Instead, his words were creating images in her head of picturesque scenes, like a field of lavender in full bloom, that Laura would be thrilled to include in her advertising of the house. Even this little car, washed and shiny and parked in front of the stone cottage, would be eye-catchingly charming. It could be included as a chattel, perhaps, in which case it would need to be in working order.

'If getting it going is as easy as putting in a new battery, it's a good idea,' she told Mike, turning away from the car. 'But I don't want to drive it.'

Her eyes were adjusting to the dim light that was such a contrast to the bright sunlight outside, and she could see garden tools like spades and rakes and hedge clippers in a corner, piled against an old hand mower. Beside the useful-looking tools was a set of shelves cluttered with objects and boxes, and there was an antique-looking rocking chair almost buried in piles of dusty books.

Personal stuff...

She drew in a deep breath. Did she want to go any closer? No... but her hand was reaching towards the closest pile of books.

It was Bert who broke the silence. 'Can't muck about in here all afternoon,' he announced. 'I've got that rotten board in the bathroom floor to replace, and if I don't get it done today, goodness only knows when I'll be able to get back. There's too many people who want jobs done yesterday at this time of year, what with so many Brits opening up their holiday homes.' He gave the car a last, lingering glance. 'Always liked these,' he nodded. 'Tin snails, we used to call them.'

Ellie picked up a book. It was just a book. Nothing personal. And how good would it be to turn real pages instead of scrolling to read on-screen?

'What does 2CV stand for?' she asked. She tucked the dusty book under her arm and stepped towards the open stable door before she changed her mind and put the book back.

'*Deux chevaux-vapeur.*' Mike's French accent sounded impressively good. 'Literally, two steam horses.' He was blinking as he followed Bert and Ellie out into the garden. 'About as much power as a decent-sized lawnmower – which is something else you could do with, come to think of it.'

They both watched Pascal disappearing into the jungle of

poppies and daisies still blooming in the long grass she hadn't had time to tackle yet.

Coquelicots and *Marguerites.*

The French words sounded in her head in Julien's voice and came with a knot of sensation in her belly that felt like... longing. Almost like loss?

Oh, help... Was all this effort in distracting herself from that attraction only making things worse?

Pascal suddenly emerged from the grass with a daisy between his teeth and a look of triumph in those dark, button eyes, and Ellie could feel a smile start with her lips but then spread all the way to her heart. She'd decided it was safe to love this little dog and embrace the joy he was bringing into her life because she knew it was only temporary. What she hadn't expected was that it would grow strong enough to bring *this* much delight. That, all on its own, was making a significant contribution to the gentle nudge life was giving her to get back to the business of making the most of what it had to offer. To start really living again.

And there it was...

The thought that she might be avoiding something that would take her much closer to embracing life properly. The thought that avoiding intimacy might be having far more of an effect on her mental health than she realised.

That it might be a big mistake to be running away from the opportunity to find out.

* * *

Ellie only remembered the book she'd found in the shed much later that day, after she'd spent the rest of the day wrestling with the ivy that was, indeed, hiding a tilting, garage door.

The book had no dust jacket, but embossed onto the fabric of its hard, blue cover was the silver outline of a small sailing boat heading into a sunset, and she had to turn the book to find the title on its spine. Ellie had never read the classic story of *Swallows and Amazons*, but she'd seen the movie a few years ago and remembered it was about a group of unsupervised children who were let loose to have a great adventure.

It felt like a sign. A 'thumbs up' for any decisions she was making that could expand the boundaries of her own freedom – like learning to drive on the other side of the road, if they did get the red tin snail going again? Ellie could remember the pride she'd felt when she'd got past the fear of the bats that first night to go up the stairs and find a blanket. In retrospect, that had been something so small, yet it had been a big step into feeling better about herself. About life.

Driving would be a much bigger step.

As for something as huge as being open to getting closer to Julien, even if it was only a kiss… well, that could be…

Big enough to change the whole direction of her life?

Her heart was doing that skipping thing again – missing a beat and then making up for it with a thump and a bit more speed. And, okay, there might be a bit of fear in that reaction, but there was also anticipation. Excitement.

Longing?

A longing to break through the protective barriers she'd been pulling around herself, even if it was just making a window so that she could see what was there?

This felt like an acceptable extension of giving herself permission to enjoy Pascal's contribution to her new life. Because, even if Julien was interested in exploring the attraction between them, it didn't have to mean that she was in danger of falling in love with him. Why would she, when she knew that it was only ever going to be a temporary thing?

It didn't even have to be a 'thing', in fact. Just a one-off experience might be all Ellie needed to answer the question of what difference it might make. To remind herself of how it made her feel. Just that kiss that she'd run away from might have been enough.

Not that she had any way of gauging any interest Julien might have in the idea. How could she, when she'd been avoiding him so successfully since that moment in his office? Perhaps *he'd* also been avoiding her?

No. Deep down, Ellie knew that he'd been about to kiss her. And that he'd wanted to just as much as she'd wanted him to. So maybe all she needed to do was to stop avoiding him, and let fate decide what would happen.

And maybe fate had already decided. Pascal suddenly leapt off the couch with a warning bark that made Ellie drop the book she was holding. She was on her feet by the time she saw the figure on the terrace, but she wasn't alarmed. She knew who it was.

Who *they* were.

Julien wasn't alone. He put his son gently down on the kitchen floor.

'Ellie? I need your help. Please?'

12

———

Perhaps it was the deep breath Julien took before he spoke again that made Ellie's heart sink so fast. Or the way he gave Theo's curly hair a reassuring stroke as the little boy turned to wrap his arms around his father's legs and bury his face.

Theo knew what was coming. Ellie knew what Julien was about to ask of her, and... she couldn't do it.

She couldn't believe he would even be thinking of asking her to do it, because... he knew, didn't he?

She'd been so sure, in those first moments when he had stormed into her life as she was holding Theo in her arms, that somehow, on some level, he'd known as well as she did that she shouldn't be trusted to keep a child safe. It didn't matter how many people had told her it wasn't her fault, there was a part of her soul that refused to believe it.

But Julien's voice was interrupting the thought even as it formed.

'My grandmother has had a fall,' he told her. 'She's being taken to a hospital in Nice by ambulance.'

'Oh, I'm sorry to hear that. I hope she's not badly hurt.'

'We don't know anything more yet. But I need to be there. My mother needs to be there.'

Ellie swallowed hard. 'Of course.'

'I don't want to take Theo. I know he was too young to remember being taken in to see his mother for the last time but just the smell of a hospital seems to be enough to scare him.'

He was already scared. Ellie didn't know how much English Theo could speak or understand, but the way he was clinging to Julien's legs made it seem as if he thought his only remaining parent was about to disappear forever, and it broke her heart.

She couldn't do this.

But she couldn't *not* do it, either. Julien needed her. He was asking for her help.

Ellie pushed a rising bubble of fear down as hard as she could. 'I'll look after him.'

This was another of those moments, wasn't it?

Like the one when she had been caught by the stone mosaic flowers and knew that she needed to stay in France. When she'd opened her heart to caring for a little stray dog. And, only minutes ago, when she'd decided she might be brave enough to learn to drive on the wrong side of the road?

This was another challenge she might look back on as a cross-roads that helped define the direction she was capable of taking for the rest of her life, but even though this one was so much bigger than any of the others – or possibly even *because* of that – Ellie wasn't about to let herself back down.

'I'll keep him safe,' she added quietly.

It was a promise to herself as well as Julien. She *could* do this.

The relief in his eyes was as palpable as a physical touch. There was admiration there as well, because he had to know that this wasn't easy for her. He crouched to talk to Theo, and she could hear reassurance in the soft, rapid stream of French. But

Theo's big brown eyes filled with tears, and his response was all too clear. He didn't want to be left alone with Ellie.

'*Noo, Papa. Prends-moi aussi, Papa. Prends-moi...*'

Julien's tone in response was firmer this time, and Ellie's heart broke all over again as she saw the way Theo bravely let go of his father to let him leave and stood there with his head down making no further protest.

'I'll get back as soon as I can, but I don't know how long it will be,' Julien told her quietly. 'If it gets late or you need anything, take him back to our house, and he can go to bed. I'll leave the kitchen door open.'

'Okay.'

'And...' It was obvious Julien wanted to leave as quickly as possible. He'd probably be running as soon as he got to the terrace, to get through the orchard and paddock and back to where his mother was waiting for him, but he hesitated for a heartbeat longer. Long enough to touch Theo's curls again. And then to touch Ellie's cheek. A brush of his fingers that was as soft as his words as he turned away.

'...*merci mille fois*. Thank you so much.'

* * *

So... here she was.

With the small boy who didn't want to be here with her.

The first child she'd held in her arms since she'd lost her own son, that evening when she believed she was saving him from being trampled by the donkeys. The child who'd called her '*Maman*'. And, while remembering that deepened the crack in her heart, it also gave Ellie strength, because making comparisons between Theo and Jack wasn't going to happen. Jack had only been six months old when he died. He'd never called her 'Mammy'.

He never would...

That sting would have been more than enough to reduce Ellie to a sobbing wreck not so long ago, but, right now, it felt as if she could simply step back from the thought. That she could pull a mental curtain so she wasn't even tempted to peer through that particular window. She had a small boy in front of her who might be astonishingly brave for his age, but he was still too frightened to lift his head and look at her. Ellie wasn't about to make this experience any worse for Theo by dissolving into tears herself.

'Are you hungry, Theo?'

Theo didn't move. Ellie opened the little fridge. He might not understand what she was saying but, if she showed him some food, perhaps he'd be interested? Pascal was certainly interested. Ellie smiled as her little dog trotted into the kitchen and sat down to watch what she was about to take out of the fridge. She knew he was hoping that cheese might be on the menu.

Theo's head moved as he looked at Pascal. Pascal looked up at Theo and wagged his tail. He wriggled closer and licked the boy's hand. Ellie heard Theo's gasp as he pulled it away, but, watching out of the corner of her eye, she saw him slowly lower his hand a moment later so that Pascal could lick it again. She remembered what Julien had told her when she'd thanked him for looking after the donkeys.

'Theo was very taken with the animals when we arrived and... and he needed something to be happy about...'

He needed something to be happy about again, didn't he? Ellie bypassed the cheese in the fridge and took out a couple of carrots.

'Shall we go and say "hullo" to Coquelicot and Marguerite? And give them a carrot?'

Theo finally looked up at her. His face was still very serious and his eyes wary, but he'd understood something.

'Coquelicot,' he said. And nodded. 'Marguerite.' He pointed at the carrots. '*Ils aiment les carottes.*'

Ellie understood something as well. Her French practice today had included things she liked. Like cheese and wine and lemons.

J'aime le fromage.

J'aime le vin.

J'aime les citrons.

She smiled at Theo. '*J'aime les carottes,*' she told him.

He stared at her, still wary.

Ellie changed her intonation into a question. '*Theo aime les carottes?*'

He was still staring at her, and he didn't smile back. But, after a long, long moment, he shook his head. Just one slow shake, but it was enough to delight Ellie. It might be on a very basic level, but they could communicate. That made it easier on more than one level, because it reminded Ellie that Theo was a little boy, not a baby. His hair was dark and curly, so unlike the red-haired genes that were strong in her own family. This was Julien's child, not her own.

She could do this.

Pascal helped. He came with them to feed carrots to the donkeys and waited while they collected some lemons on the way back. He ate the crust of Theo's bread that got dropped accidentally on purpose when Ellie offered her unexpected guest a bit of supper, and wagged his tail when Theo put out a tentative finger to touch his ear.

Time ticked on and the light was fading. Ellie wondered if she should take Theo back to his own house and put him to bed but, despite being curious about what it was like, the thought of being alone in Julien's house was daunting enough to keep her in her own safe space. Besides, she had a pair of dark eyes, remarkably similar to his father's, watching her carefully with no sign of their owner being tired.

There was no television in the house, but she knew how easy it would be to find something online that might entertain Theo, like a cartoon or a funny animal video. Reaching for her phone, however, she spotted something else. The paper and pencils she'd used to create her limoncello recipe. She put a blank piece of paper on the table in front of Theo, picked up a pencil and began a rapid sketch, leaving some exaggerated ears until last.

The little boy's eyes widened dramatically. '*C'est Coquelicot...*'

Ellie nodded, smiling. And kept sketching.

'*C'est Pascal,*' she told Theo, as she worked. It was an easy portrait to do, with that distinctive, droopy ear. 'Yes?'

This time it was Theo who nodded. 'Yes,' he said.

Ellie wondered if his mother had spoken English with him. Or maybe Julien was bringing him up to be bilingual. How tragic was it that he'd lost his mother at such an early age. And that Julien had lost the woman he'd loved so much. Ellie tore off another sheet of paper.

'Your turn,' she said to Theo. She piled the differently coloured pencils in front of him. 'What can you draw? Marguerite? Theo? Papa? Or shall I draw something for you, and you can colour it in?'

If Theo understood what she was saying, he gave no sign of it, but he did pick up a pencil and make a mark on the paper that turned into a laboriously drawn circle. Two uneven dots near the top of the circle came next, and then a wobbly line near the bottom. It was, almost, a smiley face.

Theo put his pencil down and looked up at Ellie.

'*Papa,*' he said.

'That's...' Ellie searched through the French phrases she was trying to commit to memory. '*C'est génial*,' she told Theo, with sincerity, because it *was* awesome.

And then Theo smiled at her for the first time, and it went straight to Ellie's heart and wrapped itself into something so tight it felt like it was cutting too deep, and she had to stand up and turn away.

Maybe she couldn't do this, after all.

Noticing the book that she'd dropped gave her a reason to move, and Ellie had learned long ago that moving physically was always the best way to get past a disturbing thought. As she picked up the old book, she noticed the corner of a bookmark poking out. It wasn't a traditional kind of bookmark: it was a rather dog-eared, small envelope that had several photographs inside it. Ellie pulled one of them out – an old black and white photograph of two young boys.

For a moment, Ellie forgot where she was and what she was doing. Was this what she'd both hoped and feared she would find in the shed? A link to the forbidden side of her own family? She turned the photograph over to find faded words written in ink, the date at the end too blurred to decipher.

Jeremy and Gordon. Cornwall.

Ellie sank onto the couch as she stared at the image again. The boys both looked younger than ten years old. They were sitting on a stone wall, grinning at whoever was taking the photograph, holding ice cream cones and looking happy enough to be on a summer holiday in Cornwall. One of those children was her father, but Ellie didn't know which one. She hadn't even known he had a brother let alone whether he was older or younger.

And yes... as she'd feared, there were memories trying to

surface, along with emotions that held streaks of pain. This was very different to the sore place in her heart that Theo's smile had just touched. This was so deep that it was like trying to capture a fragment of a dream that was already evaporating. On one level, Ellie didn't want to catch it at all. On another level, however, it felt like she had no choice.

Because there'd always been an element of something like doubt that Ellie had never even tried to resolve. She didn't want to remember the man whose violent temper had become increasingly unpredictable or that many people had regarded the disappearance of Gordon Gilchrist as a blessing in disguise. She'd rather remember being held by a gentle man who had loved her as dearly as she'd loved him, but was that just wishful thinking? A fantasy of what it could have been like to have a father?

It seemed like another kind of fantasy as Ellie felt the cushions of the sofa moving and found that a small boy was climbing up to sit beside her. To lean against her arm, even, as he reached to touch the front of the book she had discarded on her lap as she was mesmerised by the photograph. She looked down at the tumble of dark curls on Theo's head and watched as he used a finger to trace the embossed outline of the yacht on the cover. Exactly the way Ellie loved to touch things, like she had with the carving in the wood of the cupboard doors in the kitchen and the stone flowers in the streets of St Paul de Vence.

Without thinking, she dipped her head to press a kiss onto those dark curls, moving her arm to make a circle around that small body. This was what she needed to think about right now, not any ghosts of her own childhood. She slipped the photograph back into the envelope and slid it inside the back cover of the book as Theo was opening the front cover. He looked at the words on the first page. And then he looked up at Ellie, and no words were needed for this communication. He wanted to be read to,

and that made another memory fight its way to the surface of
Ellie's brain. Or maybe it was coming from her heart.

Her father used to read to her. From the newspaper he was
reading himself, and it didn't matter at all that she didn't understand what it was about, because it was just the sound of his voice
that she wanted to hear. Both in her ears and in her body, through
the rumble of his chest that she could feel because she was
tucked in under his arm. Ellie could almost feel what it had
provided enfolding her now – the security of being loved.

Safety.

Comfort.

Still without thinking, simply following instinct, Ellie started
reading the book to Theo. And Pascal, who'd jumped onto the
sofa to snuggle in as close as he could get to the small boy. It
clearly didn't matter that Theo couldn't understand, because the
sound of the words was weaving a spell that was comforting.
She could feel his head getting heavier and heavier as it rested
on her arm, and she could feel when he gave in completely to
the pull of sleep. Very gently, she took her arm away and laid
him flat on the sofa and made a cocoon with the blanket she'd
used that first night when she'd slept here, folding part of it to
be a pillow and using the rest as a cover. Pascal only moved to
let her tuck Theo in and then curled up again to guard the
small boy.

Ellie stayed where she was for a long, long moment.

Looking at Theo's still face and the fans of black lashes
against pale cheeks.

So pale.

She stared at the blanket covering him, watching for any tiny
movement that would reassure her he was still breathing. He was.
Of course he was, but it wasn't enough to stop that bubble of fear
returning now that she had nothing to distract herself with.

Fear that was threatening to spiral into something worse as unwanted thoughts crowded in on her.

What would she do if Theo stopped breathing?

What could she do to make sure it *didn't* happen?

What should she have done that might have stopped it happening to wee Jack?

Surely there had been something, however tiny. Any one of the millions of things that had occurred to her in those agonising days and weeks after losing her baby.

The pain could still be as fierce as ever, but something had changed, because Ellie didn't want to hide right now. She wanted... comfort.

Like the comfort Julien had offered by holding her after she'd witnessed the fight for the life of that little French girl?

Julien wasn't here, but Ellie realised she needed the comfort that had always been there for her entire life, even if there'd been times she hadn't wanted to cling to that rock. Moving quietly away from the couch into the kitchen and then just outside the doors on the terrace, where she could still see Theo just as clearly, she called her mother.

'I'm looking after the wee boy from next door,' she said. 'And... I'm a bit scared, Mam... What if... what if something happens?'

'Nothing's going to happen,' Jeannie Gilchrist said. 'Oh, *m'eu-dail*... it's alright. Everything's going to be alright...'

The catch in her mother's voice and the way she used the Gaelic of her own childhood to call Ellie 'sweetheart' cut through the loneliness that the alchemy of her fear and remnants of her grief was creating.

Her mother understood exactly what that fear was about, and she kept talking softly. 'It wasn't your fault, Ellie. It was never your fault. You do know that, don't you?'

'Yes...' The word was only a whisper – as if Ellie was still tiptoeing around the idea of believing it.

'You were such a lovely mother,' Jeannie said. 'Nobody could have cared for wee Jack any better than you did. He knew he was so safe and so loved for every minute of his life. I was so proud of you... I am still so proud of you...'

The words were a balm. The bond between Ellie and her mother was even more of a comfort. Ellie had been the first of the Gilchrist girls to have a baby. The first to truly know what it was like to be a mother. To discover how limitless love could be. And she knew, deep down, that having an utterly pure, unconditional love like that in her life was – and had been – a blessing like no other, even if, at times, it now felt like a pain like no other.

Ellie breathed in the cool evening air as she watched Theo stir and then slip back into his sleep.

The threat of panic had evaporated. The fear had vanished to leave her feeling a little drained but... surprisingly good. With a feeling of peace that was as much of a balm as the love in her mother's voice had been when she'd said how proud she was of Ellie.

She was proud of herself, she decided. She'd been ambushed by a barrage of memories and emotions in the last few hours, and they hadn't defeated her. Was part of how good she was feeling now because she'd allowed herself to soak in that almost indescribable softness and joy that a child cuddled against you could bestow?

Ellie could still feel that touch, wrapped around her heart, as she stood there on the terrace looking in to where Theo lay sleeping with Pascal still glued to his side. Her wee dog was awake. She could see his black, button eyes looking back at her and the twitch of his upright ear that told her there was nothing to worry about. He had her back and was taking his guard dog duties seriously.

It made Ellie smile, and that feeling of an internal hug around her heart grew big enough to shed tendrils of warmth that reached every cell in her body.

* * *

Maybe that warmth and the feeling of that child's touch, still imprinted on her heart, was somehow visible in her body language, or on her face, or simply being breathed out into the air on this terrace. Maybe that was why Julien was so silent as he walked towards her from the orchard.

Why it felt as though there was a completely new and a much more meaningful connection between them as her gaze met his. Why Julien looked into the house to where he could see Theo asleep on the sofa, but he didn't immediately go inside to pick him up.

'Theo's fine,' Ellie told him. 'I didn't want to wake him up to take him home to his own bed.'

Julien's gaze was on her face as she spoke. 'Thank you so much,' he said quietly.

'How's your grandmother?'

'Not badly injured, thank goodness. A few bruises, but no bones broken. And they haven't found any medical problem that might have caused the fall, but they're going to keep her in hospital to do more tests.'

He sounded so calm. Doctors probably had special training to be able to stand back and not be emotionally overwhelmed by an emergency, Ellie thought. And perhaps, in Julien's case, personal tragedy had taught him how to take that to an even higher level?

How good must he be at reassuring his young patients and their frightened families?

'When the tests are finished,' he added, 'We will need to make arrangements for my mother to take her home and stay with her for a little while. A week or two, perhaps, so she can be sure that her mother is safe from falling again. She will take Theo with her.'

Saying his son's name seemed to prompt Julien to turn his head again. The light on inside was like a soft spotlight illuminating the sofa with the young boy curled up and sound asleep in his nest of blanket, a small hand resting on the scruffy coat of the little, white dog lying close enough to be guarding him, and it looked like an image begging to be captured in a photograph or painting. A scene that would tug at heartstrings because of the bond between the child and the dog, both asleep but not alone. And not lonely.

Ellie's breath caught somewhere deep in her chest. From tomorrow, Julien, like herself, would be alone for some time. Would he be lonely? Might he want some company...?

It was another question that must have been leaking into the late evening stillness on the terrace, because Julien's gaze had slowly drifted back to settle on Ellie's face.

'Thank you,' he said to her again. 'I know that it was a lot to ask. I was afraid it might be too much...'

Had he guessed – like her mother had – how afraid she *had* been?

That a part of her might always blame herself for Jack's death?

It felt as if a door that had been kept so firmly locked had been left ajar in the wake of that conversation with her mother. She might only be circling that truth, that she was not to blame, but it was so close and so bright she was tempted to reach out and see if she could feel its glow.

'Why did you do that?' she asked softly. 'What made you so sure?'

Muscles around Julien's eyes tightened as he focused on her words. 'About what?'

'That you could trust me to care for your son...'

Julien's voice was just as quiet, but his words were far less hesitant.

'Why wouldn't I?'

Ellie opened her mouth, but no words emerged. How could she even begin to explain how it felt to have him make it sound as if there was no reason why she shouldn't be trusted? As if it would never occur to him to think it had been her fault that her baby had died?

Or that being alone with Theo – something she would never have chosen to be if Julien hadn't needed her help so urgently – had generated fear and determination, courage and joy all enclosed in a poignancy that was now layered with a sense of... what was it? Being free from being trapped in the past? Hope for the future? The idea that, yet again, being in this place at this time was exactly where she needed to be because things were changing.

Big things.

Julien said nothing more, either. What he did do, without breaking eye contact with her, was to raise his hand to touch her cheek with his first two fingers. She felt the gentle pressure on her cheekbone, and then it moved towards her ear and slowly, softly – like a brush from a feather – traced the outline of her jaw until it reached her chin, where it stopped, to be joined by an equally gentle pressure from his thumb on the other side of her chin.

It felt like her face was being held still, and she couldn't move, even though she knew perfectly well that the touch was so light it would take no more than a sigh of movement to escape. She could no more break that touch than to look away from those dark, dark eyes that were holding her own.

Time had stopped along with her ability to move. Or even breathe, it seemed. The need to kiss this man had suddenly become overwhelming, because it seemed that Ellie had totally forgotten what it would be like to have someone's lips touch her own. It was forever ago. In another lifetime. What was it she saw in his eyes? Was he wondering the same thing, or was it just her own need she could see in the reflection?

What would it be like...?

Was it wise, or safe, to even try to find out?

Not that it felt like there was any choice. Time was moving again, very, very slowly, and Ellie couldn't have said who was actually moving, but the gap between her face and Julien's was closing. And, even though what she could see became blurred as it got too close to focus, she kept her eyes open as she registered his warmth before their lips actually touched. Because this was too important to risk not using all her senses to experience it.

The touch was so light, so evocative, it was like the fragment of a barely remembered dream or a scent that invoked a childhood memory. Whatever it was like, it was so compelling that Ellie found herself moving her head just a fraction, from side to side – parting her lips slightly as she responded to a subtle increase in pressure from Julien's lips – trying to capture a little more of that feeling and find out what was eluding her.

If she closed her eyes, Ellie knew she could sink into the physical response her body was experiencing as a flicker of new life seemed to be igniting in cells throughout her entire body, right down to the tips of her toes, even. Instinct warned her not to, however. If things became too intense too soon, it could well be enough to shatter the illusion of safety.

So she pulled back, to find that Julien also had his eyes open and, for a long, long moment, they were staring at each other again. Communicating silently but not in any recognisable words. It felt more like ripples of emotions.

Delight.

Astonishment.

Yearning for more. A lot more...

One thing was certain. There *would* be more. But not right now. Not with a small boy who was nearby and stirring, again, in his sleep – this time to the point of wakefulness.

'*Papa?*'

'*Oui, c'est moi, mon poussin.*'

But Julien didn't move for another heartbeat. He touched Ellie's bottom lip, watching his finger as he traced its shape as if he was committing its shape and softness to memory.

'*Plus tard,*' he whispered. '*Bientôt...*'

Ellie had to look those words up on the dictionary on her phone after Julien had gathered Theo into his arms to carry him home, and the translation made her catch her breath. And then it made her smile.

Later, he'd said. *Soon...*

13

Anticipation.

As an emotion, it had a magic all of its own. Nothing else could allow you to be completely in the present but also give you the apparent ability to touch the future. To be able to imagine what was going to happen with such clarity and detail that it felt as if it *was* actually happening. The danger was, of course, that the reality might not live up to its promise, but that contributed to the delight of anticipation, Ellie decided, because it made the journey possibly more significant than the destination and therefore something that deserved to be savoured in its own right.

She was smiling a lot more, she realised, when she rode her bicycle down to the village to follow what was becoming a familiar route around the shops near the church in Tourrettes-sur-Loup. People smiled back at her. Perhaps they were starting to recognise the new foreigner with her bright red bike and small white dog. Or maybe it was because she was deliberately taking her time today – savouring the first steps of a new journey – that was making her more aware of everything around her.

Ellie took a moment outside the *épicerie* to simply admire the care that had been taken to display the fresh fruit and vegetables so beautifully. Today there was a rainbow arrangement of tiny cardboard punnets of wild strawberries, blackberries, raspberries and currants as a centrepiece to other fruit like small peaches shaped like doughnuts, apricots and plums and nectarines. Trusses of ripe tomatoes at the other end of the trestle table had glass jars with bunches of basil amongst them, and Ellie picked both to purchase, making a mental note to find some mozzarella at the fromagerie so that she could make her favourite salad to go with the fresh baguette she would buy at the boulangerie.

She paused to let Pascal sniff a tree and listened to someone nearby greeting a friend in passing.

'*Bonjour Bernard. Ça va?*'

'*Oui, ça va. Et toi?*'

'*Ouais... ça va. À bientôt.*'

And Ellie was smiling again as she heard the words she recognised. Words that would probably remind her of Julien Rousseau for the rest of her life. Words that might conjure up this delicious bubble of excitement that sparkled like the end of a slowly vanishing fuse.

À bientôt. See you soon.

Bientôt. Soon...

Would it be today?

Not knowing added another layer to the anticipation that became a background hum to everything else that happened that day. Ellie uncovered enough of the garage door to make her think that someone with some muscle might be able to open it, so it was timely that it turned out to be the day that Mike brought his mechanic friend, Gary, to see the car. He also brought a bottle of strong alcohol that his mate had sourced in Italy, which Ellie happily reimbursed him for.

They hauled the tilting door open despite the loud complaint from long-neglected hinges, and then they pushed the car out into the sunlight and set to work. They talked about ignition coils and fuel lines and sparkplugs, and Ellie smiled and left them to it. They were all smiling when the engine sputtered into life, with a cough and then a roar, an hour or so later. Mike added to the celebration by tooting the tin snail's surprisingly loud horn, which was no doubt why somebody stopped their car further up the road to turn and stare. And why Julien Rousseau came out of his gate to walk towards La Maisonette.

That was the point where Ellie's level of anticipation threatened to render her incapable of saying anything, but she didn't need to, because these three men were making their own introductions and bonding over the vintage car.

'My first car was one of these,' Julien said. 'I was fifteen. It was... how do you say it? My joy and pride?'

'Pride and joy,' Mike nodded.

'Where did it come from?' Julien turned to Ellie, his gaze catching and then holding hers. 'Have you bought a car, Ellie?'

She could only shake her head. Still smiling. Still holding that eye contact.

'It's been locked away in this garage for goodness knows how long,' Mike told him.

'But it sounds like it's going well.'

Gary was wiping his hands on a rag. 'This car's a beauty,' he said. 'All she needed was a tune up.' He glanced at his watch. 'We've got time to take her for a bit of a road test. Why don't you come along?'

Julien shook his head. 'Thank you, but I have my own driving to do. I'm off to Roquebillière in a few minutes.'

'Ellie? You want to come?' Mike peered into the car. 'Or maybe not. Needs a bit of a clean, that back seat. And I suppose we should make sure it's not going to conk out first.'

'Good idea.' Ellie was trying to find a balance between savouring the anticipation and fending off the disappointment that clearly today wasn't going to be the day. 'I'll put the kettle on for a cup of tea when you get back.'

Julien waited with Ellie just until the little red car was moving up the road. They could both see that someone was standing near his gate.

'My mother's anxious to leave,' Julien said. 'I'm taking her and my grandmother and Theo up to Roquebillière now, and I'll be staying there tonight.'

Disappointment had definitely taken the lead in the battle for balance.

'But I will be back tomorrow,' Julien added, as he turned to leave. He glanced over his shoulder at Ellie. 'And I am hoping I could take you out to dinner.'

Anticipation totally obliterated disappointment.

'I'd like that.'

Her words sounded shy. Hesitant, almost? Maybe that was why Julien simply nodded and began to walk away.

Ellie searched for something else to add and remembered what she'd overheard this morning in the village square. '*À bientôt*, Julien.' She also remembered to pronounce his name with a soft *J*.

He looked back again, and this time there was a lopsided smile tilting his lips. '*À demain*, Ellie. Yes... see you soon.'

* * *

Even if she'd had an entire wardrobe full of dresses, Ellie would have chosen to wear the pretty blue one with the tiny white daisies, puffed sleeves, and buttons all the way down the front because she could remember wishing she'd been wearing it when she'd met Julien for the very first time.

When he'd been so angry. So protective of his tiny son. So dark and passionate and... so incredibly drop-dead *sexy*...

She washed her hair, letting it dry in the warmth of the late afternoon sun and then brushing the curls into soft waves that she intended to leave loose, as she had also done that night she'd worn the dress for the first time in so long. She changed her mind, however, and twisted a thick tress along each side of her head to keep the hair away from her face, leaving the length rippling over her back. A compromise between looking tidy but having the comfort of what felt like a shield protecting her back. A shield against the scary part of an anticipation that was like nothing she'd ever experienced before.

A touch of mascara and lip gloss was the only makeup she chose, having never been as concerned as Laura about covering up her generous sprinkling of freckles. She brushed Pascal, too, in case he was included in this invitation for dinner. For this... date.

Oh... there were nerves hovering in the wings with their talent for creating doubt, but Ellie wasn't about to let them spoil what might be the last of this particular shade of anticipation. Because there could only ever be one first time with someone, couldn't there? But that thought, cloaked in the knowledge of what was almost inevitably going to happen later this evening, only added a much sharper edge to that anticipation. The kind of edge you might find on a metal sign warning of danger?

Luckily, distraction was close at hand, and, by the time Julien knocked on her front door, Ellie had finished both a glass of wine and a session of practising her French phrases.

'*Salut*,' she said, as she opened the door, because 'hi' seemed a friendlier way to greet him than 'good day'. '*Ça va?*'

'*Oui. Ça va. Et toi?*'

Lost already, Ellie just smiled as she picked up her shoulder bag. At the signal she was leaving, Pascal came to sit in front of her. She glanced at Julien. 'Can he come too?'

'Of course. Dogs are welcome everywhere in France.' He was already heading for his car, which was parked by the gate. 'Except in supermarkets.'

He took a route that Ellie didn't recognise, to circle the old walls of Vence and arrive on the far side of the city, where they parked near the cemetery.

'It's the first summer evening market,' he told her. 'I thought you might like to walk through it.'

Traffic had been blocked from the old town because the evening market was set along the cobbled main street that led towards the central square – where Ellie and Laura had walked together after that first visit to La Maisonette and their lunch in the tiny square hidden behind the cathedral. There were tables set along the footpaths, but the shops on the street were also participating, staying open longer and putting racks of clothing or other goods outside to attract customers. There was music, with a live band and a stall where children could get their faces painted, and there was a bouncy castle and whole families and many dogs – a slow-moving river of people out to enjoy a long summer evening.

Ellie was drawn to a table of handmade leather items, like belts and bags, and she bought a small, dark brown bag with just enough room for her phone and a few small items and a strap long enough to wear across her body, which would make it easy to use when she rode her bike.

Pascal stayed very close to Ellie's feet. When a child tried to race between them, Julien reached out to take Ellie's hand, perhaps to protect the little dog from being stepped on, but then he didn't let it go. They strolled past the offerings of jewellery and dreamcatchers, polished gemstones and lavender oil, hand in hand, as if they'd known each other for ever and were totally comfortable in each other's company. Amazingly, that's what it felt like to Ellie. Comfortable.

Safe.

Safe enough to soften those sharp edges that could have destroyed the delicious flicker of butterflies still dancing in her belly. If anything, the feeling of her hand enclosed within his had increased their number.

'Oh... *look*...' The table tucked against a stone wall at the opening of a side street was very different to any around it. Paintings were propped against the wall. Big, colourful paintings with textures that gave the images a choppy, three-dimensional look. Images that were utterly Provençal, capturing not only the soft colours of the stone buildings and flower-studded fields but that light that was so distinctive here. More than that, even. This artist, if that's who the man sitting on a stool behind the table was, had managed to capture that sense of peace that Ellie had been so aware of. She actually had to blink back sudden moisture in her eyes as she found herself drawn so far into this work she didn't even notice when Julien let go of her hand.

The biggest painting, which had to be well over a square metre of canvas, had a smudged stone building that could have been a small chapel to one side and the shadow of mountains in the background, but the focus was the colours of the flowers in front. Blood red and clear white against the gold of dry summer grass and stony ground. The colours of her own tiny front garden. The flowers that were pretty much the first French words Ellie had learned since high school.

Coquelicots and *Marguerites*.

'That's... *magnifique*,' she said softly. But then she turned to

Julien. Saying '*J'aime ça*' this time was not going to be enough. 'How can I say I *really* love this?' she asked in a whisper.

'You could say "*J'adore ça tellement*",' he whispered back.

But the man was half hidden beneath a wide-brimmed hat, and Ellie suddenly felt too shy to try out her French on a complete stranger, so it was Julien who said something, and then the man looked up. He had a bushy grey beard and eyebrows that he could hide behind, but he stared at Ellie for a long moment. Long enough to make the moment so awkward that she actually stepped back as she broke eye contact.

'Do you want me to ask how much it is?'

'No.' Ellie shook her head. 'It would be too much. And it's far too big. How on earth would I ever get it back to Scotland?'

Julien's nod was an agreement. 'We've run out of time in any case. I have a reservation for dinner.'

He led her through a stone archway onto a cobbled street with crowded footpaths as customers spilled out of busy eateries and then into narrower pathways between buildings. It wasn't until they emerged into a wider space that Ellie recognised where she was.

'I know this place,' she exclaimed. 'I had lunch near that tree with my sister on my very first day here. That's the back of the cathedral, isn't it?'

'It is. Did you eat at the vegetarian restaurant?'

'No. I had a slow-cooked beef stew that was the most delicious meal ever.'

'Daube de boeuf,' Julien smiled. 'One of my favourites, also. And that is where we have a table waiting for us.'

The restaurant looked completely different at night. The huge chestnut tree had fairy lights woven amongst its branches, and candles flickered on every table. A man with a top hat and a piano accordion was wandering through the large group of diners, and there were peals of laughter that suggested the song was an amusing story. It didn't look as if there was any space at all, but the owner had spotted Julien and ushered them to a small table almost hidden beneath the tree. Pascal curled up, out of sight, behind the drooping corners of the white tablecloth.

A short time later the propriétaire was back, carrying two glasses of champagne, and began to talk about the special black-board menu for the evening. His words flowed around Ellie, competing with the music, and conversation from a nearby table for six. With the addition of the warmth of the summer evening, the aroma of the food around them and the myriad tiny lights and flames, this was not only the essence of what Ellie was coming to love so much about France, it was also the most romantic setting imaginable. The crisp tingle of champagne on her tongue was the final touch, and Ellie almost had to blink away a prickle of embryonic tears.

She was happy, she realised.

Really happy. It felt like the first time she'd ever felt quite like this. There wasn't a single thing she would change about this moment, and, even if it only lasted a heartbeat, she would remember it for ever.

Okay... maybe it wasn't the champagne that was adding the final drops to a happiness that was quite unlike any she could ever remember experiencing. Maybe that final touch was that she had Julien sitting on the other side of the table. Or the way he was smiling at her.

This was as full of promise as any first date could aspire to be.

Except... this wasn't really a first date, was it? Not in the usual sense. She wasn't hoping it might turn into anything more than a... what was it, exactly? A friendship with the benefits that could come from a mutual attraction? An opportunity to find out if male companionship could provide something that would enhance the quality of her life?

But was Julien on the same page?

Perhaps he'd seen that flicker of doubt on her face, because he put down his wine glass. 'What are you thinking?' he asked.

'That I'm only here in France for a short time,' she said, quietly. 'And that this might be the only time I'm ever here.'

He understood exactly that she was saying she didn't want this to be the beginning of a significant relationship. Was it a wash of relief she could see in *his* eyes?

'Which is what makes this so perfect,' he said. 'You have your own life to go back to, and I will never try to replace Theo's mother – for his sake or my own. It simply isn't going to happen. This is a moment in our lifetimes that *will* never happen again, *ma chérie*, so... *on devrait en profiter tant que ça dure...* we should enjoy it while it lasts.'

Ma chérie? Didn't that mean 'darling'? The tone of Julien's voice certainly made it an endearment that sent a prickle of sensation from Ellie's ears right down to her toes.

And Julien was right. This *was* perfect.

What they had together had a shape. A beginning, a middle and, most importantly, an end.

And that made it safe.

Perhaps he could see relief in *her* face now, because he was smiling.

'Have you been driving in your car yet?' he asked, changing the subject as if it was no big deal to discuss the time frame of an affair.

'The tin snail?'

'The...' Julien blinked. 'I'm not sure I understand.'

'It's the shape,' Ellie said. 'That's what Mike the builder said they used to call them, because they look like snails.'

'Ah... *un escargot*. I see that.' Julien laughed. 'Perhaps you should call her Margot?'

'Margot the *escargot*?' Ellie was laughing now, too. 'I love it.'

Their laughter was lost amongst the sounds of the restaurant, but Ellie knew she would hear the echoes of it later.

You could fall in love so easily with a man who could make you laugh.

Maybe she already had – just a little bit.

Because it wasn't going to last very long, and that made it so much safer.

* * *

Her house.

Her room.

Her bed.

It was the choice Ellie would have made because this was her safe place in this new, very different life, and there was still enough of an edge of danger in doing this to make it daunting. So daunting that the butterflies in her stomach were battering themselves senseless by the time Julien had driven them home, and it was impossible to find the words to tell him she didn't want to go to his house.

And she didn't need to.

It seemed that Julien knew where she would feel most safe. That he knew there was a fine line between wanting this and being scared enough to run from it. That had to be why he paused just inside her front door, holding her gaze with his own. Why he reached out to touch her face, stroking her cheek with his fingers before cupping her chin gently, bending his head as her eyes drifted shut, to touch her lips with his.

A soft touch. A question that needed no words.

Did she want this?

As much as he did?

Oh... *yes...*

This was the point that Ellie had anticipated above all else. The moment when it was absolutely clear that this was what they both wanted. The moment when the need to touch – and be touched – could be released from any restraints. After being stoked so slowly by sharing a long, summer evening of food and laughter and being so physically close without being able to touch, Ellie had been sure that, given its freedom, anticipation would explode into reality as an uncontrollable force.

She couldn't have been more wrong. and it couldn't have been any more perfect because of that. Instead of passionate flames that would burn themselves out far too quickly, it seemed that time slowed to a point where its passage became meaningless. Every moment stretched far enough to be aware of details that Ellie might never have thought of before, and each one of those impressions added to an intensity that was unprecedented.

She could hear the rub of fabric as Julien undid the tiny buttons on the front of her dress, and she could feel goosebumps forming on her skin as she felt his breath on the side of her neck. His lips found hers again at the same moment the pad of his thumb stroked one of her nipples through the lace of her bra, making it harden so fast it almost hurt. The sound that escaped Ellie's mouth was a mixture of ecstasy and a need so deep she had no idea where it came from.

She pressed into the hand cupping her breast, but she could feel the chill of his warmth leaving her skin, and she pulled away from the kiss to search his face. Oh, God... it would be unbearable if he'd changed his mind.

His eyes were so dark she couldn't tell where the pupil ended and the iris began. Sinfully black. Bottomless pools that Ellie was being pulled into.

'We have all night,' he murmured. 'And we can never have this first time again, can we?'

Ellie had to lick her suddenly dry lips as anticipation reached a level that was completely off any charts she'd ever been aware of. In danger of drowning in that gaze, her voice deserted her, so all she could do was shake her head. Slowly. As slowly as the astonishingly arousing circles Julien was making with his thumbs just below her collarbones as his hands rested on her shoulders.

She tipped her head back, her eyes closed so that she could sink into the sensation. Created on such a small patch of her skin, it was astonishing that it could be felt so far through the rest of her body even her toes were tingling.

And then she felt Julien's lips on the side of her neck – a trail of featherlike kisses – the strap of her bra pushed aside as they reached her shoulder. Her hands skimmed over the hard contours of the muscles in his back and shoulders, her fingers brushing the soft skin on the sides of *his* neck – which she was aching to press her lips to – and then burying themselves in the soft, silky waves of his hair. The ache of unleashed passion was sharpening the pain in her nipples, so she pressed her breasts against his chest as she rose to her tiptoes to beg for another kiss.

He made a sound that Ellie could interpret instantly, and she knew the battle to slow this foreplay down was being lost. But did it matter? As Julien had said himself, they had a whole night together before anyone, or anything, from a forgotten world beyond this room could pull them apart. Perhaps this first, insane need to be as close as it was humanly possible to be had to be sated before they could take the time to savour discovering each other's bodies. To touch and taste and hear the sounds of pure pleasure.

Ellie heard a tiny whimper of need escape from her throat, and Julien's response was so swift she barely felt her feet leave the floor, her dress slithering from her body before she was lying on her bed. And then Julien was kneeling between her legs, his gaze touching her own with the same fierce, hard heat she could feel so tantalisingly close to that most private space in her body.

Her cry might have been his name.

Or perhaps it was simply a wordless plea to give her something she needed so badly that it felt as if she might die if it didn't happen. She was already drowning in that look in his eyes, so she saw the reflection of what her body was feeling as that space was filled.

She could see that he wanted – *needed* – this as much as she did.

And Ellie held out her arms to welcome him.

14

Julien was kissing Ellie again.

The dream was so intense she could feel everything. The touch of his lips against hers, his warmth, the whisper of his breath on her skin. The scent that was as distinctive as a fingerprint and an echo of the delicious taste of him...

When she woke abruptly, just as those dream hands were sliding down her body, Ellie was aware of two things. One was that a shaft of sheer desire could actually be physically painful, and the other was that memories of such exquisite love making, especially when combined with the anticipation of repeating the experience in the very near future, could overwhelm absolutely anything else.

She wasn't about to let it stop her doing the things that she was planning to do this morning, like the bike ride to the *bricolage* to buy some car polish as her contribution to Margot the *escargot*'s makeover. But, if the last few days were anything to go by, this anticipation would be there every moment, humming through her body like an electrical current that was both exhilarating and a bit scary at the same time.

Because it felt as if life was unexpectedly speeding up, and, generally, if things kept speeding up, they would start going too fast, and then it was too easy to lose control and if that happened... well...

'It could end in tears, Pascal, that's what.' About to tip dog food into his bowl when they got downstairs, Ellie paused, her hand in mid-air. 'Except, if you know it's going to end – even *when* it's going to end – doesn't that mean you've actually got nothing to lose, because you know you're going to lose it anyway?'

Her little dog tilted his head obligingly and wagged his stumpy little tail, but he was far more interested in his breakfast arriving than any question that was far too convoluted to be comprehensible.

Ellie was still thinking about it as she sipped her coffee, however, while she sat out on the terrace to enjoy the early morning stillness and a light that was soft but completely different to the other end of the day. Could she do what Julien had suggested they do and enjoy the ride for as long as it lasted? If it was going too fast, did that mean it would end sooner?

But, if it did, wasn't quality something to be valued over quantity?

She'd certainly never found qualities in any previous relationship quite like those that seemed to be intrinsic to Julien Rousseau.

That physical hum strengthened more than a few notches as Ellie let her mind drift back to that first night with him. And the next. He hadn't stayed last night because he had an early start with a clinic at the hospital in Nice, but it was a half-day for Julien today, and he was planning to be back early this afternoon. He had insisted, in fact, that he was going to give her a driving lesson in her own car.

'You're braver than you think you are,' he'd told her. 'You should know that.'

He wouldn't be saying that if he knew the thought of being behind the wheel of a car on the wrong side of the road was enough to send a shiver of terror down her spine. Ellie wondered if she could find an excuse plausible enough to wriggle out of the offer when the time came. She felt her lips curving into a smile. Maybe she could persuade Julien that an afternoon in bed might be far more pleasurable for both of them?

That thought sent a much more welcome shimmer down Ellie's spine. One that culminated in a tingle she could feel quite distinctly in the tips of her toes, which was something she'd never experienced in any previous physical attraction. Was it because the quality of Julien's lovemaking was also like nothing she'd ever discovered before, or was this a chicken and egg kind of question and it was something about the man, rather than any sexual skills he possessed, that made it so very different?

With a resurgence of that delightful hum in her body that almost made it feel like she was floating, rather than a far more mundane kind of movement, Ellie got on with her morning. Even if she wasn't going to drive Margot, the little car needed sprucing up so that she could star in Laura's marketing photo shoot.

* * *

Julien could see just how scared Ellie was. He was about to rescue her by saying it really didn't matter if she learned to drive on a different side of the road because she wasn't going to be in France for much longer, anyway.

But, as he held her gaze, he could see the moment that she decided she *could* be that brave after all, and it gave him a surprising glow deep in his chest. Around his heart. The kind of feeling he got when Theo surprised him with the effort he'd put into doing something new.

Je l'ai fait. Je l'ai fait pour toi, Papa...

Pride, that's what it was.

Even if they didn't get any further than the end of this road, he was proud of Ellie for taking up the challenge. What he really wanted, however, was for Ellie to feel proud of herself.

'First things first,' he told her, when she was sitting in the driver's seat, clutching the steering wheel, her seat belt fastened. Pascal was sitting on the back seat, watching proceedings with interest. 'Have you driven a car that is not automatic before? I forget the word for it.'

Ellie nodded. 'My first car was an old Mini, and that was manual.'

'Manual... pfft...' Julien shook his head at his own error. 'How could I have forgotten that? It's exactly the same in French. *Manuel*. Of the hand. *Main* is hand.'

Ellie clearly wasn't interested in a language lesson.

'Where's the gear stick?'

'It comes out of the dashboard. Here, see? Put your foot on the clutch and just try the different positions. Pull it out, go left and up for reverse.'

'Is the clutch in a different place on this side of the car?'

'No. It is always the same. Clutch on the left, brake in the middle and the accelerator on the right.'

It took Ellie two tries to move the stick into the reverse position, and, on the second attempt, Julien was watching her face rather than what she was doing with her hands. She had deep frown lines as she concentrated hard, and she had the tip of her tongue between her top teeth and her bottom lip.

Adorable... that's what it was. Like everything he was discovering about her.

Julien had to clear his throat. '*Bien...* Push down to the left and then pull towards you for first gear. Push in for neutral and then push again for second gear. Pull straight back towards you for third.'

It was getting easier for Ellie now.

'The top gear is fourth, and you twist to the right and push in – the opposite to reverse.' But Julien smiled at Ellie. 'You probably won't need the top gear today. We'll just go quietly. To Grasse, maybe?'

He saw Ellie's chest rise as she took a deep breath. 'Okay.' She glanced sideways. 'What's "okay" in French?'

'*D'accord.*'

'*D'accord,*' Ellie was still looking very serious. 'Do I just turn the key to start?'

'You might need a little bit of the starter.'

'The what?' Ellie tilted her head to see the knob he was pulling out of the dashboard. 'Oh... yes... I had a choke on my Mini. I had to be careful not to pull it out too far or it flooded the engine, and then I was stuck.'

The engine chugged into life. Julien reminded Ellie to release the hand brake and use the indicator, and then they made their way, rather appropriately at the pace of a snail, down to the village, past the tiny chapel of Saint Jean.

'Turn right at the end of this road, beside the *Café du Midi.* Have you eaten there yet?'

'No.'

It sounded as if Ellie was speaking through gritted teeth. Julien hid his smile. 'We will go there soon. Theo thinks they have the best *frites* in the world, especially when he has an egg to dip them into. It's a lovely place to sit and watch what's happening in the square.'

But Ellie was only interested in watching what was happening on the road, so Julien stayed quiet apart from complimenting her use of the gears and brakes as she completed the tight turn that put them on the main road to Grasse and even picked up speed a little as they left the village behind them. He didn't hide his smile as he saw Ellie hunch her shoulders as they drove through a patch of road carved from rock and even under an overhang as the winding road continued.

'There is a place you can stop, coming up,' he told her. 'Just before a road to the right. There is a bus stop.'

'You want me to stop?'

'*Oui.*'

Ellie was silent as she pulled onto the side of the road, but then her gaze slid sideways. 'You want to get out?' she asked. 'To catch a *bus*? Is my driving that bad?'

Julien laughed. '*Pas du tout* – not at all. I thought you might like to take a breath, that's all. And this is the best view of Tourrettes-sur-Loup. You might like to take a photo.'

She did. Then Julien took one of Ellie standing to one side of the distant view of the village over the huge, forest-filled gully. And then someone else who had stopped to admire the view offered to take a picture of the two of them. Julien put his arm around her shoulders, and he knew she was smiling up at him rather than at the camera when the photos were being taken because he was smiling down at her. The tourist who handed back the phone was also smiling.

'*Votre copine est si belle*,' he murmured.

Julien was not about to deny that Ellie was very beautiful. But his *girlfriend*? Is that what Ellie was?

She was most certainly his lover, but could she be considered a girlfriend when it was only going to be for such a short amount of time?

What did labels matter, anyway? It was a beautiful day, and this was fun. He hadn't had fun with an adult, let alone such an attractive woman, since... maybe he didn't want to remember the last time, because this was new. Different.

Better...

'I wonder if I can remember how to roll up the roof,' he said, taking Ellie's hand as they ran back across the road to where Margot was parked. 'Would you like to have the wind in your hair?'

'I might not be able to see where I'm driving. Then we might *both* want to catch a bus home.'

'I could drive.' Julien was grinning. 'I would rather like to feel like a teenager again.'

He disconnected brackets and undid oversized domes to fold back the front flap of the soft roof and roll the fabric until he could find the leather straps at the back and secure the roll with more domes. With Ellie strapped into the passenger seat, he could put his foot down and show her what fun this little car could be, with its quirky suspension, as they bounced over any bumps in the road and rolled around corners.

He *did* feel like a teenager again.

Out with his *copine...*

And he did like it. He liked it enough to suggest another outing when he was clipping the roof back into place. Ellie was trying to find the clip on her side of the car, but she had to push back curls of her hair that the wind had teased free of her pony-tail to see what she was doing properly.

'Ouch.' She scrunched up her face in pained surprise as her fingers caught in knots in her hair. 'It's sad that there's such a downside to having your hair blowing in the wind when it's such fun to do.'

'*C'est la vie.*' But Julien smiled. 'You could wear a scarf like the old-time movie stars. Brigette Bardot? Lauren Bacall?'

'I could never be so stylish. But a scarf is a good idea for next time.'

Next time...

'Would you like to come with me when I go up to Roquebillière to visit Theo and see how my grandmother is doing?' Julien spoke without thinking. 'It would be good driving practice for you, and there are some wonderful places to see. We could even take Theo up to the wolf park in the mountains. He's been begging to go there again.'

Ellie was still trying to untangle her hair, and Julien leaned into the car to fold down the last clip to fasten the roof. Out of sight, he found himself making a face not unlike the one Ellie had made when she'd tugged her hair so sharply.

He was suggesting a family outing? That Ellie spend time with Theo by choice and not the necessity it had been on the night of his grandmother's accident?

He could hear an echo of his son's sleepy voice the first time he'd laid eyes on Ellie. When she'd been holding Theo in her arms, and he'd woken up and smiled at her.

'*Maman?*'

Theo was already aware that something was missing in his life. How easy would it be for such a young child to get attached to someone who looked as though they could fill that space?

He remembered the way Ellie had been watching Theo as he slept that night, too. Watching him breathe? The intensity of what was in the air around her had made him catch his own breath. How overwhelming would it be for a mother who had lost her child to feel that soul-deep need to care and protect?

He could hear an echo of that heartbreaking question she'd asked about why he'd been so sure he could trust her to look after his son, and he understood the depth of her pain. He knew how he would feel if something happened to Theo. How he would choose to die himself if it could prevent that happening to his child.

So he understood why Ellie didn't think that she deserved to be trusted with caring for a child. He just wished there was some way he could let her know that not only could she care for one, but – if she let herself – she could find that kind of love again in her life.

But not yet.

And not with *his* son, when it was only for a short time and would end up causing heartache for everyone involved.

As Julien straightened, he found himself meeting Ellie's gaze. His thoughts had, of course, been in French, but it felt like every word had been understood, and he felt a need to protect Ellie that was almost as fierce as the need to protect his son from that heartache.

'*Désolé*,' he said quietly. 'That was thoughtless of me.'

She understood the apology, as well, and the poignant curl of her lips told him that she appreciated *his* understanding. His protection? It was all the confirmation he needed that it was far too soon for Ellie to imagine including a child in her life in any significant way. But it was that poignancy that touched his own heart and drew him to her with a force that was irresistible. He had to touch her lips with his own before that curl finally faded, and, while the lack of any desire to keep an eye on protective boundaries should have been a warning, Julien couldn't have cared less.

This... whatever it was between them was only going to last until Ellie went home. Until the last summer market, which was only a matter of weeks away. It was something that was just between the two of them, and it didn't need to involve something like a family outing with Theo.

Surely it wouldn't do any harm to simply enjoy it for what it was? To feel this alive again and regain hope for any future joy he might be lucky enough to find in his life? It felt as if Ellie could also find that hope again, and that made this even more special. Important, even.

'I will go and visit Roquebillière by myself,' he told her. 'But, after that, we can give you more driving practice.'

'*D'accord...*'

Her pride in remembering her new word made Julien smile. He loved the joy he could see in her face. That he was, more and more, coming to see the real Ellie as she gained enough confidence to emerge from where she'd been hiding.

It made kissing her as they stood in this dusty old garage as necessary as taking his next breath. He carefully smoothed his hands over the tangles in her hair so that he could hold her head and find the perfect angle to let his tongue dance with hers and taste every astonishingly delicious corner of her mouth.

She was *so* different to any woman he'd ever been with.

Was it because he could *feel* what she was thinking so often? Like her pride in remembering a new word or overcoming her fear of driving? Sharing her appreciation of a view or a painting that captured some of the colours and light of Provence was a gift. She had taught him to love the smell of sunshine on sheets that had just been washed. The sound of an accordion playing a classic French song. The taste of simple food like fresh tomatoes and basil. He would never ever forget the sigh of pleasure that he could invoke by touching her bare skin...

It would be so easy to fall in love with this woman.

Not that that was going to happen, *bien sûr*. The boundaries of this *brève liaison* were what was making it possible to be this close to her, because *they* were making it safe.

But he was going to remember this time with Eleanor Gilchrist for the rest of his life.

Oddly, that thought gave Julien a wash of something that felt like sadness.

Was he missing her already?

15

The curls of lemon rind had been in the bottle of alcohol for seven days now, religiously taken out of the cupboard and shaken every day by Ellie. Days during which she found she was putting the final touches on some of the bigger projects of renovating La Maisonette.

The interior stone walls were completely clear of the crumbling whitewashed plaster, and every particle of dust had been removed. The *tomettes* on the floor were gleaming, and she had sanded down and repainted the repaired shutters in a lovely shade of Paris blue with a lavender undertone. On a trip to the local *bricolage* to find some white paint to freshen up the wrought-iron table and chairs on the terrace, Ellie had discovered that her now-favourite shop had all sorts of unexpected things for sale. She had been able to find tiny tubes of oil paint in a craft section that were just what she needed to restore the ceramic tile with the name of the house. And she had spotted pretty pale-green glass bottles with embossed flowers and flip-top wire clasps that were perfect for the next stage of making her limoncello.

This evening, she had boiled the water and sugar into a syrup and let it cool, and now she was adding it to the alcohol to filter into the bottles through a funnel and a clean scrap of cotton fabric. A summer storm was brewing outside, with dramatic, black-tinged clouds crowding the sky and rumbles of thunder in the distance. Pascal was hiding under the table, close to Julien's feet, and, as Ellie carefully poured the syrup into the two pretty bottles and then clipped the stoppers into place with the wire clasp, she noticed the way he reached down to give her dog's ears a reassuring scratch every now and then.

It was another tiny sliver of the jigsaw she was putting together of who this man was, and it was, piece by piece, a picture of... a kind man. An attribute that might not be considered particularly sexy, maybe, but – along with the ability to make someone laugh – it was, without doubt, the most attractive attribute any man could possess.

Ellie put the bottles back into the cupboard, where they needed to sit for twenty days before the limoncello would be ready to drink. She didn't want to think of what day it would be. She knew it would be in August. Far too close to the date she'd set as the time to go home to Scotland.

Laura was arriving in just a few days, and when the photographs were taken the marketing campaign would begin in earnest. Surely it wouldn't take very long at all to sell the little house in its orchard setting that Ellie now knew was a small patch of paradise. Would she have the chance to do anything more than taste her own effort to create limoncello, or would it end up being a farewell gift for Julien?

Ellie pushed that thought away even more firmly as she sat beside him with a glass of her favourite rosé. She loved that he would drop in after work for a glass of wine. Sometimes they ate dinner together. Sometimes Julien stayed the night. Other times he needed to go home to do some work or to make a video call to his mother and his son if he hadn't had time to do it earlier in the day.

Today it felt as if he was planning to stay. Right now he was looking through her sketch pad.

'When did you do these?'

'Just today. I spent the morning picking up old fruit in the orchard and cutting long grass with the shears I found in the garage, but I needed a break, so I took Pascal to St Paul de Vence and we wandered around all afternoon. I tried to find and draw all the different patterns of flowers I could find in the cobbles.'

'I must look more carefully the next time I go there. I'll take Theo and make sure he can see the flowers and how beautiful they are.'

Oh... Ellie wanted to go with them. To be out with Julien and Theo and Pascal. Finding things to do that would bring them all joy in being together.

Like a family...?

It was lucky that Julien was absorbed in turning the pages of the pad and couldn't guess her thoughts. Ellie could hear an echo of his words from the night they'd first made love.

'*...I will never try to replace Theo's mother – for his sake or my own. It simply isn't going to happen...*'

'I've never seen this one, with the flowerpot and the flowers inside it.' Another page was turning, and Julien made an appreciative sound. 'These are very good, Ellie,' he said. 'Will you sell the pictures?'

'No.' Ellie shook her head. 'Well... maybe. Eventually. I have other plans for things I want to do first.'

'Oh?' Julien's glance was keen. Interested. He picked up his own glass of wine to drink, his gaze still on Ellie, and any shyness in sharing a plan that was only just coming together in her own head evaporated.

'I want to make paving stones,' she told him. 'Like fragments of the old pathways, with these flowers in them.'

Julien nodded. '*Sympa*,' he murmured. 'Nice. For people to make their own pathways?'

'Yes. But they could be stepping stones in a grassed area. Or a whole courtyard. Or even a wall that could be a background for a vertical garden. How good would it be to sprinkle a little bit of medieval France in other places? In Scotland and England... maybe in other countries, too. All over the world, even.'

'Think big,' Julien smiled. 'I like it.'

'I'm even thinking of a name for my studio.' Ellie hunched her shoulders, in a mix of shyness and delight. 'I'm going to call it "Stone Flowers". Or maybe "A Touch of France".'

Like applause from the universe, a flash of lightning flickered outside, followed a few seconds later by a roll of thunder that ended in a crack that Ellie could feel right into her bones. Almost immediately, rain started to fall. Fat, heavy drops that rapidly gathered force until they were drumming on the roof and bouncing off the stones on the terrace.

'I *love* thunderstorms,' Ellie confessed. 'But poor Pascal. Look... he's shivering.' She gathered the little dog into her arms. 'Good grief, can you hear that rain?'

'*Il pleut comme une vache qui pisse*,' Julien said.

Ellie only had to catch Julien's glance to ask for a translation. He grinned.

'It rains like a cow pissing,' he said.

Ellie laughed aloud. 'I am so going to remember that. It will be very useful in Scotland.'

Maybe it was the reminder that their time together was limited. Or maybe it was another crack of bone-tingling thunder, but the electricity in the room was suddenly less about the weather and all about the irresistible physical attraction between them. With Pascal still in her arms, Ellie raised her face to meet Julien's kiss, but, before the next crash of thunder, the little dog found himself being put gently down on the floor. Neither Ellie nor Julien noticed him following them up the stairs and wiggling under Ellie's bed so he could stay safe in a stormy world.

Ellie had never felt so safe, herself, in Julien's arms. Safe enough to allow a crack of thunder to open a door to a vulnerability she'd never exposed before. To open herself, body and soul, to the man she knew had stolen so much of her heart it could never be whole again on its own. To give him everything she could without saying a word. And then to give even more.

Maybe it was the magic of the storm surrounding La Maisonette that night. Maybe Julien was aware of that cocoon of safety in the pretty brass bed with the soft duvet that smelt of sunshine and lemons. Maybe it was because he felt safe enough that he seemed to accept the invitation to enter the intimate space Ellie was offering. He did so with respect. Gentleness. And a fierce passion that touched her, quite literally, in way she'd never ever felt before. But it was the touch that had nothing to do with anything physical that she was going to remember from that night.

Emotionally, it was a touch that felt like it was holding out a hand.

Welcoming her home…

And it was then that Ellie realised she had fallen, head over heels, in love with Julien Rousseau.

* * *

Falling in love was a drug, wasn't it?

Potent enough not to wear off, even hours after Julien had left to go to work the next morning. If it was fading at all, Ellie simply needed to close her eyes and remember how it had felt falling asleep in his arms last night to top up the effect enough for it to colour absolutely everything. Her coffee tasted wonderful. The sky, washed clean after last night's storm, was a shade of blue she was quite sure she had never seen before. The soft fabric of her now well-worn summer dress, with its daisy print, brushed her body with a caress that ramped up the addictiveness of this drug because it made her think of Julien's touch.

Ellie knew she was in trouble. Despite her hope that knowing this time with Julien was only temporary could mitigate the risk of heartbreak, it could just as easily undo the healing that had crept up on her thanks to that impulsive decision to stay in the south of France for summer. It felt like she'd only just rediscovered that life was not only worth living, but that it could actually turn out to be better than she'd ever dreamed it could be.

She'd started feeling the first stirrings of a new happiness before she'd met Julien Rousseau, but falling in love with him was taking it to an extraordinary new level. If imminent heart-break was the price she needed to pay to feel like this at all, it had to be well worth it, because nothing, *nothing* else could feel *this* good – as if anything was possible. No... as if *everything* was possible. There was no point in even thinking about future bridges, much less crossing them before she was forced to.

Thinking about the tasks that still needed to be done before Laura's visit was not appealing either, because everything Ellie did to finish the renovations and get the house ready for its marketing photographs was taking her one step closer to the time she had to leave. So, instead of working in the garden or starting to sand down the wrought-iron furniture ready for its new coat of paint, or perhaps even finding the courage to go and do something about the neglected space of the child's bedroom, Ellie put

Pascal's harness on and slipped the strap of her small bag over her head.

'I think I need a new dress,' she told him. 'Let's go down to that little shop at the bottom of the hill, past the ice cream shop.'

It was a habit that had once been automatic, so Ellie thought nothing of picking up her sketch pad and some pencils and putting them into the basket on her bike. It didn't matter that Pascal would be sitting on top of them.

As much as Ellie loved Vence and St Paul de Vence, it was the small medieval village of Tourrettes-sur-Loup that was claiming her heart as her favourite. Her hometown. Nicknamed 'City of Violets', the cobbled streets had reminders of the tiny purple flowers it had been famous for since the nineteenth century. She left her bike in the square, under the shade of one of the huge plane trees, and walked past a group of men engrossed in what appeared to be a very serious game of boules. Glancing up, she saw the restaurant that Julien had mentioned – the one that had the best *frites* in the world, which Theo loved to dip into egg yolks.

She could almost see Julien and Theo sitting under an umbrella at one of those tables overlooking the square. Not just Julien and Theo. Ellie could imagine herself sitting there with them, and they were laughing because Theo had egg yolk on his chin and the happiest smile on his face as he enjoyed a favourite food.

Maybe it was the happiness that Ellie was so aware of today that cushioned her from being ambushed by grief, with the reminder that she would never see her own son's smile again. There was a poignancy there, but a sweetness as well that made the squeeze on her heart one that was nowhere near fierce enough to end in tears.

From the first steps through the archway onto the cobbled

walkways, there were reminders everywhere of the celebration of violets. Shops were selling postcards and tiles, violet-scented soap and oil, and even wine, candied violets and countless other items that were decorated with the unpretentious little flowers.

A poster advertising the annual violet festival in early March was still attached to a wall. The ice cream shop further down the hill was famous for its violet-flavoured ice cream, and Ellie bought one because... well, it was a gorgeous summer day. And what could be better than enjoying a pale-purple ice cream with a sugary flower on top and wandering down to the ramparts to admire the dramatic view of the gorges and forests and the distant sea?

The shop Ellie had walked past many times was open when they headed back up the hill, and Pascal was happy to sit on the stone step while Ellie looked at racks crowded with pretty summer dresses and shirts. The garment that caught her eye instantly was a long dress in white muslin, printed with small, bright red poppies and tiny green leaves.

On closer inspection, she found the poppies were actually heart-shaped, but that only made it more appealing. It had spaghetti straps, a smocked yoke and a layered skirt, and Ellie knew how unlikely it was that she would ever be able to wear it back in Scotland. Being white, it was also highly impractical, but it was too pretty not to try on. She already had a dress with daisies on it that would remind her of Marguerite the donkey. Surely it was only fair to have a dress with poppies on it for Coquelicot?

Putting it on made it so impossible to resist that Ellie decided she would wear it and had her blue dress wrapped up to carry home. She walked slowly up the cobbled slopes, enjoying the swish of the long skirt against her legs and the sun kissing her bare shoulders, reminding herself to buy a bunch of carrots for the donkeys at the *épicerie* before heading home.

Ellie put her parcel into the basket of her bike, which was in the shade of one of the huge plane trees around the square, and noticed the sketch book and pencils she'd put in there earlier. A glance towards the *épicerie* showed her that the shop was currently busy, and it seemed like the perfect excuse to sit in the shade for a few minutes and capture a fraction of this quiet summer morning in the village that was becoming something so special to her.

The church, on the other side of the square, had always caught her gaze. An ancient stone building with a picturesque bell tower and quirky architecture that suggested additions during different centuries was typical of a medieval French village, but, as Ellie began outlining her sketch, she was paying more attention to what made the Église Saint-Grégoire so appealing. Maybe it was the central, octagonal-shaped section. Or the seemingly random placement of arch-shaped windows on some walls and square ones on others. A chimney seemed out of place, but the tower with its spire and glimpses of the old bell was everything you could ask for in a church.

Ellie moved so that she could see the entrance to the church, which was a remarkably plain wall with a small cross on the roofline, a round window directly beneath and, in the same line, an archway-shaped depression in the wall that held a statue above weathered-looking wooden doors. Only one of the doors was visible because the other was opened inwards, leaving a shadowed gap in the wall.

An invitation to go inside?

'Wait here,' Ellie told Pascal as she tied his lead to the iron rack. 'Guard the bike for me. I won't be long.'

For some reason, Ellie hadn't taken the time to go inside the church before. As she stepped inside to see the light pouring into the richly decorated space, creating wide, misty rays beneath the dramatic curves of a vaulted ceiling, she caught her breath. Beneath her feet she could feel the unevenness of huge flagstones that had been worn smooth by centuries of footsteps, and the rows of wooden chairs were begging for someone to sit and take it all in with an appropriate reverence.

There were small bunches of white gypsophila tied onto the chairs at the aisle end of the rows with silk ribbons, and Ellie realised there must have been a wedding in here very recently. She moved slowly and quietly further into the church as, more and more, the vibrant artwork, numerous statues, gilding and wrought iron added to her initial impression of a remarkable space, and she wondered how many couples might have been blessed to exchange their vows in this holy place. She could almost hear echoes of the promises of commitment and fidelity and love for the rest of their lives.

That was when Ellie finally sat down on one of the chairs with its fluff of white blossom and soft ribbon. Just for a moment. Because there was deep sense of yearning that was bringing a lump to her throat and the threat of tears to the back of her eyes. And her imagination was pushing her into a space that hadn't even existed a few minutes ago. Because she could see herself in a white dress, maybe even *this* white dress with its tiny poppies and green leaves. She was holding a bunch of simple white daisies, and she had flowers in her hair. Beside her, Julien was looking impossibly gorgeous in a dark suit, and little Theo was walking in front of them, scattering rose petals from the small basket he was carrying.

Ellie and Julien were walking towards the front of the church, where the altar and lectern were behind the intricate ironwork of the railing.

Getting married...

She'd never dreamed of getting married before. Even to Liam when she found out she was carrying his baby.

But this was different.

Julien was different, and, in this fantasy moment, the wedding she was imagining was the most perfect event of her life. She had never wanted anything quite this much. And then she blinked and it was gone, and she got to her feet and walked back out of this magical place knowing that it had been nothing more than fantasy. That it was something that could never happen in real life.

And, however much she wanted to hang on to that tiny scrap of something so perfect, it was already fading – just a final glimpse of a dream evaporating into wakeful reality, swept along by a painful twinge of... oh, yes... had she actually begun to forget what grief felt like?

Perhaps it had been the addition of Theo into the fantasy that had been the reminder that grief could still be sharp enough to hurt despite this new happiness. Reality meant that if Julien ever imagined *her* as his bride, he would, no doubt, feel the same grief for the wife he'd loved and lost and would never try to replace. Grief had no timetable, and there was no point in longing for a future that was never going to happen.

Except... Ellie could feel the caress of this soft new dress against her legs as she blinked in the bright sunshine outside. If she was lucky, perhaps a fragment of that fantasy might have caught somewhere in the folds of this pretty fabric, and she might be able to catch another frisson the next time she put it on. Even for a heartbeat would be long enough to remember it was possible to feel as if you'd found the holy grail of life, which was so very simple yet so complicated at the same time.

To be happy.

To love. And be loved.

16

The first hint that there was something a little different about Laura was her reaction when Ellie video called her, early in the morning before she would be at work, with an offer to pick her up from the airport in Nice.

Not that she noticed anything odd straight away. The initial, acerbic response was an echo of the bossy, older sister she remembered so well from her childhood.

'What?' Laura's incredulous huff suggested she was offended. 'In that antique rust bucket that looks like it could break down at any moment?'

'Margot is totally trustworthy,' Ellie assured her.

'You've *named* the car?'

Ellie came very close to rolling her eyes. 'Wait till you meet her,' she said. 'You'll find out just how much of a personality she has. Want to change your mind and meet her at the airport? There's a 'Kiss and Fly' lane at Terminal Two which is supposed to be for dropping people off, but apparently, if you time it well, it's okay to pick people up there too.'

'Thanks, but it's already organised.'

'But you don't need to go to the expense of renting a car this time.'

'I'm not.'

'Taxis are even more expensive.'

'I'm not renting a car or getting a taxi.' Laura's increasingly impatient tone was a warning that Ellie was getting out of line. And then she visibly sucked in a breath and broke eye contact. 'Noah's picking me up, okay?'

'*Noah*? The estate agent?' Ellie was blinking in astonishment now. 'You're not going on the back of his motorbike, are you?'

'What if I am?'

'What about your suitcase?'

'I'm only coming for a couple of days. I could put my toothbrush and some clean knickers in my handbag if I need to.'

Ellie was silent now. Laura had never done anything remotely impetuous in her life, let alone something as wild as putting a pair of knickers in her handbag and climbing on the back of what she remembered being a rather large and powerful motorbike.

'Oh...' It was Laura who broke the stunned silence. 'I meant to tell you – don't worry about dinner for me that night. Noah's taking me to some posh restaurant that he thinks I should see. He says it's famous enough to be worth mentioning in the advertising blurb for the house.'

'He's taking you out to dinner? Have you been online dating without telling me?'

'Don't be ridiculous.' Laura's laugh sounded perfectly genuine, and she had no hesitation in rolling *her* eyes. She even tossed in a shake of her head, making her silky, straight bob shimmer as it brushed her shoulders. 'Even if I was desperate enough to do something like online dating, do you really think I'd ever be remotely interested in someone like Noah Dufour?'

Ellie echoed her laughter. 'Not in a million years,' she agreed.

'He's being helpful, that's all. And the sooner we get it all sorted and the house sold, the better, yes?'

'Mmm...' Ellie tried to sound enthusiastic, but it was too difficult.

She wasn't ready to leave yet. The weather was glorious. The limoncello wasn't ready to drink, and she'd thought of half a dozen more things that she could be doing to the little house and garden to make it even more appealing. She hadn't given any thought to what arrangements might be necessary to take Pascal back to Scotland with her, and... and what about Julien...?

She was nowhere near ready to leave him yet.

But she turned her half-hearted agreement into a bright smile.

'Wait till you see how it's looking,' she told Laura. 'There's a reason I haven't been sending you any photos lately. I want it to be a surprise.'

* * *

The biggest surprise of all was that she wanted to spare Laura the task of dealing with the second bedroom. Because she wanted her sister to know that she had found the courage to do it herself. Not just to thank her for her support – and the push – she had given Ellie, as well as the inspired gift of the wonderful red bicycle, but to show her that being here *had* been exactly what she'd needed. That she was healing. That it felt like she was really starting to live again. And, for that, she would owe her big sister a debt of gratitude for ever.

But time had almost run out. She would be arriving in only a couple of days.

So Ellie didn't give herself time to even remind herself of the get-out-of-jail-free card Laura had offered by saying she would sort that room. As soon as she ended the call with her sister, she walked straight up the stairs to open the door.

With her knuckles white from the strength in her determined grip, Ellie twisted the brass doorknob and almost flung the door of that room open – as if she was about to confront an intruder.

But had merely opening the door drained the reserves of her courage?

Ellie had taken only a single step into the room before she stopped. She could feel the thump of her heart against her ribs, and her throat was tight. Too tight to release the air in her lungs. She knew the cot was there, of course, but if she stared straight ahead at the newly replaced pane of glass in the window, the baby's bed was only a pale blur in her peripheral vision, so it was possible to ignore. Then she looked down at the mess the glazier had left on the floor, which included some shards of the old glass amongst a scattering of bat droppings.

Sharp, dangerous shards, which Pascal was heading straight towards.

'Oh *no*...' Ellie stepped forwards to scoop a surprised little dog up into her arms. 'You can't walk there,' she told him. 'You'll cut your paws. And those bat droppings might be poisonous, for all I know. That's the first thing we need to clean up, isn't it? Let's go downstairs and find our dustpan and broom. And you'll have to stay down there until it's safe.' She held Pascal close, resting her cheek against his head, more grateful than ever for the warmth of the little creature who was sharing so much of her life. '*D'accord*?'

It was easier to walk into the room the second time, but Ellie still avoided looking directly at the cot by keeping her gaze down. There was an old rag rug in the middle of the floor. Handmade, with braided strips of fabric carefully stitched into an oval shape with scalloped edges like a big flower, and another flower, with petals, in its centre. It was so dirty that it was hard to see what the original colours might have been, and Ellie might have been tempted to throw it away except... except that the flower in the centre of the rug reminded her of the stone mosaics in the paths of St Paul de Vence.

The flowers that had been the reason she'd stayed here in the first place.

The spark that had slowly but steadily become a glow of happiness.

If she hadn't stayed, she wouldn't have Pascal in her life now. She might never have picked up her paints or pencils again. She wouldn't have limoncello maturing in her cupboard.

She might never have found out what it felt like to fall in love more deeply than she'd ever known was possible.

Ellie picked up the rug and carefully shook out the bat dirt. She took it to the bathroom and put it in the tub, running enough water to let it soak for a while. She would wash it later. If it needed mending, she would do that, too. She would, in fact, take it back to Scotland with her when she left, she decided. Because looking at that flower shape would remind her of everything about this patch of the planet, and Ellie had the feeling that she might need reminders of what it had felt like to have been *this* happy.

She went back into the bedroom and swept the floor, starting at the window to get rid of the glass splinters. She moved the small bed, which had a simple white, curved metal frame with bars, like an antique hospital bed. She swept underneath, and then, again without giving herself time to think about it, she took hold of the cot and dragged it away from its corner of the room to sweep the last part of the floor.

It was safe to let Pascal come upstairs again after that, and he padded after her as she took all the folded bedding, and even the mattresses, outside to air. She used a broom to get dust and cobwebs from the beams on the ceiling and then filled the first of the several buckets of hot water that were needed to wash the wooden floorboards and wipe down the slightly cracked white paintwork on the bed. The walls of the room were also painted white and needed a thorough clean. The only thing left to wipe down after that was the cot, and it wasn't as difficult as Ellie thought it was going to be, because the seeds of a distraction had been planted while she'd been cleaning the walls.

The plain, bare white walls that looked like an oversized canvas.

If she were a child on her first visit to France and had gone running up those stairs to find where she was going to sleep, what would make this space as magical as everything else about her holiday?

By the time she had wiped down every square inch of that cot, Ellie knew what she was going to do. She'd paint a frieze on the walls just above the level of the bed frame and the sides of the cot. Tendrils of green ivy and scattered blooms of daisies and poppies and spears of lavender. It would be easy, but she had limited time, so perhaps it was just as well that Julien was away visiting Theo. Ellie could stay up all night, if that was what it took, because she could imagine the look on Laura's face when she saw that not only had she been brave enough to tackle this room, she had rediscovered her passion for art.

When Ellie opened the window to let in more of the warmth from the sunshine outside to dry everything, she was still planning the frieze. The window was a bonus. She could make the ivy scramble around its outline on the walls but have leaves and flowers dangling onto the casing that framed the glass. As she walked out to take a break to sort and wash the bedding and the rag rug, she was leaving a room that already looked – and even smelt – very different.

* * *

Lunch had been postponed in favour of a quick trip to the *bricolage* for a range of small pots of quick-drying, water-based paints. The staff in the hardware store recognised Ellie as a new, loyal customer, and the girl at the checkout counter smiled at her.

'*Ça va?*'

'*Ça va,*' Ellie responded. '*Et vous?*'

The girl shrugged as she handed over the purchases. '*Ah, tu sais... le train-train...*'

The tone suggested that a sympathetic smile was in order, but Ellie had no idea what had been said. Or why a stranger was using the less formal address for her. She found herself talking to Pascal about it as she pedalled home.

'*Le train*? Isn't that, like, a railway train? Or is it something completely different when it's two of them?'

Pascal wasn't interested. Riding in the basket of the bicycle was one of his favourite things these days, and he sat very still and upright, with his ears flapping a little in the breeze their speed created and his nose lifted so that he didn't miss anything worth sniffing.

'Fine...' Ellie smiled. 'I'll remember to ask Julien.'

Dinner had almost been forgotten as Ellie used pencils to draw the pattern of the frieze before starting to paint. She had filled in the dark green of every single ivy leaf before Pascal's sad sigh broke her focus long enough for her to realise it was way past time to feed him. She also needed to turn a light on so that she could start painting the flowers. White daisies with yellow centres, and blood-red poppies, would be easy, but there had been no small pots of purple paint available, so now was a good time to take a break. She could mess about with some blue, red and white paint to create a lilac shade for the lavender while both she and Pascal had a bite of dinner.

Ellie had no idea what time it was when she finally finished her work many hours later. She felt drunk with fatigue, but she stood in the middle of the room she'd been too afraid to come into until this morning and found tears rolling down her cheeks.

Happy tears. Because she had made this bedroom a beautiful space. Or perhaps they were sad tears because she had, on impulse, finished this enormous task by quickly painting three tiny daisies on the curved wooden top at the head of the cot and, increasingly, had been aware of an echo of the emptiness of this small bed in her heart. An emptiness that was heavy enough to feel like a stone that would be too big to carry. As heavy as a baby who'd spent six months happily growing as fast as he could?

Ellie knew exactly how heavy that was. She could *feel* the weight as she remembered the last time she had gently tucked Jack into his cot for the night. As she had pulled him out in complete panic the next morning so that she could try and breathe life back into her precious baby.

It hurt.

So much.

But when Ellie raised her gaze and followed the garland of flowers and leaves right around the room, there was pleasure to be found to dilute at least some of that pain.

And pride, because Ellie knew that she'd taken another step into her new future and it had been a big one. And now she was so tired that even big emotions or heartbreaking memories were not going to keep her awake a minute longer.

* * *

Sunshine streaming through the window woke Ellie the next morning, along with a bark from Pascal to let her know that he was waiting by the French doors and it was getting urgent to be let outside.

It was only when she was feeling a lot more awake – thanks to the strong coffee she had sipped, sitting out on the terrace, still wearing the shorts and paint-stained tee shirt she'd fallen asleep in last night – that she remembered she'd left the bedding outside. Luckily, it hadn't rained, and she found the mattresses and bedding dry and smelling fresh. Even the rag rug, hanging over the branch of a lemon tree, had dried in the warm temperatures during the night.

She dragged the mattress for the bed up the stairs first, slightly nervous about entering the room after the emotional ambush when she'd left it in the early hours of the morning. But, amazingly, with the sun coming in through the window and the bright colours of the flowers, there were no unbearable emotions lurking. She worked for the next hour to put the room back together, making up the bed with sheets and a lace cover similar to the one on her larger bed. The handmade patchwork quilt with the classic 'grandmother's garden' pattern was the perfect finishing touch. Or perhaps it was the pale yellow centre of the flower on the rag rug, which had been invisible under the years of dust and grime. Fresh and clean against the darkness of old wood, it was as much a work of art as the latest contribution that Ellie had made to this house.

In the end, it was the very final touch that had to be the most significant. When she completed making up the cot by smoothing a soft, yellow blanket over the mattress. When she found she wasn't remembering the horror of finding her baby had died. Instead, she was remembering how Jack would be lying there awake first thing in the morning. Hungry but keeping himself happy by sucking his fists. And then he would kick his feet and gurgle with his version of laughter as he saw his mammy for the first time that day – as if it were the best thing that could possibly be happening in his world. He would hold up his arms, with the total confidence that he was about to be picked up and cuddled, and it was always the best thing that could possibly be happening in Ellie's life, because her heart would be melting – overflowing with the pure love she had for this tiny person.

Her eyes were, yet again, filling with tears that were also about to overflow. But she was smiling at the same time.

And maybe... just maybe... the balance had shifted a little. Because this was the first time that Ellie could see even a shred of truth in what people had been telling her for months. That time would heal the pain. That one day there would be joy to be found in her memories. The joy had always been there, but somehow it had been able to feed rather than override that unbearable sense of loss.

Until now...?

17

_____

Julien never knew quite what to expect when he took the private route to La Maisonette and walked through his garden to climb over the fence and into the olive grove. Ellie knew he was coming back from Roquebillière this evening, and he rather hoped she might be sitting out on her terrace waiting for him. He had a bottle of wine in his hands, and they could *prend un verre* before he took her out to dinner.

There was a Michelin-starred restaurant in Vence that he hadn't taken her to yet, and he knew she would love the intimate feeling of the small tables in the garden courtyard. He wanted to see her reaction to the stunning food they served, as well. Would she close her eyes and tilt her head back a little to focus on how delicious something was? The way he'd first seen her do when she was eating her favourite cheese?

The way she did when he kissed her? Or ran his fingers over her body with a gentle, teasing touch as a prelude to so much more?

Oh, *mon Dieu*... he'd been looking forward to getting home all day, and the anticipation of making love to Ellie had just reached an almost unbearable pitch. Perhaps a late dinner would be a good idea.

There was always the possibility that she would be oblivious to the time of day and in the middle of a task she was too passionate about to want to be interrupted. Something artistic perhaps, like her sketches. Or messy, like chipping plaster from stone walls. His mouth curved into a lopsided smile as he remembered the first time he'd taken this route to find her and he'd been concerned she was deathly ill, with the pallor the plaster dust on her skin had created. She might be out driving in her little red car, of course. Or riding her bicycle. Or...

Oh, la vache... what on earth was Ellie *doing*?

Julien could see her on the other side of the olive grove as soon as he climbed over the fence. Pascal was keeping a safe distance away from her. One of the donkeys – Marguerite, it looked like – was standing right behind her, looking over her shoulder. Coquelicot was... almost unrecognisable because she was covered with a white, foamy substance. Ellie had a bucket at her feet and a large sponge in her hands and she, too, was covered in...

Soap suds, that's what the substance was.

Ellie was also very damp. She had shorts on, with suds dripping down those gorgeous legs of hers, and a tee shirt that was covered in paint stains and... *oh...* it was wet enough to be very obvious that she wasn't wearing a bra.

She was also laughing.

'I'm sorry, Coquelicot. I put too much shampoo in the water. I'll have to go and get another bucket to rinse you off with. Probably lots of buckets. Don't go anywhere.'

Ellie picked up the bucket, turned to see Julien coming towards her and promptly put it down again. Her face lit up with joy. She pushed curls back from her face, which left soap suds in her hair, and came towards him.

Julien, having had the idea of taking Ellie somewhere very elegant for dinner, was wearing a favourite pair of chinos and a freshly ironed linen shirt, but it didn't occur to him not to put down the bottle he was carrying and take Ellie into his arms.

And kiss her.

Thoroughly.

So thoroughly they could well have ended up making love in the olive grove, except that Ellie pulled away with a sound of frustration.

'I can't leave Coquelicot all soapy. And I still need to shampoo Marguerite.'

'Why?'

'It seemed like a good idea. My sister Laura is arriving tomorrow to take photos of the house to use for the marketing campaign, and I thought the donkeys should look their best so they can be in the photos, too. I've left it a bit late in the day, though, and I'll need to get them as dry as I can with the old towels. I can brush them in the morning.'

Several thoughts were competing for prominence in Julien's head as he tried to listen. The reminder that this property would soon be sold, so the end point of his time with her was getting closer, was a bit of a shock. He couldn't intrude on the time she would have with her sister, which meant that being with her was off the agenda for the duration of the visit, and his body was letting him know in no uncertain terms just how much he wanted to be with Ellie. Right now. And for as long as possible.

The awareness of how much he was going to miss this was trying to push its way in; right on its heels was the desire to make the most of every single moment that was left.

But he loved that she wanted to wash the donkeys so they

would look good in photographs. He loved that she loved the donkeys and was no longer afraid of them, the way she had been when she'd thought she was rescuing Theo from certain death.

It would be so easy to love *her*, it was as simple as that – or as simple as it would have been in another time and place, before his world had changed beyond recognition. But that didn't mean he couldn't make the most of these moments of escape with Ellie. If anything, it made it more important to gather memories he would be able to treasure.

'I have a...' The word in English escaped him, perhaps because his brain was still trying to grapple with an underlying sense of urgency that came with the reminder that their time together was limited. '*Un tuyau d'arrosage*. You know?'

'No...' Ellie was laughing. 'I have no idea what that is.'

'It might help get the soap off. It's for putting water on the garden.'

'Oh... a *hose*?'

'*Oui, c'est ça.*'

'Perfect.' Ellie stood on tiptoes to press a kiss to his lips. 'I couldn't find one, and I didn't want to go to the *bricolage* two days in a row.'

It was Julien who pulled away this time. Because if he didn't, he wouldn't want to move at all, and the sooner they got those donkeys clean, the sooner he could give making love to Ellie his undivided attention.

'You start making Marguerite soapy,' he said. 'I'll get the 'ose.'

The donkeys seemed to like getting soapy with the vigorous massage that went with it. They weren't so keen on getting drenched with cold water from the hose. They were too polite to walk away, but they shook themselves repeatedly, initially creating cloudbursts of soap suds that covered both Julien and

Ellie and were, inexplicably, the funniest thing that had ever happened to him.

Or perhaps he just *wanted* it to be the funniest thing ever because he wanted to hear the sound of Ellie's laughter. To imprint it in his memory so that he could find it whenever he needed to.

Because it made him feel, also inexplicably but undeniably, the happiest he'd ever been in his life.

The scattered soap suds became much colder sprays of water as the donkeys were rinsed and, by the time Ellie was rubbing them down with towels and Julien was rolling up the hose that had gathered a layer of sticky mud, it was obvious that they would not be going out anywhere for dinner.

'I'm sorry about your clothes,' she said.

He shrugged. He could actually feel the touch of her gaze as if it were roaming over his bare skin instead of clothes that were not only soggy, but were now liberally streaked with mud from rolling up the hose.

Ellie kept a straight face as she lifted her gaze to his.

'I'll wash them for you,' she offered. 'But you'll have to take them off.'

Julien's lips twitched despite his own attempt to keep a straight face. '*D'accord...*'

'Come with me, then.' Ellie gathered up the towels. 'It's still more than warm enough out here to dry out damp donkeys, but I'm getting cold.'

'You need a hot shower.' Julien nodded. 'And so do I.'

The mental image he suddenly had of soaping every inch of Ellie's body was enough for him to decide that the pleasure of anticipation had run its course. He was more than ready for the real thing, so he turned to start walking towards where Pascal was still patiently waiting on the lemon orchard side of the fence.

'I don't have a shower,' he heard Ellie say behind him. 'But I do have a lovely old bath.'

* * *

The last time Ellie had shared a bath with anyone had been when she was small enough to fit between her older sisters. It seemed like a romantic thing to do now, but she was finding herself oddly nervous as she started filling the tub and went out to the terrace to borrow some of the large candles she had recently placed inside the ornate holders. Julien had poured wine into two glasses, and he followed her upstairs.

With a window that was small enough not to let in much of the fading daylight, the candlelight made it less daunting to remove every stitch of her clothing without the distraction of spiralling arousal, but this still felt... odd.

Intimate but so ordinary at the same time.

Also awkward. Bathtubs weren't really designed to hold two adults, so it wasn't easy to find a way to arrange their legs as they sat facing each other, and Ellie needed to be careful of the taps behind her back. But then Julien leaned over the edge to pick up the wine glasses and handed one to Ellie. The water stopped sloshing and the flickering light from the candles was suddenly perfect.

As perfect as the way Julien was smiling at her.

'Ça va?' he murmured.

Ellie took a sip of her wine. The query had reminded her of the exchange in the *bricolage* yesterday. So she shrugged.

'Ah, tu sais...' She managed to find just the right note of nonchalance. '*Le train-train...*'

Julien almost choked on his wine as he burst into laughter.

'What? What did I say?'

'*Le train-train...*' Julien managed to stifle both his laughter and his coughing. 'It means... *pas grand-chose* – nothing special. Just the same as usual. You might say "same old, same old"?'

Ellie was grinning now. Any awkwardness had been swallowed by the laughter.

'My bad,' she admitted. 'I've never, ever done this before.'

Julien's foot moved to stroke her thigh as they both took a sip of their wine, studying each other's face over the rim of the glasses.

'And is it good?'

'I like it,' Ellie smiled. 'Apart from the taps.'

'Ah...' Julien took their glasses and put them on the floor beside the bath. 'Turn around,' he commanded. 'So you have your back to me.'

The candles flickered and small waves threatened to splash over the rim of the tub as Ellie turned herself around. Julien put his arms around her and drew her against his body, where she nestled between his legs. When she tilted her head back to rest it in the dip just under his collar bone she could look up and see his face.

He wasn't looking down at her. He was reaching behind him now, to where the lavender-scented soap she had bought in Tourrettes-sur-Loup was sitting, along with an artificial spray of lavender bloom, in the small ceramic saucer that had come with it. She had a heartbeat to simply soak in the profile of his face, feeling his skin slip against hers at the same time. She was also feeling something very similar to that overwhelming rush of emotion she had been reintroduced to only a matter of hours ago. That warm, liquid, totally heart-melting sensation of pure love.

The words almost escaped her.

I love you, Julien...

But Ellie pressed her lips together to stop them being heard.

Because she didn't want to spoil this moment by reminding him of what he'd lost in his life. By creating an echo of what his wife must have told him a thousand times.

Besides, coherent words were about to get a lot harder to find. Julien had soaped his hands and placed them on her shoulders and was stroking them down the front of her body to cover and outline the shape of her breasts, just above the level of the water in the bath. He bent his head at the same time, and she could feel his lips and his tongue against her neck.

Her breath came out in a sigh that became a groan of pleasure as one of Julien's hands slipped below the level of the water so that his touch became breathtakingly intimate. He knew exactly where to find what he knew would coax her over the edge very quickly, but she knew he was probably just teasing her a little now. He had a gift for taking her right to that edge and then slowing things down so that, the next time, it would become even more intense.

It felt like he had the ability to slow down time itself. Ellie could only hope that when it was her turn to give him this kind of pleasure – which might have to wait until they were out of the bath and in her bed – he would feel the same way. As if, for whatever time they had together, the outside world ceased to exist and the passage of time became completely irrelevant.

Le train-train?

Aye... that was going to be a joke for ever, because this was so special that Ellie knew she was never going to find it again.

18

Julien stayed away from La Maisonette while Ellie's sister was visiting.

Had that been because he didn't want to watch them getting ready to sell the house, which would make the ticking of that clock feel even louder? Or was it that meeting a member of her family might make it feel that things between them were more significant than they were and would mean it was time to escape?

Julien wasn't ready to escape.

Not yet. Not until he had to.

Sitting on this terrace with Ellie close enough to touch without even having to reach for her, savouring the last drops of an excellent glass of wine, with a small, white dog sound asleep in shade that was merging with the fading light of sunset, was...

It was perfect, that's what it was.

It felt like Julien had come home after being away for too long, which was strange because it had only been a couple of days.

Not that he was about to try and analyse why it felt like this. He simply wanted to enjoy it.

'So it was good? To have your sister here? She must have been very happy with what you've done to the house.'

'She was.' Ellie opened a big envelope that was on the table. 'She printed out some of the photographs she took while she was here. Look... here's one of the donkeys asleep under the olive trees. And one of my bicycle.'

Julien smiled, remembering the day that Ellie had fallen off that bicycle because Pascal had run out in front of her. He, shifted his hand just enough to brush the skin of her arm with the back of his hand. He knew it would still be there. The sensation that was like a faint electric current. Something he'd never felt with any other woman, no matter how attracted to them he'd been.

But this was Ellie.

And she was different.

'Here's one of Margot. And I love these close-ups of the flowers on the front door, and the door-knocker.'

The door-knocker, shaped like a delicate female hand holding an apple, was shinier than Julien had remembered it being.

'Did you polish it?'

Ellie nodded. 'Laura thought it was new, but I said it had just needed a bit of love. Like everything else in La Maisonette.'

She was tilting her head towards Julien, although they were too far apart to kiss. She turned her arm so that when his hand reached her wrist she could cup her fingers around it. When Julien turned his hand over, it felt like the most natural thing in the world for their fingers to interlace. Loosely, so that they could still move and play with each other in a slow, gentle dance.

'And she took so many photos of the flowers I painted on the walls in the other bedroom. She knew why I'd avoided going in there for so long. She almost cried... and Laura never cries.'

The child's bedroom.

Julien said nothing for a moment, but he knew she would feel the change in the pressure of his fingers against hers. That she already knew he'd understood how significant her caring for Theo had been that night and that he'd been so proud of everything she'd achieved in her time in his country. That he would always be in awe of her courage and her creativity and her ability to offer love. He couldn't go there again, knowing how hard it would be to survive the aftermath, but he was confident that Ellie would be brave enough one day – not just with a lover but as a mother as well. That she would find all the love she so deserved to receive in return.

'She must be so proud of everything you've done here.'

'I think so.' Ellie smiled. 'I didn't really see much of her, though. She spent more time with the estate agent than me. She said it was business – they were making up the marketing information for the property and he was taking her to some of the highlights this area has to offer. They even went as far as the lavender fields in Provence so that she could include them in the brochure, but I think there was more to it than that.' Ellie shook her head. 'Not that Laura would admit it. Quite the opposite, in fact. She even told me that she never wanted to be in any kind of serious relationship. Ever.'

'Oh?' Had Ellie's oldest sister been through as much of a disastrous marriage as he had himself? 'Why not?' he asked. 'Has she had her heart broken?'

'It's more that she's afraid of relationships, I think. She's seen too many examples of how bad they can be.'

'Like yours?'

'Mmm.' Ellie was biting her lip. 'But it goes deeper than that. It was about what happened in our family and how we lost our father. She was the oldest, so she was far more a part of it than me, or my other sister, Fiona.'

'You had trouble? With your father?' A chill ran down Julien's spine. Had Ellie been abused in some way? Physically? Sexually? The thought made him feel ill.

Ellie caught his gaze for a heartbeat. 'It's a long time ago. I won't bore you with it.'

She began to slide her hand away from his but it felt like it was stretching something important. Something that would break as soon as he couldn't feel her skin against his, so he caught her hand and held it tightly. As if he could protect her from what had happened so long ago?

'I want to know,' he said. 'Please... tell me.'

He let her sit in silence for a long minute while he refilled their glasses. And then he waited patiently, and Ellie began to fill that silence with her memories of happiness and hurt from her early childhood. It was clear that she had adored her father and had the kind of pleasure Julien hoped Theo would remember from playing with his papa or listening to him reading a story.

'But he was an alcoholic,' Ellie continued softly. 'He was getting drunk in the daytime and he lost his job. He got angry a lot, and I know Mam and Laura got scared. And then something happened. He hit another man and hurt him badly, and then... he just disappeared. He ran away...'

Julien could feel the confusion that the child Ellie had been left with. The fear and grief when her father simply vanished from her life, but the relief that was mixed into the emotional turmoil, that her mother and sisters didn't need to be scared any longer. Thank goodness Theo had been too young to have memories of his mother that would last a lifetime. And that he had no knowledge of what might have created his father's – guilty – sense of relief. He never would. Julien would make sure that he believed his mother had loved him so much that the thought of leaving him would have been incomprehensible.

'Look...' Ellie pulled a smaller envelope from amongst the newly printed photographs. 'These were inside a book I found in the garage. This is my father and his brother. It was taken in Cornwall in the nineteen-fifties.' She put another couple of faded photographs on the table. 'This one's really old. We thought the woman might be our grandmother on our father's side of the family. She was French. We didn't know that until we heard about this house that my uncle had owned and we had inherited. The church looks French, doesn't it?'

It was a wedding photograph of a couple standing in front of a church. There was a bell tower to one side and the rest of the church was quite plain apart from a round image of a saint painted on the highest part of the front walls and a gilded figure on the roof above it.

Julien frowned. There was something familiar about the church. He picked up the other photograph. Perhaps these were the same two boys from the photo taken in Cornwall, but this was when they were much younger. One of them looked no more than Theo's age here, squatting beside a small channel of fast running water in the middle of a cobbled street, watching his brother put a toy boat into its current. A woman was watching them, seated in a café amongst other shops on the street, and she seemed to be laughing.

Julien's eyes widened. 'I know this place.'

'You *do*?'

'It's a small town called Saint-Martin-Vésubie. It's very close to where my grandmother lives in Roquebillière.'

'Are you sure?'

'*Oui*... I thought I recognised that church in the other photo, but this...' Julien pointed at the small boys and their boat, which they were about to float down the tiny man-made river in the cobbled street. 'I know that café. I have eaten there. And this *gargouille* in the main street is very distinctive.'

Ellie tried to repeat the word but stumbled.

'A *gargouille*,' he repeated slowly for her to copy. 'It's a channel. An old word for a throat, I believe.'

'Oh...' Ellie's interest had been caught, which was a good thing. The sad memories of her childhood were being pushed to one side. 'That'll be where gargle comes from. And gurgle?'

Julien nodded. 'And gargoyle. That's why the creatures were placed on the roofs of buildings – to channel the water away when it rains.'

'When *il pleut comme une vache qui pisse*?'

Julien's laughter faded into a smile. He usually only felt this soft sensation in his chest when Theo did or said something so adorable it made his heart melt.

He loved the way Ellie could do this...

The way she could notice or remember – and capture – a tiny thing that could touch others was part of the way she looked at life and one of the things that made her so good to be near.

'*Oh là là... tu es adorable*,' he said. He didn't bother translating his words. Instead, he reached out to touch her cheek. The way his fingers traced the outline of her face felt so familiar now – like the way something caught in his chest when Ellie tilted her face into his touch. Her chin was the perfect fit for the cup his hand could create, and her eyes were closing already in anticipation of his kiss as he leaned towards her.

A long, slow, delicious kiss...

And then another.

But then Ellie rested her head on his shoulder and Julien moved his arm to provide a protective circle. Because he didn't want her to move anytime soon. When they did move to go upstairs to her bedroom, it was quite possible that she wouldn't want to make love in the aftermath of remembered trauma and sadness, and that would be fine by him. He would be more than happy to simply hold her like this and feel her fall asleep in his arms. To keep her company.

And to keep her safe.

Maybe that was why he responded the way he did when she spoke again.

'I'd like to go there,' she said quietly. 'To where these photographs were taken. Would it be hard for me to find?'

'Saint-Martin-Vésubie? I'm going near there myself,' he found himself saying. 'I'm collecting Theo from Roquebillière on Saturday afternoon because he's been invited to the birthday party of a school friend in Vence on Sunday. I've been promising to take him to that wolf park for such a long time, and this is the day we can finally go. Saint-Martin-Vésubie is on the way. I could drop you there for an hour or two and pick you up on the way back.'

Except... he didn't want to abandon Ellie to explore the village alone. He would know exactly how she felt about seeing the background of old family photographs come to life because it would be written all over her face. He wanted to share the warmth of something that made her feel good. Or offer comfort if it was something tinged with sadness.

'Or...' he added. 'You could come with us and we could all explore Saint-Martin-Vésubie on the way home? The wolf park is in a beautiful part of the mountains.'

What was he doing? Inviting Ellie to spend time with his son again? Taking her into a part of his life that he had been protecting so fiercely – for Ellie's sake as much as Theo's? But this was important, too.

This was about Ellie's family. And the unknown part of her heritage that was French. It would only be a tiny piece of the puzzle that represented a missing part of her life but perhaps it might help, in the same way that visiting the grave of someone lost could bring a sense of connection. Peace, even...?

And who knew when, or even if, he would get another chance to take Ellie to that town alone? Preparations were being made to put this house on the market very soon. Summer was drawing to a close.

At least this time he could give her the choice of whether she wanted to spend time with his son, on an outing that could cause pain by reminding her of her own loss. This wasn't simply a thoughtless invitation.

'They don't allow dogs in the wolf park, of course, and you might not be happy to leave Pascal at home alone for half a day?'

The look in Ellie's eyes told him that she understood the escape route he had just offered, but he could see something else there as well. Something that hadn't been there the first time he'd suggested she spent time with him and his son. He'd known all along that she was courageous, but there was a strength there that felt new. Had making that child's bedroom so beautiful changed something for her?

The hint of something like surprise – or wonder – on her face made him think that she was just discovering that new strength for herself as well.

'I'd love to come,' she said softly.

19

It was only an hour or so's drive to the small town of Roquebillière, but Ellie had never been this far up into the mountains, and the scenery – not to mention the road, which appeared to be carved into the side of an enormous cliff with a drop on the other side to the river at the bottom of the canyon – was spectacular. Several times she found herself holding her breath and, when Julien slowed to negotiate a narrow tunnel, she let out a gasp.

'Don't worry,' he told her. 'I know this road like... what's that expression? Ah, *oui* – the back of my hand. You're perfectly safe.'

Ellie nodded. 'It's an astonishing road. I've never seen nets like that attached to cliffs.'

'Rockfall protection,' Julien told her. 'This is one of the more scenic roads in France. The river below us is the Vésubie, which is a tributary of the Var. Do you remember the terrible storm a few years ago where so much damage was done and many people killed?'

'I do,' Ellie said. 'It caused problems in Scotland, too, but nothing as bad as in France. It was a real weather bomb.'

'It was this river that caused the damage with the flooding

here after such torrential rain. It wasn't long after I was married, so I wasn't here, but there were pictures on the news of houses being washed into the river as the banks collapsed. Sometimes with people still inside...' Julien cleared his throat as if the memory was overwhelming.

'It must have been terrifying,' Ellie said. She could feel herself trying – and failing – to push away an image of Julien and his new bride on their honeymoon before it could spark a pang of envy. 'And so awful to be a long way away and feel helpless.'

'Sometimes it feels like it only happened yesterday.' Julien seemed intently focused on the road ahead of them. 'But it was before Theo was born. And there's been so much done to repair the damage, but there are always reminders when I drive this road. There will always be the scars on the land in this area.'

'And for the people,' Ellie agreed quietly. 'Life can leave so many scars.' She wanted Julien to know that she understood – and shared – the loss he had to live with for the rest of his life. 'Sometimes,' she added softly, 'it can be the scars you can't see that are the hardest to heal.'

Julien's gaze only left the road for a fraction of a moment. Just long enough to make contact with Ellie's and for the connection between them to become that tiny bit stronger.

For her to know that Julien could see her own invisible scars. He could feel them.

And he cared.

If they never saw each other again after she left at the end of summer, Ellie knew that, as much as he could, Julien loved her, even if he didn't recognise it – or chose to acknowledge it – himself.

It was enough.

Because it had to be.

* * *

Julien parked his car outside his grandmother's house.

'I'll only be a moment,' he said. 'If I take you in, we'll have to make it a visit and that won't leave enough time to get to the wolf park.'

Ellie nodded but she could feel the chill of an undercurrent that told her they weren't close enough for her to be meeting his family. That perhaps this was the reason she hadn't seen him while Laura had been visiting.

She could feel herself being watched from the windows of the small house as Julien disappeared inside to fetch his son, and the chill intensified enough to give her a shiver.

But then he reappeared and Theo was running towards the car. He climbed inside and gave her a folded piece of paper before Julien fastened his seat belt.

'Theo's drawn a picture for you,' he explained. 'He said that's what he does when he's with you.'

Knowing that Theo not only remembered the night she'd looked after him but had wanted to repeat the connection that had come from drawing pictures together made any lingering chill evaporate instantly.

'For me?' she asked. '*Merci*, Theo.' Ellie unfolded the paper and admired the image, which seemed to have quite distinctive ears and teeth on a round ball with stick legs. '*C'est magnifique*,' she told him. 'Is it a wolf?'

'*C'est un loup?*' Julien translated when his son looked blank.

'*Non...*' Theo's face lit up in the biggest smile Ellie had ever seen from this rather solemn little boy. '*C'est Pascal...*'

* * *

Julien pointed out the turning to the village of Saint-Martin-Vésubie as they passed it to get to the wolf park, high in the mountain forests towards the Italian border. Ellie turned her head as if she was trying to get a better glimpse of the village.

'Stopping on the way home will be much better,' he told her. 'There's a falconry show at two o'clock and it's a favourite for Theo. He loves the owls most of all. I'm sorry; I know seeing the town is the real reason you wanted to come today, so I hope you don't mind waiting a little longer.'

Ellie shook her head. 'I love owls, too,' she said. 'I can't wait to see them.'

There was something about her smile that made Julien think she was only being polite, and she seemed quieter than usual as she bent her head to scroll on her phone. Was it because of Theo in the back of the car? Had she overestimated her strength in coping with the reminder of having lost something so precious?

The reason for her scrolling became obvious, however, as he pulled into a car park beside the chalet that sold tickets to the park. She had been using her translation app to find out what *owl* was in French.

'*J'aime les hiboux*,' she said as Julien lifted Theo out of his car seat.

'*Moi aussi*,' he shouted. '*Dépêche-toi, papa. Allons-y!*'

'He's telling us to hurry up,' Julien told her. He held out his hand to his son. 'Come on, then.'

He purchased their tickets, and then they had a short walk through the forest to reach the bridge that formed the entrance to the park. He knew the old wood and stone buildings on the other side provided audiovisual presentations that depicted the history of wolves and their interactions with humans, but those were in French and he didn't want Ellie to feel excluded. Besides, he could see people gathering to sit on the bank around the large, grassed area where the falconry show would take place very soon. He turned it that direction, but Ellie wasn't watching and kept going straight ahead.

'Ellie!' Theo called. '*Viens avec nous. Par ici.*' He held his hand out to make the invitation obvious.

To Julien's surprise, Ellie took hold of Theo's hand, and they walked on either side of his son – like any parents of a small child.

Initially, he was shocked that Ellie, to outward appearances, was taking the place of his son's mother, but then Theo looked up at him and the smile on his face was so happy it almost broke his heart. Could a child so young be aware that, for the moment, Ellie was filling the enormous gap in their lives?

But was it breaking Ellie's heart as well?

Should he pick Theo up, perhaps, and give him a piggyback so that he wasn't able to hold Ellie's hand?

As if she'd caught his thought, or felt his gaze, she glanced up and there was reassurance in her eyes. There might have been a tiny tremble in her lips as they curved into a small smile that was definitely poignant, but she wasn't distressed. She was, however, completely silent as they sat amongst the crowd a minute or two later. But that could simply have been because she was as mesmerised as Theo by the huge birds of prey soaring and swooping between handlers who were dressed in traditional costumes, with white shirts beneath leather jerkins and breeches tucked into high boots.

They moved on after the performance to find one of the viewing platforms where they could try and spot some members of the wolf packs and watch a feeding time, and Julien knew he had to check that Ellie was really okay with Theo wanting to hold her hand again.

'I'm sorry,' he said softly, when Theo had let go of Ellie so that he could press his hands and his nose to the glass of a viewing area and couldn't hear him speaking. 'It was an... imposition, perhaps? For you to come here with Theo?'

'It's fine,' Ellie said quietly. 'Theo is adorable. I love that he's not shy with me any longer.'

Julien hesitated. He wasn't surprised that his son liked Ellie so much: he felt the same way himself. But could he say that? Or that he envied the way the little boy had taken hold of her hand, as if it was the most natural thing in the world to do. He would have liked to be holding her hand himself right now, to be honest, but he would never do that in front of Theo. As he'd reassured his mother and grandmother, when they'd been peering through the window at the woman sitting in his car, Ellie was his neighbour. A friend. Nothing more.

'I'm sorry I didn't take you in to introduce you to my mother and grandmother,' he said quietly. 'That was rude of me.'

Ellie shrugged. 'It doesn't matter,' she said. 'I understand.'

But Julien could sense that it did matter. That there was a barrier that he didn't want to be there today.

Theo had spotted a wolf and was excitedly looking back at his father and pointing. Julien nodded and gave him a thumbs up, but he was thinking of something very different.

If he told Ellie the truth, she would really understand why they could never be anything more than friends. Knowing the truth might mean she could look back, when this *affaire* was over, on what they had had together without any regret for what they didn't have. And it would be over soon. Very soon.

Theo was completely focused on the park attendants walking in the enclosure with buckets of food to leave for the wolves. Not that he would have understood what Julien was saying in English, anyway.

'My mother and my *grand-mère* have never forgiven Sarah,' he told Ellie quietly. 'I knew they might not make you feel welcome.'

Ellie's eyes widened. 'They've never *forgiven* her?' she echoed. 'Why? Was the accident her fault?'

'She wasn't driving,' Julien said, his voice without expression. 'It was her lover's car. She was leaving and, as far as I know, she had no intention of ever coming back to me. Or to Theo.'

He could see the total shock in Ellie's eyes. He wanted to confess that he believed it had been a good thing Sarah had never come back, because she hadn't loved him. She'd only married him because she was pregnant. He hadn't loved her, either. Not the way you should love the person you were choosing to spend the rest of your life with.

Sarah hadn't even loved her son enough to take him with her.

And maybe that was why Ellie was looking so shocked. Because she would do anything to have her own son with her again. She would never ever have left him behind.

But Julien hesitated before admitting that guilty secret and the opportunity was lost. As if he knew he was being talked about, Theo's head turned swiftly, his eyes shining with happiness. A small finger was pointing into the wolf enclosure.

'*Regardez, regardez...*' he called. '*Les loups viennent manger maintenant.*'

Julien smiled back at Theo. Maybe part of that smile was relief that he could shut the past away again – in that locked space where it belonged.

'The wolves are hungry,' he said to Ellie. 'Here they come...'

* * *

It wasn't until they had driven to Saint-Martin-Vésubie, parked the car and started walking down the main street – with its distinctive channel creating a downhill stream that was running fast enough to create tiny waves and delight Theo – that the implications of what Julien had told her began to surface from the shock it had given Ellie.

She had been so sure it was because he'd lost the love of his life that there could never be a future for her with Julien.

But if it was because he wasn't ready to trust again, that felt like... like a light at the end of a tunnel.

A glimmer of hope...

Theo found a small branch, like a miniature tree with a bunch of shiny green leaves at the top, broken off a laurel or bay tree that was growing in a huge urn outside a shop. He dipped the leafy end into the *gargouille* and watched the water rippling around it as he walked beside it, holding the sharp, snapped-off end with care. And then he dropped the whole branch into the stream and trotted after it as the current swept it downhill.

Keeping up with Theo meant there was no time to look around and try to spot the café that would have been where her father and uncle had been playing in the *gargouille* so many years ago, but when they reached the church where her grandparents had been married, there was plenty of time to let the moment sink in. Oddly, Ellie found herself thinking about a completely different church.

The beautiful Église Saint-Grégoire in Tourrettes-sur-Loup that was forever embedded in her memory due to having become lost in the fantasy of something too good to be true – that she had been marrying Julien there.

She had yearned for that future hard enough for it to hurt, assuming that it could never happen in real life. But was it possible that it could? That glimmer of hope became a little brighter. Bright enough to make her eyes water, but Ellie was smiling as she blinked and took out one of the two photos she'd put in her pocket that morning.

She could feel Julien looking over her shoulder as she glanced up from the black and white image to the soft, Mediterranean colours of the church in front of her and the faded painting in the circle. At the same moment, the bell in the ancient tower to one side began to strike the hour. Five slow notes that filled the air and echoed between the stone walls of surrounding buildings.

Ellie tilted her head to smile up at Julien. 'This is magic,' she said. 'It's like I've stepped into this photograph or gone back in time, or someone has just waved a wand and made a picture come to life.' She pulled in a deep breath. 'Thank you so much for bringing me here. I think I know why I love France so much – it feels like at least part of me belongs here.'

'Of course it does.' Julien sounded matter-of-fact. 'You have French blood in your veins. Part of you *does* belong here. Maybe...' He was holding her gaze. '...you should stay?'

Ellie's breath caught somewhere deep in her chest. Did Julien *want* her to stay?

Hope was as much of a drug as falling in love, wasn't it? Ellie knew she might be in danger of instant addiction.

'Why don't you keep La Maisonette?' Julien added. 'You already own a third of it.'

Oh... Could it be this easy to remain a part of his life? For long enough to win his trust? To earn at least acceptance if not approval from the women in his family?

'It's a good house,' he added. 'I thought of buying it myself if it ever came on the market, so that my grandmother could live closer, but when I talked to her about it, she made it very clear that she would never leave the village she's lived in all her life.' He was watching Theo, who was being drawn back to the miniature river on the main street. 'You and your sisters could use it for a holiday house, perhaps, if you didn't want to live here?'

Did he think there could be any reason why she *wouldn't* want to live here? Like, how awkward it might be to have an ex-lover as a neighbour?

The thought didn't get a chance to embed itself in her head, fortunately. Julien was looking up at the sky.

'We should go,' he said. 'Those clouds might be a long way away, but the weather forecast did have a warning for a possible thunderstorm today and they can be quite violent at this time of year, with lightning and thunder and hailstones.'

They walked back up the hill towards the car. Theo clung to his father's back with his arms and legs as he was piggybacked, still holding the branch he'd found. It wasn't easy to keep up with Julien's long strides, but Ellie could understand why he was in a hurry. Was Theo afraid of thunderstorms, like Pascal? She wanted to get home herself and make sure her little dog had been okay on his own all afternoon.

But even that underlying sense of urgency couldn't prevent her stopping, so fast she almost lost her balance, outside a window she hadn't noticed on the way down to the church.

'Oh, look!' she exclaimed.

Julien was several steps ahead of her, but he turned and, when he saw Ellie's face, he came back.

'*Oh là là...* It's the painting you liked.'

It was.

It was the big painting that she had fallen so instantly in love with when she'd seen it at the first summer market she'd been to in Vence. The one with the chapel-esque stone building. The one with the mountains as an indistinct background to the brightness of red and white flowers in the grass and stones in the fore-ground, made even more stunning by the impasto technique of layering the paint – probably with a knife or just fingers – to give it both a three-dimensional effect and the suggestion of movement, as if a breeze were blowing across the meadow.

There was a link here that felt important: that this artist, whose work touched her heart so much, might come from the same village that the unknown side of her family might have lived in.

'Is this where he works, do you think?'

Julien looked at the sign hanging over the door. 'It's a gallery rather than a workshop, so it may just be in here for sale. Have you changed your mind about buying it?'

Ellie shook her head. Reluctantly. Because if this painting wasn't way out of any price range she could afford, it should be.

'Why don't I ask?' Julien suggested, as if he'd read her thoughts. 'Or there might be a smaller version in the gallery?'

So they went inside, but the other paintings on display were clearly by very different artists. Julien spoke, at some length, to the woman behind the counter.

'I don't think the artist wants to sell the painting,' he told Ellie. 'He's asking over a thousand euros.'

'Someone will buy it,' Ellie said. 'And he deserves to be paid that much.' She led the way to the door, knowing that she'd held them up long enough.

'Apparently no one knows his real name,' Julien said as he stopped outside the gallery to pick Theo up again. 'He lived on the streets for a long time but now he lives in an old stable on a farm. Nobody sees him during the winter, and that's when he does his paintings. And then he comes out in summer and takes them to the market to earn money for more paints and food. People call him *l'ermite*.'

'The hermit?'

'*Oui*. The 'ermit.'

Sometimes Julien's accent was just too gorgeous. So cute it made him as adorable as his son. Ellie heard herself sigh, which was a sound of pure happiness.

'That's a good story,' she said quickly, in case Julien guessed the real reason she sounded so happy. 'Maybe he was living on the streets because he felt lost, and now he's found where he needs to be and he's doing what he loves.' Ellie took one last glance behind her at the painting. Had that been, unknowingly, why she'd felt such a connection to this artwork? Because she had been lost herself but lucky enough to have come to what might be the only part of the world that could have made it possible to find herself again?

The storm was much closer as they followed the mountain road towards the canyon that had been carved out by the Vésubie river. Gigantic fluffy clouds were filling the sky, intermittently blocking out the sun, giving them a shockingly bright halo around an inky blackness in their centres that made them look like bottomless holes.

The first flash of lightning came as they went through one of the tunnels in the gorge. When Theo cried out in fright, Ellie put her hand though the gap between the front seats of the car so that he could hold onto it when the crash of thunder followed only seconds later, but he was clutching the tree branch which he had insisted he had to take home with him, so she just rubbed his arm instead.

The storm was right on top of them. Fat raindrops hit the windscreen a minute later with such ferocity that Julien had to put the wipers on a frantic speed. When the rain changed to hail after another blinding flash of light and a crack of thunder that she could feel in her bones, Ellie was as frightened as Theo.

'We need to find somewhere to pull over.' Julien's voice was calm but grim. 'I don't like this.'

With the river down a steep bank on their left and a sheer rock wall on their right, there was nowhere *to* pull over, but Julien was driving very carefully as he went into the next bend. It didn't matter how careful he was being, however, when he found himself facing a large vehicle that was passing a small peloton of cyclists huddled together as they battled the elements.

They were only moments away from a head-on collision with the truck. In the space of a heartbeat, Ellie could feel the impossible choice Julien was having to make. Should he swerve towards the cliff and collide with the cyclists? Take the chance that the truck was also going so slowly a collision might be the safest option? Or should he pull the wheel the other way and hope that the low concrete wall would be enough to prevent them going over the bank?

Ellie also felt the moment that the concrete wall gave way as the screech of the car's hubcaps on the hard surface competed with another rumble of thunder. The car tipped so far she was sure they were about to roll, but then it hit the bank and somehow stayed upright but gathered speed on the steep slope.

The scream of pure terror from Theo as they hurtled towards the river was a sound she was never ever going to forget. But worse was to come. The crunch of hitting the huge boulders in the river was so jarring, Ellie was convinced this was the last thing she would ever be aware of.

Except it wasn't.

That shrill scream of a small child had been cut off as if a switch had been flicked.

Despite the roar of rushing water around them, another crack of thunder, and the horrific gunshot sounds of airbags deploying, the silence from the back seat of Julien's car was deafening.

20

'Are you hurt?' Julien's voice snapped the silence like the crack of a whip.

'I... don't think so...'

How could she know? Ellie couldn't identify any immediate pain but she could barely catch a coherent thought. And Julien wasn't listening now, anyway. He had unclipped his safety belt and was twisting in his seat to see into the back of the car.

'Theo? *Theo...? Oh, mon Dieu...*'

The note of horror in Julien's voice made Ellie's blood run cold. She twisted herself to try and see what he was seeing, but was it her movement that made the car shift and scrape as it moved against the boulders? No... Julien was trying to wrench open the driver's door, but it was clearly jammed.

'*Ne bouge pas, Theo, Ne bouge pas...*'

There were people outside the car now. Some were the Lycra-clad cyclists. A burly man – the truck driver, perhaps? – was shouting into a phone. Julien was shouting as well. Ellie couldn't understand a word, but someone was picking up a small rock. Julien turned and held out his arms to shield her as the rock was used to smash the window of the driver's seat and then clear the shattered glass until he could put his arms through the frame for people to pull him from the vehicle.

Ellie unclipped her own safety belt as she felt the first lap of icy water around her feet, and a new terror dug its claws into her. She had to get to Theo. Maybe she could fit through the gap between the front seats and release him from his safety belts to pass him out through the empty window frame in the front?

She turned.

And then she froze.

Theo wasn't unconscious, as she'd thought he would be when that scream had been so abruptly terminated. He was staring back at her, his little face as white as a sheet and his eyes wide and terrified. He was as frozen as she was, and she could see what had made Julien's voice so frighteningly raw.

Theo was still holding that branch he'd wanted to bring home with him. The glossy, green leaves looked exactly as they had when he'd picked it up to dip into the *gargouille*. The other end – the jagged, sharp end where the branch had broken from the tree – was nowhere to be seen.

Because it was inside Theo. The shocking jolt against rocks that had stopped the car's momentum so suddenly must have turned the branch into the spear that was now lodged in his stomach.

'It's okay, darling. We'll get you out. We're going to look after you and make it all better.'

Ellie heard the words coming out of her mouth and knew that she couldn't possibly know that anything she was saying was true. She knew that Theo wouldn't even understand what she was saying, but surely he would hear the comfort she was trying to give him?

The love...?

It was in that horrible moment that Ellie realised she had done the one thing she'd tried so hard to protect herself from. She had fallen in love with Theo Rousseau as much as she had fallen in love with his father. This small, solemn boy had captured her heart – probably from the moment she'd first held him in her arms to save him from what she'd believed was a serious risk from dangerous donkeys. From the moment he'd opened his eyes and called her *Maman*...

She had been able to keep it safely below a conscious admission, however. Even when he'd climbed up onto the couch beside her on the night she'd been looking after him and she'd felt that curly-topped head against her arm get heavier and heavier as he'd fallen asleep.

Even when he'd taken hold of her hand at the wolf park and it had felt like those small fingers had been holding her heart as much as her hand.

There was no hiding from it now.

She loved Theo.

And he was hurt.

Badly hurt.

Was she about to face losing another child?

No... she couldn't let that happen, if there was anything at all she could do to prevent it, even if it meant losing her own life.

Ellie tried to push herself into the gap between the seats, but the car was rocking now. There were so many people around the outside of the vehicle. Were they attempting to lift it over the boulders that were preventing the doors from opening? Ellie turned back. She hadn't been thinking clearly. Maybe she could open the door on her side of the car? And then open the back door?

But people were reaching in through the window where the

glass had been smashed. Shouting at her with what were clearly instructions to get close enough to the window so that they could pull her out.

The water was almost up to her knees.

And the back door of the car was opening with a screech of metal against rock. It was Julien who was climbing into the back and reaching to release the safety belt holding the car seat in place.

A man had his head and shoulders through the driver's window space now. He grabbed hold of Ellie's arm and pulled.

'*Vite, vite... il n'y a pas le temps...*'

Ellie let herself be pulled. When her own head and shoulders were through the gap she could use her feet to push against the seat and make it easier for her rescuers. She saw Julien backing out of the rear door with the car seat in his arms and, when the people who'd been supporting the car chassis let go, she saw the vehicle turn and get caught by a current strong enough to lift it away from the boulder that had jammed the driver's door. It turned further and sank on the passenger side as water filled the interior, and then it got swept into the deepest part of the river, with only the roof visible as it moved downstream.

More people had gathered to help and there were cars blocking the road in both directions. The storm had blown past with the same speed with which it had arrived, and Ellie could hear the faint sound of sirens in the distance. At the same time she saw people looking up and pointing. She could hear the sound of an approaching helicopter.

Ellie looked back at the hunched figure of Julien beside the car seat that was now safely on the tarmac of the road.

Expert help was almost here.

But was it going to be too late?

* * *

The scene was crowded already, but Julien could hear the sirens
getting louder, advertising the arrival of the people he really
needed around him.

He was aware that Ellie was somewhere behind him, amongst
the people who were trying to help. He had seen her being pulled
from the car and helped to safety. He was also aware that being
unable to understand what was being said to her might be adding
to a terrifying experience, but there was nothing he could do to
help her.

His son was the only thing that mattered in this moment.

Julien could hear the approaching helicopter and wondered
where it would land. The flashing lights of a police car could be
seen further up the canyon road, already controlling oncoming
traffic, and an ambulance was edging past to get closer to the
scene.

Thank God for that.

He would have expert assistance and, more importantly, the
equipment that would be needed to keep Theo alive until they
could get him to a hospital.

Into an operating theatre where they could remove the stick
that had penetrated that small abdomen.

They couldn't move it yet. For all he knew, without the technology
of something like a CT scan, the piece of wood inside his son might be
the only thing protecting him from a catastrophic haemorrhage –
from a ruptured artery or a laceration to his liver or spleen – which
meant that his priority was to ensure that this impaled foreign object
wasn't bumped or moved in any way. Julien had one hand around the
base of the stick, where it protruded from Theo's tee shirt, and was
using his other to shield the leafy end from an accidental nudge.

Theo was quiet and pale and not even attempting to move, which was a good thing, but it was also a warning sign for Julien that he could already be in serious trouble from internal bleeding. Children were so good at compensating for blood loss by increasing their heart and breathing rate, but they could crash fast, too. The way Theo's eyes were drifting shut, like they did when he was on the point of falling asleep, sent a chill down Julien's spine.

He caught a glimpse of Ellie as the back doors of an ambulance opened and uniformed medics came towards him carrying their packs of gear. She was standing, watching. A blanket wrapped around her shoulders and a frightened face that was almost as pale as Theo's.

And then he forgot all about her.

With Theo on the stretcher minutes later and word, via the police officers on scene, that the helicopter had landed further up the road and the crew was awaiting transfer of the patient, the work to make sure he was stable enough to travel kicked up a gear.

There were rushed introductions and a rapid collection of information about the condition of their patient and what exactly had happened in the accident. All while Julien maintained the stability of the branch. He wasn't going to let it go, he told the medical team. He was a paediatrician himself. He knew what he was doing.

The SAMU doctor put his hand on Julien's shoulder as he spoke. Did he want him to change his mind?

'*Non.*' There was no way Julien could let anyone take over this responsibility. He could do this, no matter how difficult it might be. He prepared to focus absolutely on his task as they got ready to roll the stretcher towards the ambulance and then drive to meet the helicopter. But something was interfering with his concentration.

'Ellie...'

She was still standing there, watching him. And she was close enough to hear him utter her name. She came even closer until a police officer put an arm out to stop her getting too near the stretcher.

'*Non*,' he barked. '*Arrêtez là.*'

Julien told him who Ellie was. That she'd been in the car with him. He asked for someone to make sure she got home to Tourrettes-sur-Loup.

The officer nodded. He could arrange that.

'*Ellie ne parle pas beaucoup français,*' Julien added.

'No problem,' the officer said, in English. 'I'll stay with her.'

Julien moved only his eyes to catch Ellie's attention. 'I'm going to the hospital with Theo,' he told her. 'This policeman will see that you get home safely. If you're sure you're not hurt?'

Ellie's eyes were huge and still so very frightened. She looked down at Theo and then back to Julien.

'I'm not hurt.' She shook her head for emphasis. 'But could I come with you anyway? With Theo?'

The stretcher was starting to move and Julien had to move with it. He tightened his fingers around the doughnut dressing that was providing another level of support so that the stick remained stable. He had to stay with his son. He had to summon the courage to face any upcoming decisions and be strong for Theo, and he knew that things could get a lot worse before there was any chance of them getting better.

There was no time to explain that he was part of a fight for Theo's life. That it felt like a fight for his own life as well and there was nothing Ellie could do to make that any easier, however much she might want to. That it would be better for *her* not to be there if the worst happened. He couldn't begin to try and put that into words.

All he could do was shake his head.

'You can go home, Ellie,' he said, his gaze already shifting back to Theo. 'We don't need you...'

21

Julien didn't want her to go with them.

Ellie totally understood that his focus was on Theo to the exclusion of anything or anyone else. Nobody would have the time or inclination to translate what was being said or done. She would only be in the way.

Theo had his father with him. Julien was with his precious son.

They had each other to cling to as their world was tipping upside down.

She understood that neither of them needed her, but that only made her feel more frightened.

Bereft, even...

The journey home to La Maisonette, after watching the helicopter take off and carry what felt like a large part of Ellie's heart away with it as it flew towards Nice, seemed to take an excruciatingly long time. She'd thought it was because she couldn't communicate with the silent police officers in the front seats, but it turned out that time had simply slowed to a crawl because it was just as slow after she arrived at the small house that suddenly no longer felt like a sanctuary.

She gave Pascal dinner that he wasn't remotely interested in eating. She didn't bother even thinking about getting any food for herself because she knew she wouldn't be able to swallow a thing. Ellie was uninjured, apart from a few scrapes and bruises, so it wasn't anything physical that was causing the pain she could feel. She sat outside, barely noticing the remnants of storm clouds catching the colours of the sunset, with her little dog on her lap, her arms wrapped around him, seemingly content to stay there for as long as it took to offer her comfort that couldn't be found.

What if Theo died?

It would feel like losing Jack all over again.

Ellie had known there could be pain involved in getting close to Julien Rousseau when it was never going to be for more than a summer fling, but she'd never imagined this kind of pain. Was it actually possible that it could feel just as unbearable as losing her own baby? Or even worse, somehow, because this would destroy Julien as well as Theo and... and she loved them both.

She'd thought she'd never be able to love like this again.

How wrong had she been?

Minutes ticked past and turned into an hour. And then another. It was completely dark, but Ellie didn't want to go inside and lighting candles seemed somehow inappropriate. Faint moonlight came and went through gaps in the clouds and the temperature dropped, but it wasn't cold enough to send her inside and it certainly wasn't cold enough to compete with the icy fear she was grappling with.

It was almost midnight when Ellie felt Pascal's muscles tense and the rumble of a low growl from his throat. The glow of light coming from the direction of the olive grove made her breath catch.

'It's okay, Pascal,' she said. 'It's only Julien.'

Only?

What a ridiculous word to use when the approach of this man held so much significance. When he held the power over both what her future would be and whether she had to relive a past where the wounds she'd thought were healing would be ripped wide open all over again.

But the first words Julien spoke changed everything.

'He's alive,' he told her. 'Theo's alive.' He sank onto the other wrought-iron chair beside the table, put his head in his hands and his next words were a sigh. 'He's going to be okay.'

Ellie tried to stifle a sob but it escaped. She scrubbed at her face to try and prevent tears, but she couldn't stop her voice shaking.

'I've been so scared,' she whispered.

'Me too.'

His sharp intake of breath made her think he was also fighting tears. He was sitting close enough for her to be able to reach out and touch him, but instinct told her that physical contact might be too much for him and... perhaps he was struggling for control because he needed to be strong. For himself but also for his family and most of all for Theo.

When he dropped the shield of his hands and looked up, he avoided direct eye contact.

'It was touch and go,' he said slowly. 'The worst time of my life was when they took him away from me and into theatre. Waiting for him to wake up afterwards and to hear his voice.'

'So he's awake?' Ellie tried to smile but had to bite her lip to catch another sob of relief.

'He's asleep again now. I've just come home to get some of his favourite toys and his special blanket. He'll have to stay in hospital for a few days at least.'

'But he's going to be okay...' Ellie was talking to herself but she had to say the words aloud.

'They couldn't operate until they'd done a scan to see what they would be dealing with, and there was a chance that he might bleed to death before they could repair the damage.'

'But he didn't...' Ellie breathed. 'And he's going to be okay. Oh, Julien... that's just the best news. What did he say when he woke up?'

'He wanted to know where his little tree was.' Julien's huff of breath was a pale imitation of amusement. 'I had to tell him that most of it had been cut off before he went into the machine to see what was happening inside his tummy.'

'Oh...' Ellie was trying to shake off a ripple of guilt that she knew would haunt her later. 'If only I hadn't wanted to go to that village with the *gargouille*. He wouldn't have found that branch and thought it was a good idea to make it float down the hill.' Her voice caught. 'He wouldn't have been holding it in the car when—'

'When I crashed it.' Julien's voice was rough. 'There's no point doing that, Ellie. None of this was your fault.'

'It wasn't your fault, either,' Ellie said fiercely. 'It only happened because that truck was on the wrong side of the road. Because of the storm. Because of the cyclists. You cannot blame yourself. You probably saved all of us by avoiding the truck. You certainly helped to save his life afterwards.'

Julien nodded slowly. 'I would have given my life if that was what was needed to save him.'

Ellie opened her mouth to echo the 'me too' Julien had said earlier but the words didn't emerge. That was partly because it felt far too much to tell him she had fallen in love with his son when she'd never told Julien how deep her feelings for *him* had become. It was also because he had finally met her gaze directly

230 ALISON ROBERTS

and was holding it, and what she could see in his eyes was so far from relief it was shocking.

'What is it?' she asked softly. 'What's wrong, Julien? What aren't you telling me?'

He was silent for a long, long moment.

Then he shrugged. As if it didn't really matter if he told Ellie or not. 'They had to be prepared to give Theo a transfusion if it was needed during the operation,' he said. 'So they did a test to see what his blood group was. There'd never been a reason to test him before, so I hadn't known.'

Ellie didn't want the silence that followed Julien's words to grow any deeper.

'I've never had mine tested,' she said. 'I wouldn't have any idea what it is.'

'Many people don't.' Julien nodded. 'Unless they've been blood donors, as I have. Sarah had no idea of her blood group, but she got tested because she was still alive – just – after the accident and, if they'd had time, they would have given her a transfusion. She was type O. I am also an O.'

Ellie didn't understand what the significance of this information was. What she did understand, however, was that this was why Julien still looked so shattered even though he knew his son was safe. Maybe he could feel the intensity of her gaze, because he looked directly at her again.

'Theo is type A,' he said. 'Two parents who are type O cannot have a baby that is type A. It's simply not possible.' He lowered his eyelids like shutters so that Ellie couldn't see what he preferred to hide. 'It means that Sarah got pregnant by someone else. Not by me.'

And then, as if he was having as much difficulty understanding this as Ellie was, he opened his eyes and spoke slowly. Very clearly.

'Theo is not my son.'

Ellie gasped. 'Of course he's your son,' she said in a tone that said there was no shadow of doubt about it.

'Not biologically.'

'That's not what matters.' Ellie swallowed hard. 'Love is the only thing that really matters. You love Theo. You're the only father he's ever known. And he adores you.'

'He certainly needs me right now.' It was clearly a physical fight against exhaustion as Julien pushed himself to his feet. 'I have to go back to him. And I have to call my mother and grand-mother. Will you be all right? I'm sorry... I haven't even asked how you are.'

'I'm fine,' Ellie said quietly. 'And yes, you need to go back to look after Theo. Please let me know if there's anything at all I can do to help.'

Not just to help a family in crisis because a child had been critically injured. Ellie had an urge to try and comfort Julien that was so strong it was unbearable. She had known from that first moment she'd met him, by the way Julien had held and spoken to his son, that Theo was the most precious thing in his life. How could you begin to navigate knowing that he was actually someone else's child? Ellie knew only too well that emotional injury could be just as hard – if not harder – to heal from than anything physical.

Julien nodded but he was looking at his phone, finding the torch button to tap. 'I'll let you know if anything changes,' he murmured. Stepping closer, he brushed his lips against Ellie's cheek – a light, apparently meaningless contact – and then turned to walk away. She couldn't blame him for his distraction. In fact, he wouldn't be the man she believed he was if he could distract himself by thinking of anyone other than his son right now. But it hurt that it didn't seem to have occurred to him that he might find support, if not comfort, in her arms.

Ellie watched the light of his torch flickering as it went past the trunks of lemon and then olive trees.

He would tell her if anything changed, but how could anything else change enough to be significant when it felt like absolutely everything that had become so important in her life had already changed? When it felt like there was nothing solid beneath her feet and she was slipping. As if the axis of her world was tipping and she couldn't find anything solid to hang on to.

Julien was walking back towards where he belonged. To his family. To his mother and grandmother and, most of all, to Theo, who was clearly his son in every way that mattered most, even if he couldn't see that himself quite yet.

Ellie wasn't needed. Julien had said so himself.

She didn't belong here.

Whatever magic this place – and Julien – had brought into her life was gone.

It felt like it was time to go back to where she had once belonged.

It was time to go home...

22

She didn't want to leave.

But she couldn't stay.

Up early enough to watch the sunrise, Ellie was sitting out on her terrace with a mug of hot coffee as the craggy outlines of the closest mountains – the *baous* – became visible and the deep shadows of La Maisonette's lemon orchard and olive grove lifted to reveal the now familiar shape of the trees.

So familiar. And knowing that she would soon be leaving them behind made it increasingly clear how much she loved this garden.

Yet again, the suggestion Julien had made on the day of the storm and that terrifying accident echoed in the back of Ellie's mind. There was still time. She did own a third of this property. She could talk to her sisters about the idea of the three of them keeping ownership or, if they weren't interested, looking for finance to buy them out of their shares. There was no reason not to do that, was there?

Yes, there was a reason.

She would be Julien Rousseau's neighbour and that would, quite simply, be too hard.

It had been hard enough this week, seeing him only briefly in passing on his way to or from the hospital where Theo was a patient. Even worse had been the time he'd come and knocked on her front door – the *front* door – to tell her that Theo was recovering well enough to be able to leave the hospital. He would take him back to Roquebillière so that his grandmother and great-grandmother could devote themselves to his care and Julien could tackle the mounting backlog of his own patients needing his attention. The escalating level of stress in his life had been palpable.

A sick son.

A mother who was already caring for her own mother.

Longer distances to travel to work – a stress all on its own – to treat other sick children who had frightened families needing reassurance.

Ellie had watched his face, her heart aching, as she'd stood on her doorstep and listened to his words beneath the arch of roses that had become such a profusion of pale yellow flowers she was bathed in their fragrance. It had occurred to her that, for the rest of her life, the scent of Banksia roses would remind her how it felt to have such an intimate connection with another human being but, at the same time, to see them through an invisible but totally impenetrable barrier.

Julien was holding himself – and his life – together. To anyone else, he would seem to be the epitome of an adoring, deeply concerned parent, but Ellie knew that he was struggling with that extra emotional blow: the proof that he wasn't Theo's biological father. He hadn't seen that coming. Such a formal visit, using the shiny brass knocker on the old wooden door to announce his arrival, instead of feeling comfortable enough to scale the fence and wander through the garden, had been a very clear signal that he had to come to terms with that devastating news by himself, in his own way.

She could respect that.

It would be hypocritical not to, in fact, given how she'd shut out her own friends and family for the same reason in the terrible aftermath of losing her baby.

Ellie sipped her coffee, lowering her gaze from the mountains to the small white dog lying beside her, his chin resting on her bare foot. Pascal had barely left her side since she'd come home in that police car. If he sensed that she, too, was struggling, he certainly wasn't going to allow any barrier to prevent him offering the comfort or reassurance she might need, and Ellie loved him for it. He was a big part of why she knew she was going to get through what had suddenly become a huge challenge, and it had made something else very clear. There was no way on earth she was going to leave Pascal behind when she went home.

He lifted his head, with that one floppy ear, as Ellie spoke aloud.

'I rang Mam yesterday,' she told him. 'Just to check that she won't mind you coming to live with her until we can find our own place. I think we might be able to buy a house, so we won't even have to worry about whether pets are allowed in a rental. When this place sells, my share should be more than enough for a good deposit. Maybe we can find a little fisherman's cottage in Oban. Or it might be nice to go and live on Mull. Would you like to be an island dog?'

Pascal's tail thumped the stones of the terrace, but he settled his chin on Ellie's foot again to wait for her to finish her coffee. Feeling the trusting weight of that little head made her smile.

Aye... she was going to succeed in navigating this challenge. And maybe she'd needed it to happen, because otherwise she might not have discovered the well of strength she could draw on that certainly hadn't been there when she'd arrived in the south of France. She was a very different person. One who could face life and embrace it far more than she ever had before.

Ellie had so much to be thankful for. If even one piece of this particular puzzle had been missing, she might not have discovered this new version of herself.

Even that impulsive decision to stay here for the summer had been a unique combination of puzzle pieces. The soft light here and the way stone buildings and streets seemed to have soaked in the warmth over so many centuries. The music of the language and comfort of food that could be both homely but utterly delicious at the same time – like a wedge of fresh baguette wrapped around some ham and cheese.

This little house had played such a huge part in Ellie's journey that it felt like it had a personality she'd fallen in love with as she'd coaxed – and perhaps, sometimes, bullied it a little – away from its sad, unloved submission to abandonment.

And then there was Julien...

It was still far too soon, but Ellie knew she would be forever grateful for the cracks in the protective layers around her heart that had grown wide enough to allow Julien – and Theo – to capture a part of what lay behind them. Her heart might be going to ache for a long time, but the reminder that it was love that matters most in life had been what had healed her soul.

'At least you're going to come home with me.' Ellie reached down to scratch Pascal behind his floppy ear. 'I'd better look into the rules about taking you on the plane.'

She wouldn't be able to take her beautiful red bicycle on the plane, of course. Even that rag rug from the second bedroom would be far too big to fit into her suitcase. And what about the bottles of limoncello that were still waiting to be tasted? It would be very disappointing if they got broken in transit. Ellie needed to start searching for a removal company that could help. She needed to find a new home for Marguerite and Coquelicot because it would be impossible to take them home with her. Margot might need a new home, too. Hopefully with someone who would appreciate all the quirkiness of a classic tin snail.

Unless…

'What if we drove home?' Ellie wondered aloud. 'It would take forever, and Margot might break down, but it would be… epic, wouldn't it?'

A massive challenge. An adventure. A way of turning the end of something precious into the start of something else that might be life-changing in a good way?

Was she brave enough to try?

Was it even possible?

Ellie rang Laura the next day.

'You're mad,' her oldest sister told her. 'Completely bonkers. Legally, the car doesn't belong to you, so you could run into all sorts of trouble. You'd need the registration details and owner-ship papers, and goodness only knows where they are.'

'I might be able to get a copy. I'll need to get the mechanic that came to get Margot going in the first place to come back and make sure she would be able to make the trip. He should know what I need to do. If I had the ownership papers and you emailed me a copy of Uncle Jeremy's will, I'm sure I could talk my way around any complications.'

'You're asking for trouble.'

No. Ellie was asking for a distraction from the trouble she was already in. A way to get through the pain of a heart that was threatening to shatter, like Humpty Dumpty, into too many small pieces to ever be able to be completely put back together again.

'Send me a copy of the will,' she begged. 'Please… So I can, at least, try.' She wanted to end this conversation before she could be persuaded that her idea was, indeed, crazy. 'I need to go, Laura. I've got a lot of things to do and places to go. While I've still got time…'

* * *

There was still time to go back to places that would be a part of Ellie's soul for the rest of her life.

Where it all began, in St Paul de Vence with the mosaic pebble flowers in the streets of the walled village. This time Ellie recorded every variation she could find. She was confident that she would be able to create her own new designs as well, and put together a plan and portfolio for the business she couldn't wait to start.

She drove Margot alone, for the first time, to one of the beaches near Nice and she and Pascal spent an early morning, before it got too hot, wandering beside the waves, filling a bag with flat, round and oval pebbles that were exactly what she needed. When they found a place to live with space for a studio, Ellie would make her first stepping stones and choose the best one to photograph, or perhaps paint, for her studio logo. She'd choose a font she loved with the name 'Stone Flowers' above the image and put a subtitle underneath to capture her inspiration – 'A touch of France'.

It wasn't going to be a problem finding suitable stones to work with in Scotland, but she wanted her prototypes to have genuine French stones. Maybe, in years to come, she would feel ready to come back and visit again. It was too soon to be thinking of weighing down her luggage with stones when her heart already felt too heavy, but collecting these few now was a step towards a future that Ellie was trying very hard to embrace.

On the Friday that Julien had come to tell her he was taking Theo to Roquebillière, Ellie had ridden her bicycle into Vence with Pascal in the basket and they'd queued up for socca, like they had the day that Julien had saved the life of that choking child and Ellie had known how easy it would be to fall in love with that man.

'*Une part?*' The man at the socca oven had smiled as if he recognised Ellie.

'*Oui. S'il vous plaît.*'

'*Le sel et le poivre?*'

'*Oui. Merci.*'

'*Vous mangez tout de suite?*'

'*Bien sûr.*' Ellie had grinned, happy to show off how much her French had improved. '*C'est si bon. Je veux le manger tout de suite.*'

Her words and her accent were probably far from perfect, but the tilt of the man's head and his smile had made it obvious that he'd understood perfectly well. And that he'd appreciated the compliment about the food.

More than that. It had kind of made her feel like she belonged.

* * *

Laura sent through draft copies of the brochure she and Noah were creating for La Maisonette, and Ellie helped choose the photographs to be included. The first must-have was a picture of the little stone house from the road, with Margot visible in the open garage and the iron gate open as an invitation to walk towards the front door, also ajar, under its wreath of yellow roses. Another was the view from the terrace, on which Laura had cleverly adjusted the lighting so that the streak of the Mediterranean could be clearly differentiated from the cloudless summer sky.

Ellie wanted to keep the close-up shot of the brass door-knocker, too, because she remembered telling Laura that it looked new because all it had needed was a bit of love. Like everything else in La Maisonette had.

Including herself?

Aye... including herself.

She'd fallen in love with this little house and its garden. With cobbled flowers and sunsets, the smell of lemons and the sound of the most beautiful language in the world. With a small dog and a tall man and...

There were tears gathering that were very close to falling, but they were happy tears.

Because it wasn't just this centuries-old, tiny stone house that had come back to life, was it? And okay... maybe the price she would have to pay for this happiness was getting closer every day, but right here, right now, it still felt totally worth it.

She let her breath out in a sigh that felt like one of relief. Because it felt like she was turning a corner.

The photograph that Ellie loved the most wasn't going to go in the brochure, but she was going to have it framed to go on her bedside table because it managed to encapsulate the most important aspects of what had changed her life so much. At first glance, it was simply a couple of sleepy donkeys under some olive trees and a small white dog with a floppy ear sitting at a respectful distance, watching them. For Ellie, however, there was so much more. She could see the exact spot she'd found Theo asleep that evening and the shape of Julien's house in the background and... she could still hear the echo of Theo calling her *Maman*...

She would print a small copy of this particular photograph, and perhaps she could find a heart-shaped frame to enclose it.

There was another photograph that she wanted to keep for ever, as well, although she might not be brave enough to keep it on view in a frame. The one taken by the random tourist who'd been there when she and Julien had taken Margot out for the first time and had stopped to admire the view of Tourrettes-sur-Loup. It wasn't the view of the pretty medieval village in the background that made the photo so precious, though. It was that, while she and Julien were both smiling so happily, neither of them had been looking at the photographer. They were looking at each other.

There was no time to allow herself to sink too far into how much she was leaving behind, however, and every reason to avoid even thinking about it. Distraction was, in fact, remarkably easy because there was so much to sort out. She had the practical details of her trip home to organise, using online maps to plan the long drive. Booking a ferry ticket. Finding out about and organising the requirements for vaccinations and a pet passport for Pascal.

It had been a small reprieve when Laura had passed on information from Noah that, even if they had an offer the first day La Maisonette got put on the market, it could be months before the property would actually change hands due the extensive paperwork and legal requirements for buying and selling property in France. Ellie would have time to think about how to make sure Marguerite and Coquelicot would not get separated and that they could find a home where they would be safe. And loved. Perhaps Julien wouldn't mind keeping an eye on them for a little while. He'd done it for months, after all, without anyone asking. She would write him a note and leave it in his letter box.

Her last day was rapidly approaching. The date that had been highlighted in her calendar ever since she'd decided how long she would stay.

Till the last summer market.

Next Tuesday evening.

Hurriedly, Ellie found something else to think about. She still needed to find a way to ship her red bicycle home. And, if space on a truck was going to be booked, she might as well take some other things she loved so that she could give her new home, well... a touch of France.

The rag rug was first on the list but there were other things, too. Like the half-glazed pots and the beautiful antique lace bedcovers. That huge mirror from her bedroom with its ornate brass frame, and even the rusty, old Moroccan candle holders from the terrace. She loved the bed itself, but that might be an unwise choice. How could she ever sleep in it without being reminded of every time she and Julien had made love?

Oh, *help*...

She might have been very close to happy tears only minutes ago, but the heartache was there, wasn't it? Hovering, like the menacing storm clouds had been on that fateful day of the accident that had torn everything apart with far more harshness than she was ready to deal with. Keeping so busy was saving Ellie from the storm breaking, but a few spots from the approaching clouds broke through occasionally.

... go home, Ellie... We don't need you...

23

The *gargouille* in Saint-Martin-Vésubie looked exactly as it had when Theo had first played in it two weeks or so ago.

Miraculously, Theo also looked almost exactly as he had then. Before the accident. Before the surgery and his thankfully swift recovery.

Before the shocking revelation that Julien was not his father.

The days since then had tumbled past, with even the shifts from day to night sometimes blurred beyond recognition. Julien had barely had time to visit his home in Tourrettes-sur-Loup between commitments to his practice in Vence, his rosters and on-call work in the hospital in Nice, and the travel each day to and from Roquebillière so that he could spend every possible moment with Theo.

With his son.

The realisation had come gradually from the mists of the shock and grief and... fear, even. But it had come.

Thanks to the words that Ellie had said that dreadful night. That he was the only father Theo had ever known. That, as far as Julien was concerned, he'd been his son since the moment he'd held him in his arms, and that bond would never be broken. One day he'd have to tell Theo the truth about the accident that had killed his mother. It might be possible to discover whether the man she'd been leaving with was Theo's biological father, but perhaps his son would feel the same way as Julien did – that biology was irrelevant compared to their bond.

That Ellie had spoken the truth when she said that love was the only thing that really matters.

He could hear an echo of her voice.

'*Of course he's your son...*'

He could remember the way that a soft emotion had made the golden shade in her hazel eyes more obvious, as if empathy – or possibly love – was doing the impossible and melting something internal.

But maybe anatomical melting wasn't impossible after all, because Julien could feel it happening inside himself as he remembered how much Ellie understood.

How much she cared.

He'd barely seen her since that night. He'd gone to tell her that Theo was well enough to be discharged, and he'd been about to go again recently but there had been a car parked in the road with the signage of a well-known estate agency based in St Paul de Vence and he knew that Ellie would be too busy to talk to him. It was also a reminder that the house was about to go on the market and that Ellie would return to Scotland and he would probably never see her again.

They'd both known that this *affaire* was temporary. Maybe it had ended with a jarring finality rather than a fond farewell, and Ellie certainly deserved so much better than that, but the truth was that it had always been going to end.

He hadn't needed that unforgettable moment of fear when he'd lost control of his car and thought his son was about to die to remind him that Theo was everything to him. That this precious child was the sun that his world revolved around. That it was his responsibility to protect him from harm, both physical and emotional, and that he'd let his guard down by letting Theo spend time with Ellie. Who wouldn't fall in love with Eleanor Gilchrist when they did that?

He could, at least, take comfort from the knowledge that Theo hadn't become so close to her that, when she left, he might feel as if he were losing his mother for a second time. But it had been a close call.

When they'd arrived in the village, Theo had looked around as soon as he'd climbed out of his car seat – without any noticeable discomfort for the first time since his surgery.

'*Où est Ellie? Est-elle déjà là?*'

No, Julien had told him. Ellie wasn't already here. She wasn't going to be here, either, because she was very busy getting ready to sell her house, and soon she would go back to live in Scotland, which was another country a long way away.

Theo simply accepted the information. Julien watched him crouch to dip his finger in the running water. He didn't seem upset that he wasn't going to see Ellie again.

But Julien was going to miss her.

Too much.

The sun would have gone out if he'd lost Theo in that accident, but it was also going to shine a lot less brightly when Ellie was no longer a part of his life.

After the disaster of his marriage, Julien been determined to never fall in love again. Or care about a woman so much it would hurt to lose them.

But losing Ellie *was* going to hurt. And the only comfort he could take from that was that he'd never told her that he loved her. He'd never offered up his heart, and perhaps that had helped to shield Ellie from what might have been a more intense pain.

It made it so much worse that it was ending badly, however. As Theo stood up and waggled his wet fingers at his papa with a smile that went straight into his heart, Julien remembered the look on Ellie's face when she'd asked to go to the hospital with them.

How could he have ignored the anguish he'd seen in her eyes? She'd been as afraid as he was that Theo wasn't going to survive, and she was hurting for *him* as well as Theo. She knew, better than anyone, what that pain could be like and yet she'd let them both into her life. She'd let Theo hold her hand that day, and how hard must that have been?

As hard as when she'd heard him call her *Maman*?

He hadn't had the emotional bandwidth, or possibly courage, in that moment to let her close enough to offer *her* comfort. It would be nice to find a way to make up for that. To think of something that might make this ending a little easier for both of them.

It was when they were nearing the bend in the main street that would take them towards the church that Julien spotted the sign for the gallery where that painting had been on display – the painting that Ellie loved so much – and he suddenly knew exactly how he could try and make up for letting Ellie suffer alone since the accident. For keeping himself so distant, thinking that he was protecting his family by focusing on them so completely.

To thank her for what she'd taught him. Because love was what really mattered, and the biological bond of family was not necessarily what made a particular relationship or love more significant. Or life-changing.

But when they reached the gallery the painting was no longer in the window.

Had it already been sold? Julien's heart sank like a stone. It might be only minutes since he'd thought of the perfect way he could show Ellie how much he cared without making their parting even harder, but this felt like a failure that would haunt him for ever.

Theo was tired now and was looking too pale. Julien picked his son up to carry him back up the hill and take him home.

There was nothing more he could do.

He'd left it too late.

* * *

Time had almost run out.

There was only one more day to take care of important tasks, like the appointment Ellie had with Christophe – the vet who'd looked after Pascal after she'd run him over with her bicycle – to have her little dog microchipped and vaccinated and to obtain his health certificate and pet passport.

She could go to the last summer market tomorrow evening and then have time for any final touches to leave the house looking picture-perfect. The sign had gone up on the roadside just today and the digital marketing campaign would go live tomorrow. Noah had a set of the keys and would take care of showing prospective buyers through – something that Ellie was more than happy not to have to be there for.

Mike and his mechanic friend Gary were coming to give Margot the once-over and a new MOT to make sure she was ready for the grand adventure of a three-day trip to her new home in Scotland. Ellie had meticulously planned her route and would drive down to the coast near Nice and then bypass Marseille to head inland to Lyon and Dijon and Reims. They would take the ferry from Calais to Dover, bypass London and keep heading north.

Heading home.

By the time they got to Oban the distance between Ellie and the south of France would feel like a whole world away.

So would the distance between herself and Julien, and perhaps that was when this separation would start to feel easier.

Ellie's phone rang as she was sitting out on her terrace watching one of the last sunsets she was going to see here. Laura's face filled the screen as she answered, but the expression on her sister's face was one that she had never seen before.

'You're not going to believe this, Ellie.'

'What?' she asked. She was still trying to interpret Laura's odd expression. 'What's wrong? Oh, my God... is it Mam?'

'No... No... there's nothing wrong at all.' Laura was smiling now. Grinning, even, which was so unusual it was almost scary. 'It's the most amazing news ever—'

'Tell me,' Ellie demanded.

'It's sold. The house is sold.'

'But...' Ellie could feel a shock wave rippling through her entire body. 'It can't have. It's not even on the market till tomorrow.'

'Well, it has. I've just had Noah on the phone. Somebody saw the sign and just went into the agency and offered the asking price even though we set it so much higher than we expected to get. The paperwork's all underway.'

Laura's excited words were tumbling out so fast they sounded like verbal static to Ellie. Her brain was refusing to make sense of any of this.

'I've signed the initial paperwork digitally on behalf of all sellers, like we agreed I could,' Laura continued, 'and now there's a legal check and drawing up a *Compromis de Vente*, which is the contract, but Noah says he doesn't think there'll be any hold-ups at all. It might take a couple of months to sort the final notarised deed and pay the notary costs and agency commission fees and hand over the keys to the new owner, but I can't believe how easy it was. They've even said we can keep whatever we want from the house. It's done, Ellie... It's over...'

Her final words slowed down and it felt like every one of them was a physical blow.

Ellie tried to sound as pleased as Laura was about the outcome but, as soon as her sister ended the call so that she could share the exciting news with the rest of the family, she burst into tears.

It really *was* over.

24

Sometimes you could feel that a house was empty well before a knock on the door went unanswered.

Before you lifted your hand to knock, even.

Ellie knew that Julien wasn't at home in the same way she had come to sense his presence when he was anywhere near her, before she could see or hear him. It felt like instinct. Something ethereal but at the same time very real. As if there had been something missing but you didn't realise until, suddenly, it wasn't missing any longer.

The hope that she could speak to Julien, instead of leaving an impersonal note asking him to keep an eye on the donkeys for the next few weeks, evaporated. Noah had said he'd come past every day or two and make sure the donkeys were okay, so she didn't need to ask Julien to do anything when he already had more than enough stress in his life.

It would only be polite to let him know that the house had sold, however. The 'For Sale/À Vendre' sign had already been taken down that morning, so it was quite likely that Julien would never guess the property had already changed hands. It still didn't feel right to be simply vanishing from his life leaving no more than a note, but it seemed that Ellie had no choice.

Not that it was any real surprise that he wasn't at his home. Julien hadn't stayed a night there since the accident in the canyon. He'd never come home for lunch the way he used to, either, so why on earth had Ellie thought he might have today? Why had she put on her pretty blue dress and brushed her hair long enough to make it shine and then left it loose?

The echo of her second, louder knock faded, and she knew there was no point standing there any longer but, for a long moment, her feet refused to obey her command to move.

This was the first time she'd been close enough to touch Julien's house, let alone get inside it. Because he'd never invited her to share his life, had he? Instead, he'd made himself available to share hers. Temporarily.

Until tonight – the night of the last summer market.

He had let her meet his son, but that had been an emergency, when his grandmother had been injured, hadn't it. If Ellie hadn't told him about her father and shown him those photographs, he wouldn't even have thought of taking her to the village with the *gargouille*. He and Theo wouldn't have been held up getting back home after the visit to the wolf park and they wouldn't have been caught in that storm.

Julien had told her that none of it had been her fault, but the truth was that the accident wouldn't have happened if she hadn't been there.

Everyone had said that she couldn't blame herself for Jack's death, either, but that might not have happened if she *had* been there. If she'd seen the moment that he stopped breathing.

As if recoiling from the thought, Ellie took a step backwards. She turned and walked back to the gate but then turned again to take one last look at Julien's house.

It was a much bigger house than La Maisonette. Solid and square with lots of windows divided into small panes. Was there a terrace on the other side with a view to the mountains and sea? Which rooms had windows that looked out onto the olive grove and lemon orchard on her side of the fence? Theo's bedroom – because he loved seeing the donkeys?

Julien's bedroom...?

Oh... the longing that was already morphing into the pain of loss and shaping itself into heartbreak was unbearable.

But Ellie knew there was something she had to do before getting on with the rest of her list of last-minute tasks for the day, which included a trip to Nice. Mike had messaged her to say that the paperwork they'd requested for the car had arrived but there wasn't enough time for it to be posted.

She retraced her steps, braided her hair with quick flicks of her fingers to get it out of the way and found her pad of art paper and her pencil case. She needed to leave something for Julien that was more than a request for a favour, but it took a while to decided how to begin, so she doodled around the edges of the paper. Small pictures of poppies and daisies. Of lemons and lavender and a small dog with a floppy ear.

Cher Julien,

She began the letter, finally, in French, because he had encouraged her to learn. And because, more than ever, Ellie considered it to be the most beautiful language in the world. It was the language of a country that had stolen her heart.

It was, most definitely, the language of love.

One day maybe she would be able to write a whole letter in French, but that wasn't possible yet.

The house has been sold unexpectedly quickly.

I'm leaving tomorrow to go home to Scotland. I'm sorry I won't get the chance to say goodbye.

She decided against asking him to take any responsibility for Coquelicot and Marguerite. One side of her mouth curved upwards as she remembered how their very first conversation had ended with Julien's exasperated hand gesture after telling her that she was the owner of these two donkeys.

'*Now you can finally start taking care of them yourself,*' he'd said. '*J'en ai marre.*'

Ellie knew what that meant now. He had been fed up. Pissed off. Unimpressed with absent neighbours who'd made no arrangements to care for their animals. And, to add insult to injury, she'd been speaking in a language he had every reason to detest.

Besides, she had something more important that she wanted to say.

I want to thank you for helping me take Pascal to the vet and for so much else as well. For suggesting I tasted socca and for teaching me to drive on the wrong side of the road.

I've left a bottle of the limoncello I made in the freezer for you and there's a key to the house in the smallest candle holder on the terrace. I hope you enjoy it.

Most of all, thank you for taking me to my first summer market. I will be thinking of you as I go to the last one this evening.

She would be thinking of Julien for the rest of her life, but she couldn't tell him that, could she?

I wish you and Theo nothing but the best that life can bring.

It took almost as long to decide how to finish the letter as it had to start it. Ellie wanted, so much, to tell him that she loved him, but again she decided that she couldn't. Not when there was still a faint echo of the devastating aftermath of the accident that had almost taken Theo's life.

'*...go home, Ellie... we don't need you...*'

In the end, Ellie finished the letter in the same way as she'd started it. In French.

Gros bisous

The literal translation was 'fat kisses' but it meant 'lots of love' in this context and, as far as Ellie could confirm online, it was a casual form of farewell that people who were no more than friends could say to each other. It would be as close as she could ever get to telling Julien how she really felt about him.

She folded the letter and sealed it into an envelope. She would put the key out in the candle holder before she forgot, take the letter next door and then it would be past time to head into Nice.

Pascal knew an outing was on offer as Ellie picked up his harness.

'We might have time for a walk on the beach,' she told him. 'And then we'll come back through Vence to go to the market. One last time.'

* * *

It was exactly the same.

Except it wasn't.

The crowds were the same. People walking arm in arm with their partners, or parents trying to see where their children had gone. Music and laughter and conversations happening in different languages. The smell of cigarettes and the more tempting aroma of hot food drifted in the air.

The stalls were the same. Lavender soap and leather belts and handbags for sale. The owner of the leatherwork stall recognised the brown bag Ellie was carrying and he nodded and smiled at her. She smiled back. This experience wasn't new and different now. She belonged here, at least in this moment.

There was the same face painting available for the children, and sweet treats of candy floss and ice cream and marshmallows. Clothing shops had put racks of offerings outside their doors as they stayed open late to take advantage of the last market of the season. And that was another difference. It was already getting dark – so much earlier than the first time – a reminder that summer was all but over.

Ellie had been nervous but excited at the prospect of seeing the painter whose work she loved so much. She'd even practised how she could tell him she'd seen his painting in the shop in Saint-Martin-Vésubie. But, although she knew she was looking at the same side street he'd tucked his stall into, he wasn't there, and it felt almost as disappointing as finding that she wouldn't be able to say goodbye to Julien in person.

Disappointing enough to tip the balance of this final goodbye from nostalgia to sadness. Enough to make Ellie realise that nothing was ever going to be quite the same from now on because Julien was no longer a part of her life.

And that was enough to persuade her that it was time to go home.

* * *

It all looked exactly the same when Ellie parked Margot in front of La Maisonette.

Except, of course, it wasn't.

There were no tenacious tendrils of ivy making it hard to push open the solid iron gate and no rust to leave marks on clothes. It was easy to walk up the path between the tidy lavender hedges. The poppies had long since finished flowering but, as Ellie bent down to release Pascal from his harness, she noticed a rogue daisy growing amongst the lavender, and she smiled as she shook her head before picking the bloom. The movement was enough to unravel a braid that had already been too loose, but she didn't do anything more than push the hair over her shoulder and tuck the stalk of the daisy behind her ear before opening her bag to find the big, old key to the house.

She had closed the shutters on the French doors before leaving the house earlier in the day, but Ellie knew this room well enough to move easily towards the kitchen. When Pascal suddenly stopped, however, to sniff the air, she felt a shiver run down her spine.

Something wasn't right.

'What is it, Pascal?' she whispered. 'Can you smell something? Someone?'

Her breath caught in her throat as she jerked her head up. And then she stood, frozen, staring at the wall above the fireplace. A wall that, like the others, she'd painstakingly chipped the crumbling plaster from. She'd never thought to hang anything to cover the stonework she loved, but a large part of this section of the wall was now covered.

With something she loved even more than the stones.

A painting.

The painting.

The one she'd been hoping to see tonight, but the artist

hadn't come to the market. The one she'd seen in the gallery in Saint-Martin-Vésubie. The one Julien had made enquiries about only to find it was far, far beyond her budget for buying an artwork.

There was only one person who knew how special this painting was to her.

And she'd made it easy for him to come here while she was out and hang it above the fireplace by leaving a key out for him.

If this was a farewell gift, it couldn't be more perfect. A square metre of paint on canvas that sang of everything she loved so much about France. Even in this half-light of moonbeams sneaking through the slats of the shutters, Ellie could see – and feel – this painting as clearly as she could feel tears gathering behind her eyes.

But she wanted to see it even more clearly, so she went to open the tall French doors so that she could push the shutters behind them open. The way she had the very first time she'd walked into this little house. When she'd caught her first glance of the stone-flagged terrace beneath the old candle holders of this secret garden space.

She opened the doors. She pushed open the shutters.

And, once again, Ellie found herself completely frozen. In utter disbelief.

Because it wasn't moonlight that had been sifting through tiny imperfections in those ancient shutters. It was the glow of dozens of candles. Big candles inside the metal holders that cut the light into pretty shapes. Tiny tea lights on the table and all around the edging of the terrace. Fairy lights that were strung through the tree branches above.

There was a rustic wooden board on the table, with bread and olives and a small wheel of cheese that was sagging and melty enough for Ellie to know instantly that it was her absolute favourite, Époisses. There was a bottle of champagne. There were two glasses.

And... there was the man who'd brought her fantasy to life. Who'd remembered every tiny detail of that stupid, romantic dream she'd confessed to him that evening when he'd told her about the death of Theo's mother. When she'd told him about her own devasting loss.

The evening the connection between them had begun.

And this was the evening it had to end.

Except... this didn't feel like an ending. Not the way Julien was looking at her. The way he was coming towards her and the way he took her face in his hands, so gently, before bending his head to touch her lips with his own.

So softly.

So tenderly Ellie could feel her heart breaking into tiny pieces.

But his first words took those pieces and started to put them back together again.

'I don't want you to leave, Ellie.'

'I don't want to leave,' she whispered. 'But I can't stay. This house isn't mine any longer. I have to go home.'

'*Non*...' Julien kissed her again. 'You can stay as long as you want. For ever, I hope. This house is yours.'

She caught her breath but she couldn't find any words to catch.

'I have bought La Maisonette,' he said. 'Because I want you to stay. Even if you only come here for holidays, I do not want anyone else to live beside me.'

In the flickering glow of the candles, Ellie could see the muscles of Julien's throat as he swallowed. She could see a vulnerability in his eyes that had never been there before. She could hear the unmistakeable honesty in his tone.

'I love you, Eleanor Gilchrist,' he said softly. '*Je t'aime.* I told you we didn't need you, but I couldn't have been more wrong. *Je ne veux pas vivre sans toi.*'

Ellie was fighting tears.

Happy, happy tears.

'*Je t'aime, aussi,*' she said, smiling despite the tremble she could feel in her lips. 'How can I say that better? *Je tellement t'aime?*'

'*Je t'aime tellement.*' Julien was smiling. 'Or perhaps *je t'aime à la folie*? I'm crazy about you.'

'Oh... yes...' Ellie stood on tiptoes, wrapping her arms around Julien's neck as she kissed him. 'That's the best. *Je t'aime à la folie, aussi.*'

But then she shook her head. 'I can't believe you bought this house,' she said. 'And the painting?'

'The house idea came later. You don't have to live here. It could be for your family when they come to visit. If... one day... if you can see yourself living next door, with me and Theo? As a family?'

Ellie caught her bottom lip between her teeth. One day – perhaps not that far away – she would confess her fantasy of marrying Julien in the beautiful church in Tourrettes-sur-Loup. He'd already made one romantic fantasy come true, however, and that was enough for one evening. More than she'd ever dreamed of...

'The painting was because I wanted to find something to give you. Something that would let you know how much you mean to me. To say *merci* for how much you've taught me with your courage and your joy in life and... and your ability to risk your heart and love all over again.'

'I didn't have any joy in my life when I came here.' Ellie nestled in Julien's arms, her cheek against his chest, where she could feel his heart beating. 'It was you who helped me find it again. You... and Pascal... and Marguerite and Coquelicot and... and Theo, of course, but most of all it was you, Julien. It's me who should be saying *merci*.'

Julien was resting his cheek on the top of Ellie's head, so it was easy to feel him shaking his head.

'It was what you said that made everything make sense,' he told her. 'Theo is my son. I've loved him from before he even took his first breath, and I will love and protect him until I take my last breath. In my heart, he has been and always will be my son. Like the way you said it – without any doubt at all. *Sans aucun doute.* And that's what matters.'

Ellie could only nod. Because her words were caught behind the lump in her throat.

'I knew that Theo would fall in love with you if he spent time with you,' Julien continued. 'I thought I was keeping him safe, but what I was also doing was stopping him from the joy of being able to love like that. And to be loved. Like only you could love him.'

'I do love Theo,' Ellie murmured. Their shared glance said it all. That loving a child enough for them to mean everything wasn't dependent on being their biological parent.

Julien's arms tightened around her. 'I got to the gallery,' he said. 'But the painting wasn't there, and I thought I'd left it too late. And that was when I realised...'

Ellie could feel the thump that followed a missed heartbeat and she lifted her head, alarmed, but Julien was smiling again.

'I realised what I was really leaving too late. That it wasn't just my love for Theo that mattered so much. And that if I let you leave, I might never see you again and I'd never be able to tell you that I love you.'

'*À la folie?*'

'*Oui. À la folie.*'

There was laughter now, in the soft glow of the flickering light of all those candles, and Ellie had never been this happy in her entire life.

And there was more.

There was champagne.

And cheese.

A whole night ahead with the man she was crazy about.

And a future together.

She did belong here.

To love and be loved because that was what mattered the most.

Sans aucun doute.

ACKNOWLEDGEMENTS

I fell for Provence ten years ago, when I took my first steps towards a long-held dream to learn to speak French before I die and spent a month at a language immersion school in the South of France. The first time I walked down the cobbled streets of a medieval French village, I knew I'd found the home of my soul. Two years later I packed up my life in New Zealand and moved to Vence where I lived for the next three years.

Falling for Provence is a book of the heart, written with the hope of capturing the magic that made me fall so completely in love with this part of France. To be able to share it is a privilege and I would like to acknowledge and thank everyone involved.

Team Boldwood, whose warm welcome has been very much appreciated.

Megan Haslam, whose faith in my writing, along with her editorial skills and wisdom, are inspirational.

Helen Woodhouse, the most outstanding copy editor I have ever worked with.

Carol, who gave me the working title of *The Last Summer Market* for this story – as we celebrated my birthday in my favourite restaurant in Vence – Le Michel Ange – that appears twice in this story.

Kelly, the first person to read the full manuscript of this book, wearing her editorial hat, who made me cry when she said she loved it.

Jim, my dad, who has decided – well into his nineties, bless him – that he loves reading romance novels, as long as they're written by his daughter.

And Becky – *my* daughter. I love that you're proud of me.

ABOUT THE AUTHOR

Alison Roberts is the author of over one hundred romance novels with Mills and Boon, and now writes romance and escapist fiction for Boldwood.

Sign up to Alison Robert's mailing list here for news, competitions and updates on future books.

Follow Alison on social media:

f facebook.com/rosie.richards.75
instagram.com/alison_roberts_author
X x.com/RobertsAli54060

ALSO BY ALISON ROBERTS

A Year in France Series

Falling for Provence

Medical Romances

The Doctor's Promise

Doctor Off Limits

LOVE NOTES

LOVE IN EVERY CHAPTER

WHERE ALL YOUR ROMANCE
DREAMS COME TRUE!

THE HOME OF BESTSELLING
ROMANCE AND WOMEN'S
FICTION

 WARNING:
MAY CONTAIN SPICE

SIGN UP TO OUR
NEWSLETTER

https://bit.ly/Lovenotesnews

Boldwœd

Boldwood Books is an award-winning fiction publishing company seeking out the best stories from around the world.

Find out more at www.boldwoodbooks.com

Join our reader community for brilliant books, competitions and offers!

Follow us
@BoldwoodBooks
@TheBoldBookClub

Sign up to our weekly deals newsletter

https://bit.ly/BoldwoodBNewsletter

Printed in Great Britain
by Amazon

47699007R00155